About the

Claire Boston fell in love wi
suspense at eleven when she discovered her mother's stash of Nora Roberts novels. Like Nora, she writes series set around families or groups of friends with a guaranteed happy ending.

She loves travelling and learning about new cultures and interesting vocations which she then weaves into her writing.

When Claire's not at the computer typing her stories she can be found creating her own handmade journals, swinging on a sidecar, or in the garden attempting to grow something other than weeds.

Claire lives in Western Australia with her husband, who loves even her most annoying quirks and is currently learning how to knit. You can find her complete book list on her website www.claireboston.com/books. You can connect with Claire through Facebook and Twitter, or join her reader group

(http://www.claireboston.com/pages/reader-group/).

Also by Claire Boston

Romance

The Texan Quartet

What Goes on Tour

All that Sparkles

Under the Covers

Into the Fire

The Flanagan Sisters

Break the Rules

Change of Heart

Blaze a Trail

Place to Belong

Romantic Suspense

The Blackbridge Series

Nothing to Fear

Nothing to Gain

Nothing to Hide

Nothing to Lose

Shelter

Shield

Harbour

Protect

Aussie Heroes: Retribution Bay

Return to Retribution Bay

Trapped in Retribution Bay

Escape to Retribution Bay

Secrets in Retribution Bay

Beached in Retribution Bay

Adrift in Retribution Bay

Wrecked in Retribution Bay

Captive in Retribution Bay

Captive in Retribution Bay

Aussie Heroes: Retribution Bay

Claire Boston

First published by Bantilly Publishing in 2024

Captive in Retribution Bay: Aussie Heroes: Retribution Bay

EPUB format: 9781922916105
Print: 9781922916112
Large Print: 9781922916129

Cover design by Mayhem Cover Creations
Edited by Ann Harth
Proofread by Teena Raffa-Mulligan

I would like to acknowledge the Bayungu people, Traditional Custodians of the land on which this story is based, and pay my respects to their Elders past and present.

Dedication

This book is dedicated to Bayungu Elder, Hazel Walgar and Yinggarda woman, Toni Roe. Thank you for your help, ladies.

Dear Reader,

This is the final book in the Aussie Heroes: Retribution Bay series and therefore may contain spoilers for the preceding novels. This story aims to answer any remaining questions. You will get a lot more from this book if you've read the rest of the series. I've tried to make it clear who is who, but there are a lot of characters mentioned in some scenes and a large cast which might be confusing if you haven't read the other books.

In terms of timeline, this story starts at the end of Book 6, Adrift in Retribution Bay, so you'll get some of the same scenes but from different points of view.

Just in case you want a refresher, here are the main players:

The Stokes Family (in order of age)

- Parents - Bill and Beth (deceased)
- Brandon Stokes who married Amy Hammond
- Darcy Stokes who is engaged to Faith. Darcy has a ten-year-old daughter, Lara.
- Ed Stokes whose partner is Tess
- Georgie Stokes who is engaged to Matt Roe (Nhiari's brother)

Others

- Sam Hackett - was in the same army team with Brandon and Sherlock. His partner is Penelope who works for Parks and Wildlife.
- Arthur 'Sherlock' Hammond - Brandon's army buddy and Amy's brother. He's in a relationship with Gretchen who has a ten-year-old son, Jordan.
- Sergeant Dot Campbell is engaged to Oliver Anderson

- Senior Constable Nhiari Roe
- Lee Slater/Kwong - works for Stonefish
- Lucas Fitton - suspected head of Stonefish
- Martin, Pierre and Colin - other police officers at Retribution Bay
- Lindsay - owns the local grocery store and surrogate mother to Dot

I really hope you enjoy this final Retribution Bay story.

Happy Reading!

Claire B

Chapter 1

The kidnapped boys would be terrified. Senior Constable Nhiari Roe's body ached with tension and she tugged on her braid. Beside her, Sam drove with confidence, pushing the four-wheel-drive hard as they raced towards the ranges. In the back seat Nhiari's brother, Matt, Arthur 'Sherlock' Hammond, and Gretchen sat just as tense. They were racing to rescue Gretchen's son, Jordan, and his best friend.

The ten-year-olds had been snatched from school by Jordan's father, and the man holding them was someone she'd been hunting for months.

Lee Slater.

Her gut clenched.

He had lied and seduced her with his words. She'd thought he could be the one until his lies came to light.

Now she had to stop him.

Lee was a loose-cannon. No one really knew what he was capable of, though he'd already killed at least one man.

She had to protect the people with her; Sam and Sherlock were ex-military, but Matt and Gretchen were civilians. They were all likely to go off half-cocked and get themselves injured or killed.

"Can't you drive any faster?" Gretchen called, the worry in her voice clear.

Sam's chuckle was strained. "Not with a police officer in the car."

Nhiari grunted. Like that mattered. He was pushing the car as fast as it would go. "When we get there, I go in first. You wait until I give the all-clear."

She felt the resistance to her statement as Arthur shifted in the back seat. He was as concerned as Gretchen, after protecting both her and her son, Jordan for a few days now. But it was Matt who piped up.

"Not going to happen, gunyjan. None of us are letting you in there without backup."

She flinched. Her knowledge of her native language wasn't as good as her brother's, but he always used the endearment when he wanted something. "I'm in charge. You'll do as I say."

Sam took his eyes off the track to glance at her. "With all due respect, that's not in our nature. We're a team and we protect and support the team."

Nhiari ground her teeth together. They weren't in a team any longer. They were civilians, but she knew from experience nothing she said would change their minds. And they were right. There wasn't another cop who could back her up fast enough. Though it didn't mean she had to like it. "I'm going to throw the lot of you in gaol when we get back."

"You do what you need to do," Sherlock said. "Just like we will."

Matt directed Sam onto a dirt road. Nhiari gripped the handle above the door as the car bounced over bumps, and she focused on the ranges in front of her. They ran the entire length of the peninsula, and the boys could be anywhere. Matt's fiancée, Georgie, thought she knew where they'd be. Apparently she'd met Lee there occasionally, despite him being a wanted felon. Nhiari would have words to her about that later.

As they got to the base of the ranges, they pulled up behind an abandoned Parks and Wildlife four-wheel-drive.

Matt sprang out before she could stop him and yelled, "Georgie!" He swore as his call echoed off the ranges. "I told her to stay with the car until we got here."

Which meant Nhiari might have another hostage to worry about.

"You just lost us the element of surprise," Arthur grumbled as he got out of the car, but Nhiari paid them no attention. Her gaze took in the red ranges, the shrubby bushes behind which someone could hide, and the dark openings of a few caves in the hillside. Too many options. Nhiari pulled out her gun and started forward. As she neared the closest cave, she glanced behind her.

Sam had moved to the opposite side of the gaping hole and had pulled a gun from somewhere, Arthur had Gretchen protected behind him, and Matt was right behind her. He would have been in front if he'd had any kind of weapon.

"Where are they, Lee?" Georgie's voice echoed out of the cave.

"I told you, I don't know." His voice was full of frustration, but it sent an unwanted shiver of warmth through Nhiari. That voice had promised her pleasure and understanding. A potent combination.

The man was her enemy. She needed to remember that. She held up three fingers, knowing Sam and Sherlock would understand. She lowered one at a time and on zero, they stormed into the cave. "Hands on your head, Lee."

The darkness in the cave momentarily blinded her,

but she blinked rapidly. Matt dragged Georgie out of the way, but her focus was on the slim Asian man in front of her. He held no weapon, but that didn't mean he didn't have one. A thin film of red dust covered his black slacks and wrinkled striped shirt, but he looked remarkably well considering he'd spent months living in this cave system. His dark hair was dishevelled, no longer the precision cut and style of the photographer he'd pretended to be. His lean body was even thinner, perhaps because of his inability to come into town for food. What had he been living on? Had someone been helping him, providing him with sustenance? Surely he couldn't have survived out here on his own.

No, he had to be in contact with someone if Kurt had involved him in the kidnapping.

What was Lee's role in all of this?

Not for the first time she wondered whether he was the ringleader, the person in charge of Stonefish, the crime syndicate they'd been trying to break since the start of the year. He'd not hesitated to kill when required, silencing those who may have provided information about the organisation.

He slowly raised his hands.

"Where are Jordan and Cody?" Sherlock demanded, striding forward while Nhiari kept her gun aimed at Lee. He acknowledged everyone in the cave, no fear in his eyes, but his gaze lingered on Nhiari. His chocolate brown eyes showed no emotion, but it was as if he was waiting for something from her. Finally he said, "They escaped."

It took Nhiari a second to remember the question he'd been asked.

"What?" Gretchen asked.

He moved his gaze to the frantic mother. "Your son and his friend escaped their bonds." He shook his head. "I don't know how."

The obvious surprise in his voice made Nhiari frown and reassess. This area was deserted. No roads, no tourist lookouts, no fresh water unless you knew where to look. And it was hot. It would have to be close to thirty-five degrees outside today. The boys could be in serious trouble.

"Why didn't you take better care of them?" Gretchen demanded.

"What happened?" Sherlock moved closer, his voice low and dangerous.

Nhiari glanced at him. Was she going to have to stop him from doing something stupid?

"I had the boys cable-tied in here," he said. "They were safe, but I didn't know if anyone from Stonefish was coming to get them, so I had to keep them tied." He directed the last comment to Gretchen. "I heard someone approach, so I went outside to investigate. It was Georgie. I was gone five, maybe ten minutes."

"I taught the boys how to remove cable ties," Arthur said, a hint of pride in his voice.

"How long ago did you leave?" Gretchen asked Lee.

"I've been arguing with Georgie for a few minutes, so it's been no more than fifteen minutes since I saw them."

Gretchen went to the mouth of the cave. "Jordan! Cody! Come out."

"Where were they tied?" Arthur asked.

Lee motioned to the back of the cave, which had a tunnel running off it. Matt and Arthur examined the ground, Arthur shining his phone torch to get a better look. Nhiari stayed where she was, keeping her gun trained on Lee.

"Everyone stay where you are," Matt said. He shone his light down the tunnel, and then shifted towards the entrance. He glanced at Arthur. "Did you teach them to backtrack?"

Arthur nodded.

"Good job. There are footprints leading into the tunnel and ones leaving the cave."

"They'll have left the cave," Arthur stated.

"Impossible. I would have seen them leave," Lee said, sounding offended.

She couldn't deal with egos right now. "We don't have time to argue," Nhiari stated. "We need to find those boys before it gets dark." She turned to Lee. "You know these tunnels?"

He nodded.

She holstered her gun and walked over, handcuffing him, ignoring the roughness of his palms. "You and I will search the tunnels. The rest of you search outside. We'll meet back here in an hour. If we don't find them by then, I'll call in search and rescue."

"I'll call Parks and Wildlife now. Get my colleagues to look for them," Georgie said.

Good idea. There could be rangers nearby.

Arthur joined Gretchen at the entrance. "The footprints go that way."

Nhiari waited for her friends to leave the cave, and turned her attention to the man beside her. His cuffed hands hung behind his back. Awareness and tension smothered her. "Let's go."

"It's good to see you, Nhiari."

She stiffened, ignoring the way his soft words caressed her skin. He was a killer. He had lied and used her. She would not be sucked in again.

"Move, Lee." She gave him a none too gentle shove towards the tunnel at the back of the cave. He didn't budge.

"Let me explain."

She wasn't revisiting their past now. "There's nothing to explain. We have two missing children, and you're going to help me find them." She hoped they had left the cave like Arthur suspected, because the tunnel system was a maze that few knew their way around. Though Lee was probably one of the few.

Lee nodded. "We'll talk later."

She didn't correct him. The only thing happening later was him heading straight to gaol. She switched on her torch and followed Lee to where the tunnel branched off from the cave. Two smaller sets of footprints were clear in the sand.

Nhiari was impressed by the two boys' ingenuity escaping their bonds, but right now she only wanted them found, safe and sound.

She shone the light down the tunnel, keeping a step behind Lee; far enough that he couldn't catch her unaware, close enough to catch him if he ran.

The tunnel narrowed, the rock walls closing in and the ground becoming rocky. Nhiari wiped the sweat from her forehead. It was like an oven in here. She'd thought the caves would offer relief from the heat outside, but it seemed to absorb it, locking it inside.

"The trail has stopped."

There was enough space in the tunnel for her to squeeze past Lee to see for herself. They weren't much more than fifty metres from where they started. There was enough room to slide through the gap in the rock, and the boys could have done so, but would they have? They had no light, and the sunlight didn't reach this far into the tunnel.

She shone her torch through the gap and called, "Jordan! Cody!"

Only her voice echoed back.

A light rattle like metal on metal behind her made her spin. Lee stepped closer, his body pressed against hers, and he slipped a hand down her side.

What happened to the handcuffs?

The question became insignificant as she realised

what he was doing.

Going for her gun.

Adrenaline spiked and she shoved his hand away, bringing up her knee, but he was too close for her to do any actual damage. He reached towards her, grunting as she twisted and elbowed him in the gut. The torch fell out of her hand. He released the clasp over her gun, but she stepped away and hit the hard rock wall. Pain shot down her back. Trapped between it and him.

His firm body pressed into her, reminding her of their night together. She blocked the thought as his other hand snaked out and lifted the gun from her holster.

No!

Nhiari grabbed his arm, desperate to stop him.

He shoved her back as if she weighed nothing and brought up the gun to point directly at her.

"Stop, Nhiari."

Shit. She sucked in a breath as her heart raced.

"I don't want to hurt you." His face was shadowed in the light shining from the torch which lay on the ground behind him. She couldn't see his eyes, but his tone held regret. The gun didn't waver.

"What are you going to do now?" She kept her own tone even as she cursed herself for letting him get her gun. She should have known he had the skills to get out of handcuffs.

He was quiet, as if figuring it out for himself. "If I let you go, you'll come back, won't you?"

She said nothing. No way she would let him go free.

He cursed quietly. "We're going back to the cave." He stripped her police vest of all her weapons, tucking them into various pockets, and gestured for her to move past him.

The cave would give her more manoeuvrability and was closer to the cars. She might be able to make a run for it. She walked slowly back down the tunnel, blinking as the sunlight grew brighter. She'd only get one chance to disarm him.

As she entered the cave, she spotted a day pack tucked behind a rock. That had to be Lee's.

In the distance, Gretchen called for her son. They weren't far away. Sam and Arthur had guns, but she didn't want this to become a shoot-out.

Lee went over to the backpack and rummaged around in it one-handed.

Perhaps she could tackle him while he was distracted. She stepped closer.

Lee pointed the gun at her. "Don't do it." His gaze held no emotion. He was a completely different man from the one she'd had dinner with. The photographer had been slightly awkward, sweet and open in his interest in her.

An act.

Just like with so many other men in her life.

And she'd fallen for it, again. Too dumb to realise they didn't want what she wanted; a companion, a partner, a lover. No, the men she dated only wanted sex or information. Perhaps it was time to give up on finding someone who loved her.

She never learnt.

Nhiari raised her hands in surrender and he extracted a notepad and pen from the pack.

Lee switched the gun to his other hand and wrote in the notebook.

She shifted her stance, judging how much he was paying attention. The gun straightened. Probably adept with both hands. The man was well trained. Her handcuffs dangled from one wrist. Had she locked them properly? She couldn't remember using the key. Idiot.

Lee ripped the note from the book, folded it in half

and placed it under a rock in a prominent position in the cave. Then he jimmied the other handcuff with a slip of metal he retrieved from his back pocket until it clicked open and tucked them into his back pocket.

Her police radio crackled with static and Lee held out a hand. "Radio and phone."

She stared at him a long moment before removing the radio and handing it to him. He switched it off. "Phone."

She scowled and retrieved it from her vest. He pressed the power button until the screen went black and tucked both into his backpack. "Let's go." He lifted the pack onto his back.

"Go where?"

"Camp."

She laughed. "You expect me to go with you?"

He nodded. "You don't really have a choice, do you? I'm close, Nhiari. I have to finish this." For the first time he let emotion into his voice and it sounded like desperation.

"Close to what?"

"Ending Stonefish."

She pressed her lips together. Georgie thought Lee was working against the organisation, but there was no proof. "You work for them," she pointed out. "You took Cody and Jordan."

"Only as part of my cover. I wouldn't have let them hurt the boys."

Easy to say now the boys were gone. "What would you have done if Stonefish had arrived before we did?"

He glanced towards the entrance of the cave. "They escaped on their own anyway."

"And if they hadn't?"

Lee seemed unperturbed. "I knew you would come." He sighed. "There's no way the Stokes would have let Kurt get away with the treasure. Not with Brandon,

Sam and Sherlock there. The men are skilled."

He knew too much. Was Georgie feeding him information? "What treasure?"

Lee looked at her with a bemused expression.

Right. She wasn't touching that. Besides Jordan had taken a gold coin to school, which had prompted his kidnapping and made it difficult to deny the treasure existed. Still she had no idea how he got his information. She changed the subject. "What will you do with me?"

"Keep you with me until this is over."

Over her dead body. She couldn't spend time with this man. "You're kidnapping a police officer?"

He scowled. "Add it to my list of crimes."

It would be very easy to dispose of a body in the ranges. No one had completely explored the eighty kilometre length of it.

So if she wanted to stay alive, she needed to play along. "Will you share the information you have?" He might not want to hurt her, but he would if she ran. While she bided her time, she could use his resources to put an end to Stonefish threatening her friends and using her town as its base.

"As needed."

Annoyance swept through her and she forced her hands not to clench so he didn't know she was riled. "Do I have a choice?"

"No."

If he had wanted to kill her, he could have done it in the tunnel. She would be safe for the moment at least. She'd get her opportunity to get her gun back, and then she'd be the one calling the shots.

But maybe, just maybe, he meant what he said.

And they could bring down Stonefish together.

She sighed. Still being far too trusting and optimistic. Still her options were limited. "Lead the way."

Chapter 2

Lee smothered a laugh. No way was Nhiari going behind him where he couldn't see her. He wasn't stupid. She might have agreed to go with him, but that wasn't the end. She'd given in too easily. And the one thing he'd learnt during their date was she didn't give up, and she didn't give in. It was something he admired her for, which made betraying her even more difficult.

But he had to be focused on the end game.

"After you." He pointed back to the tunnel, trying to release the tension in his shoulders. This was all Kurt Webb's fault.

Kurt was supposed to meet him to swap information, not bring two innocent boys with him, and force Lee to take them off his hands. He'd recognised Jordan and Cody immediately and knew if he hurt them, there would be nowhere he could hide. The Stokes and their friends would make it their mission to find him.

He'd already done enough to hurt them, and he might need their help to end this.

He couldn't hurt those boys.

Added to his stress was the uncertainty of whether

this was a test from Stonefish, to check if he was still loyal. His loyalty had already been questioned, but that might have been a taunt from a man who had always been jealous of him, rather than the truth from the top. Either way, he was safe as long as Stonefish didn't know for sure where his loyalties lay.

The boys escaping on their own didn't help matters.

It took a lot to surprise him, but returning to the cave to find it empty had shocked him. Then he'd been impressed by the boys' ingenuity. Neither boy had seemed scared. They'd been defiant. Jordan was certain Sherlock would come for him, and the boy had been right. Sherlock had been smart enough to recognise how much of a threat Kurt was and to teach the boys to protect themselves.

A relief, really, because Lee hadn't known what to do with them.

Lee followed Nhiari back into the tunnel, admiring how the cut of her blue police uniform pants moulded to the curves of her bottom. He suppressed the urge of longing. Their one night together had been perfect, but the memory would have to last him a lifetime, because there was no way she would trust him again.

He was a criminal and she was a cop.

Nhiari stopped at the small gap in the rock. "Where now?"

"Keep going." It was a tight squeeze, but doable.

"I'm supposed to go through there?" Her voice wavered at a slightly higher pitch than normal.

Lee kept out of her reach and shone the torch on her face. Sweat glistened on her forehead, but it was humid as hell in here. Her chest rose and fell rapidly, and her hands trembled as she clenched them. Shit. She was scared. This strong, brave woman was claustrophobic.

Or pretending to be.

The reminder gave him pause and tempered his protective instincts. They couldn't go back without risking being caught by the others. He nodded and kept the emotion out of his tone. "That's the way out. It widens on the other side."

She stared at him, ignoring the glare from the light. "No."

He raised the gun. "Do it, Nhiari. We don't have all day."

The whites of her eyes showed as her eyes widened, but he couldn't let it get to him. Couldn't show his weakness for her.

She just stood there.

He huffed out a breath. "Close your eyes and imagine you're in a large room. Feel your way through." He couldn't shoot her, couldn't end this beautiful woman's life, but he hoped she didn't realise that. He pointed the gun at her head. "If you don't go through, you're no use to me." His voice was void of emotion and he kept his gaze steady and uncaring.

She swallowed hard and turned. Her fingers shook as she placed her hands on the rock and closed her eyes. Slowly she slid through the gap. As soon as she was trapped between the two rocks, he moved closer. The tunnel widened on the other side, and she might run, whether or not she had lighting. He couldn't let her get too far ahead of him. She could get lost in here, and if she did, she would likely die.

His gut clenched.

By the time she exited the tight gap, he was halfway through. He pointed the gun at her, but she didn't notice, bent double, panting.

Perhaps he'd found her kryptonite.

He kept his distance as he entered the larger space and gave her a minute to get her breath back before saying, "We have to keep moving. There's another couple of hundred metres of caves before we get out in the open."

She glanced at him. "We're getting out of the cave?"

He nodded.

She straightened. "Which way?"

He gestured and she moved quickly, striding along the hard, sandy floor towards the exit. Lee softly exhaled. After they left this cave system, they would be fine. It exited on the western side of the ranges and those searching for the boys were on the eastern side. They wouldn't be spotted.

The walls of the cave lightened and Nhiari increased her stride, trotting towards the glow. Lee kept pace, always out of her reach in case she went for him, but it was unwarranted. Her focus was on the exit.

The bright sunlight hurt his eyes, and he kept in the cave's shadow as Nhiari burst out into the sunlight.

She inhaled deeply, turning in a circle to take in the new location, even while recovering from her panic attack.

Impressive.

They'd come out at the base of the ranges and there was sparse vegetation around; a few bushes, a couple of trees, but mostly grasses.

Lee waited until her breathing returned to normal and she started studying the surroundings more closely, before he took her arm. "This way."

It was a short walk to where he'd left his off-road motorcycle. They'd both fit on it, but Nhiari wasn't a willing passenger. He didn't know what she would try.

A frisson of excitement shot through him and he tamped it down. At any other time he'd revel in the challenge, the idea she could give as good as she got, but right now he needed simple and easy. Lucas was getting desperate. He would make a mistake and Lee would be there to trap him in it.

Then Lucas would pay for what he'd done.

Lee smiled and directed Nhiari through some bushes and the few hundred metres to where he'd left the bike. He'd been careful to use a different path each time he came this way so as not to leave an obvious trail that someone could stumble on. He was certain Georgie was trying to keep tabs on where he was and she'd found him once already.

Nhiari eyed the dirt bike. "Want me to drive?"

He raised his eyebrows. "Do you know how?"

She laughed, the sound a little sarcastic and disbelieving. "I've been riding motorbikes since I was a child."

Good to know. He'd keep the key in his pocket so she didn't steal it when he wasn't looking. "You can drive." That way he could keep hold of the gun and hopefully she wouldn't do something stupid.

She straddled the bike, her pants tightening as she sat and put her hand out for the key. He got on behind her, using his free hand to pass her the key and then pressed close, wrapping an arm around her.

She smelled like honey and although she wore an equipment vest, he felt her warmth underneath. Memories of the softness of her skin swept over him. Running his hands over her body, hearing her moans… He stifled a groan.

Not for the first time he wished things had turned out differently. He hadn't expected to connect so deeply with her when he'd taken her to dinner.

But she'd been so different from what he'd expected. Underneath that tough police exterior she'd been sensitive, shy and well-read. They'd discussed everything from Shakespeare and Chaucer to E.L. James and Lee Child. He'd spent the entire night so intrigued and entertained that he'd almost forgotten the reason he'd invited her in the first place.

To get information.

As the bike roared to life, he leaned closer and murmured into her ear, "That way." He pointed.

She shivered and pressed her lips together. Was she repulsed by his presence? Probably. He wasn't stupid enough to hope her reaction was proof she wasn't immune to him. Not after the way he'd behaved. There was no love lost on Nhiari's side.

He directed Nhiari along the ranges and into one canyon, across rocky terrain until they reached their destination. "Stop there."

She did as he asked and shut off the bike, pocketing the key. He grinned briefly before controlling his expression and held out a hand. "I'll take that."

A sullen expression as she fished it out and slapped it into his palm. He got off, keeping his gun pointed loosely at her as she dismounted.

"Is this where you shoot me and hide the body?" Nhiari asked.

He kept the surprise off his face. "If I was going to kill you, I would have done it in the cave." He thought she understood. "I can't let you free only to have you hunting me."

"You really think whatever you need to do will be easier with me as a reluctant participant?"

She was right, though he wouldn't admit it. When he'd freed himself of the handcuffs and pressed into Nhiari, his only thought was to keep her with him. To steal more time with her. Idiotic. He'd been trained to ignore his feelings. "You might have useful information."

She snorted. "As if I would give it to you." The derision in her eyes was clear. He had hurt her, which meant this was going to be twice as difficult.

"Nhi, please. I know I've hurt you, but I promise you, the man in charge is within my grasp."

"Give me a name."

He hesitated. If she escaped and then started monitoring Lucas, Lucas would know. The traitors at the Retribution Bay police station would tell him. "I can't. Not yet."

"What can you tell me?"

He pressed his lips together and moved the motorbike so it was next to a bush, and then added branches on top of it to hide it further. "We can talk when we get to camp."

She crossed her arms and her stare was hard, but rather than intimidating Lee, he itched to pick up his camera and photograph her just like that. He'd call the photo, Gives No Shit.

It would be some time before he could go back to taking photographs for enjoyment—if ever. When he'd started this, he hadn't thought past stopping Stonefish. But he had killed people. Both men had threatened the lives of innocent people and would have continued to make lives miserable, but that might not count.

His justification sounded weak in his head. Who was he kidding? He had hurt people and committed enough crimes to send him to gaol. He pushed down the guilt and gestured with his head. "This way." He moved towards one of his campsites, not looking back as if sure Nhiari would follow. He'd gone a couple of metres before her footsteps crunched behind him. Lee exhaled softly, relief filling him, and continued on his way.

***

They climbed for about ten minutes before they reached an overhang on the side of the ranges. It was high enough to stand upright, and hopefully wide enough not to freak out Nhiari. Inside was his larger backpack with some emergency supplies.

"Cosy," Nhiari snarked.

"It's not too narrow in here for you?" he asked.

She hesitated and crossed her arms, hugging herself. "It's fine. Surely you haven't stayed here all this time."

He debated not answering, but it was something he could tell her and maybe it would help to soften her, show her he would share what he could. "No. I've got camps all along the ranges."

"Is your car at one of them?"

He nodded. One of the first things he'd done on arriving in Retribution Bay was to set up his bolt holes. He knew if his involvement with Stonefish had been exposed, he'd have to run and the peninsula didn't give him a lot of options. Particularly if Lucas wasn't willing to bail him out.

He'd figured lying low until the heat faded would be his best bet. And posing as a nature photographer gave him plenty of reasons to spend time in the ranges scoping out the best locations.

That had definitely paid off.

"Have you got any water?" Nhiari sat on the rock he used as a seat.

Lee dug in his backpack and pulled out a flask, handing it to her. She gulped down the liquid without hesitation and he moved across to the entrance. From this height he could see down the canyon, but aside from a kangaroo lazing in the shade below, nothing moved. The ranges were perfect for hiding as there were very few roads in.

"So what now?"

It was a good question and not one Lee had a good answer for.

"Can we search for the boys from here?" Nhiari added.

Lee shook his head. They'd come too far north and west. There was no way the boys could have made it this far. "They would have found the boys by now."

"You can't know that."

He glanced at her. "Do you think any of them will give up before they find them?" He didn't wait for her to answer. "The boys couldn't have gone more than a couple of kilometres and if Sherlock trained them as he said he did, they would stick to shade and cover until they could find help." He hoped he was right. He hated the idea of the two children out there alone, but he had to look at the bigger picture.

Nhiari scowled as if she was building her argument.

"Those boys weren't scared, even when Kurt handed them over and drove away. They whispered together, but I heard Jordan reassure Cody that Sherlock would come for them." The only person to show him that amount of faith had been his father.

The stabbing pain hadn't lessened in the past year, but he could ignore it. "Will they mount a search party for you?"

"Matt will search even if no one else does."

"Your brother is a pain in the arse." Matt had been in the wrong place at the wrong time on a number of occasions and had almost blown Lee's cover. And he was continuing to be a pain even now. It didn't matter that Lee had saved his and Georgie's life.

Nhiari barked out a laugh and then smothered it as if realising she shouldn't agree with him. She swallowed. "Did you kill Clark?"

The question was unexpected, but how should he answer it? He couldn't forget Nhiari was a police officer, and she could put him behind bars.

Though she knew enough of his crimes to arrest him now. He hadn't cared what happened to him when he first started his mission. He had only wanted Lucas to pay.

Now, he wished he'd done things differently.

"Yes. Georgie is innocent."

Nhiari leaned forward. "Why did she say she killed him?"

"Because I asked her to. If Stonefish knew I had killed Clark, they would have stopped trusting me and I need their trust."

"So you let her be accused of murder?"

He narrowed his eyes, annoyed she was trying to push his buttons. "Self-defence not murder, and you know it."

"Tell me what happened."

An order, not a request. Lee clenched his teeth. He should have just left her tied up in the cave. Should have ignored the small part of him that hoped if they spent time together, she would see who he truly was, not who he'd had to become.

He kept his eyes on hers as he crossed to the other side of the cave and leaned against the cave wall. "Clark kidnapped Matt and called Georgie to come to his rescue. His plan was to kill them both."

"Why?"

"Clark was a spoilt child who had watched too many movies. He only got involved in the business at the beginning of the year after I did. He couldn't stand the praise his father gave me for my work."

Nhiari's eyebrows raised, but she didn't speak.

"He embraced being the bad guy and discovered he enjoyed the power that came with killing. So when Matt and Georgie messed up his smuggling ring, he decided they needed to pay."

"How did you get involved?"

"He called me and told me to meet him. I thought he wanted to gloat about how good he was, but he said his father wasn't sure about my loyalty and I had to prove it by killing Matt and Georgie." It hadn't been a difficult choice. Matt and Georgie had been kind to him from the day he'd met them, whereas Clark had been the bully of his childhood. "Georgie turned up with a rifle. I retrieved it from her, shot Clark and asked her to take the blame until I could finish building a case against Stonefish."

"That was over two months ago."

His failure ate at him, but he was so much closer now. "I know."

Nhiari was silent for a long moment. "Thank you for saving them."

"I care for them too."

Her eyes shuttered and she crossed her arms, leaning away from him. Right, too much touchy-feely. He moved over to his larger pack and took out another water flask and a couple of ration bars. "Catch." He tossed her one, forcing her to move, and let him in.

She caught it, watched him for a moment and then ripped open the packet, taking a bite. Yeah, it was going to take a lot more to get her to open up to him.

He'd made a mistake bringing her here. He should have taken her to his main site, where he could share all his information if he wanted her to work with him. But letting her in also exposed her to danger and showed her just how much of himself he'd compromised in the past year.

Then there would be no hope for them.

He wasn't ready to admit he had lost her yet.

Chapter 3

Nhiari chewed on the surprisingly tasty ration bar. She wasn't a patient person, but she dug up some patience from deep within her and settled in for the long game. Lee wanted to pretend they were friends, that there was something between them, but he'd shattered that opportunity months ago. She was here to discover what he knew and then to arrest his arse and everyone involved in Stonefish.

She hunched over, peering out the cave mouth. This was smaller than the cave the boys had been in and she had no distractions. Above her was hundreds of tonnes of earth. Her muscles tensed. The urge to flee was strong—not only because of the enclosed space, but also because she was being held against her will by a man who triggered so many mixed emotions in her.

She wouldn't get far while he was awake. Focusing on her breathing she tried to calm her anxiety.

Lee had been living in these caves for months and nothing had happened.

She could wait this out.

Lee's phone beeped and he checked the message. "The boys have been found."

She raised her eyebrows, glad for the distraction. "Who told you?"

He shoved his phone in his back pocket. "Someone who knows."

She rolled her eyes. Still not willing to share his sources. He was tempting her to stay by promises of information he wasn't delivering.

Darkness fell and Lee handed her an MRE—meal ready to eat—or army ration, which was some kind of curry. Edible and considering her circumstances, better than nothing. She didn't like the idea of hunting for her dinner. Besides, Matt had learned more about hunting when her parents had taught them about the land and their heritage, and she'd been expected to learn about the women's work—gathering things to eat. Not that she would show Lee what around them he could eat. He seemed to be doing fine on his own.

"We'll sleep here tonight." Lee dug through his larger hiking pack and pulled out a thin mattress and a cover. "You can sleep on this."

"Where will you sleep?"

"I'll manage."

No. This fake gentleman shit would not work on her. He was trying to lull her, make her believe in him, but even her claustrophobia hadn't swayed him. He didn't care for her wellbeing. "I'll be fine on the ground."

"Nhiari, don't be stubborn. You'll be more comfortable on my mattress."

"I'd be more comfortable in my own bed, but since you denied me that option, I'll make do with what I've got."

He didn't wince, didn't show any kind of emotion in response to her words. Where had the expressive, open, sweet photographer she'd dated gone?

This man was military through and through. How

had she missed it?

"Suit yourself."

She moved over to the entrance of the cave, needing a glimpse of the sky, and Lee snorted. "You can sleep at the back."

Nhiari inhaled deeply, but without complaint she changed direction and found a spot nearer the back. Her skin tightened and she focused on her breathing. Lee was biding his time with her, probably still deciding what to do, otherwise he would have taken her straight to his main camp. There was no trust lost on either side.

She didn't blame him. The second he fell asleep, she was out of here. She couldn't stay here in this cave, couldn't continue being his hostage.

"Take this." Lee handed her his day pack and she used it as a slightly lumpy pillow.

Lee laid out his mattress between her and the entrance and there wasn't a lot of room on either side for her to pass by.

But she'd manage it somehow. She turned her back to him and pretended to go to sleep.

They'd travelled about ten kilometres from the cave where Jordan and Cody had been held. Still too far away to hike into town overnight. Her parents lived south of the ranges, but she didn't want to risk them coming into contact with Lee. He might view them as collateral damage.

So her other option was heading for the coast, which was only a couple of kilometres away. Camp sites dotted the shoreline, and though they were quieter at this time of year than during peak season, they always had campers. She could borrow a car and be in Retribution Bay within the hour. She could return with backup, arrest Lee and force him to give them his information.

Lee switched off the torch and the cave plunged into darkness.

Nhiari stared into the dark and slowly the pitch black faded to grey and shapes were discernible.

Her escape would have to be timed perfectly.

Lee would disappear the moment he noticed she had gone and it would take more manpower to search the ranges for him.

She hesitated. Would she lose a vital opportunity to learn things about Stonefish by leaving?

Lee's steady breathing seemed loud in the cave, but it lacked the heaviness of someone who was asleep. The sound reminded her of their night together, of lying wrapped in his arms, sated from their lovemaking, feeling as if she had finally found someone who understood her.

Her stomach cramped.

Wrong again.

Too desperate or idiotic to realise no one wanted to be with her. Not the boys at high school who only noticed her early-onset boobs. Not the men at the academy who were threatened by her competency. Not this man lying only a few metres away who had just wanted her information.

Nhiari itched to get up and run. To get as far away as possible from this man and the emotions he made her feel.

He was holding her against her will.

Though he'd tucked the gun away after they'd arrived here and promised her information.

If she could sneak out, she might return with backup before he woke. She needed to end this. Stonefish had harassed her town for far too long.

She smothered her groan at her indecision and turned so she faced the exit. Lee was just a lump on the ground, but outside was far lighter. The moon had another week before it was full, but it still lit the night, giving trees and shrubs shape.

Nhiari watched Lee, looking for a sign he'd fallen asleep. He was well-trained—she suspected military, but her queries to both the Australian and Singaporean governments had revealed no Lee Slater had ever enlisted. Which meant he had either lied about his name, or his training had been less legitimate.

He would be foolish to fall asleep immediately—if at all—and he wasn't foolish. She would have to be quick. Her hand closed around a fist-sized rock. Her heart quailed, but she ignored it. She wasn't planning to kill him, just knock him unconscious for long enough to restrain him.

"I won't attack you in your sleep, Nhiari." His warm voice slid over her skin like a blanket. Another reminder of the night they'd spent together. Talking late into the night, sharing their hopes and dreams.

Lies, all of it.

At least on his side.

She'd opened up to him and told him things she hadn't even told her best friend, Dot. He'd been so open, so sweet in his desire to learn all about her.

She flinched, the urge to flee these feelings almost overpowered her.

"You can put the rock down."

She didn't reply but gripped the rock tighter.

"I still have your gun loaded and pointing at you. You wouldn't be able to so much as twitch before I could shoot you." He sounded sad along with bemused.

Nhiari closed her eyes and ignored him. He would fall asleep eventually, and when he did, she would be ready.

Lee sighed. "Sweet dreams."

The words pierced her heart, wounding her. Nhiari exhaled through the pain. She would lull him the way he had lulled her.

She counted in her head, trying to keep track of how much time had passed. After two hours she loosened the grip on the rock, allowing her hand to come open as if she'd fallen asleep. She couldn't discern any difference in his breathing.

At the next hour mark Lee snorted as if asleep and she held her breath, waiting for more. He shifted, but soon his breath was low and even.

Too easy.

He had to be faking.

She gave it another hour and clenched the rock again. No change in his breathing.

What were her chances? She opened her eyes a slit and glanced around without moving. Lee lay across the entrance, but there was space to get around him.

The rock felt heavy in her hand. As much as she disliked the man, she didn't want to hurt him, and hitting him over the head might do more damage than she wanted.

So maybe escape was the better option than restraining him.

The dirt would be a problem. It was more rocky than sandy and each step would make a noise. Stealth would work if he was asleep, but speed would give her the element of surprise if he was awake.

Maybe she should wrestle the gun from him.

She didn't really believe he would shoot her. Not unless he reacted in his sleep.

Stealth was her best option. If he was awake, she could use the stone and then run for it.

Bit by bit she shifted to a better position, waited for a response, and then shifted again. When she couldn't wait any longer, she crouched and then crept towards the entrance.

"Where are you going, Nhiari?"

She gasped. Damn him. He had probably been watching her with amusement, waiting for her to make her move. "To the bathroom."

He grunted and sat up.

"I can go by myself." She moved to the front of the cave, slipping past him.

"I'm sure you can, but I'd hate for you to get lost coming back."

The caring in his voice lured her. Stuff it. It was now or never. She hurled the rock at him and heard his satisfying yelp as she ran down the rocky slope, praying she didn't twist her ankle or trip on something in the dark.

Rocks clattered above her and she pushed herself harder as she hit the flat ground and put some bushes between her and Lee. Her heart raced as she darted left and then right, moving west, past where Lee had dumped the bike.

No time to disable it. She'd have to keep to thick shrub so he couldn't use the bike to catch her.

"Nhiari, you're not getting away." Lee was close behind her, not sounding at all puffed.

She kept running, tripping over a low shrub, and stumbling before picking herself up again and continuing to lengthen her stride.

Fingers brushed her top. No. She couldn't let him stop her. She jerked away and the movement shifted her off balance. She stumbled again and her ankle twisted, pain spearing through her. Nhiari yelled and fell hard, her wrists jarring as they stopped her from face-planting in the dirt. She gasped as the pain throbbed in her ankle.

Lee stopped next to her as she clutched her ankle and groaned. He kept his distance. "Did you hurt yourself?"

"Twisted my ankle."

"No offence, Nhiari, but I don't believe you right now."

She couldn't blame him. Not addressing the comment, she elevated her foot, placing it on top of her other ankle to give it a bit of height. She squeezed her eyes closed as her ankle throbbed. "I'm not going anywhere fast." She huffed out a breath.

"What were you hoping to achieve?"

"Escape, borrow a car to get to town, return with backup, and arrest your arse."

He chuckled. "Even if you had slipped away, I would have left the moment I noticed you were missing."

She knew that, but despite what he'd done to her, she hadn't been able to really attack him. Her thoughts were too emotional. That's what he did to her. It still hurt to know she'd been so easily manipulated by him. She couldn't reconcile the photographer with this killer in front of her. The one who'd done awful things to her friends, and who had killed people in the name of Stonefish.

"If you can't work with me, I'll have to tie you up until this is over." He sounded resigned, as if she'd disappointed him.

Arsehole.

But what were her choices? Continuing to try to escape wouldn't get her anywhere. She had to move from the hurt of the past and think like a police officer. What facts did she have?

He hadn't pulled a gun on her this time.

He'd asked for her help.

He seemed genuine in his need to stop Stonefish.

Why was that?

The question made her pause. She hadn't considered it before, hadn't wanted to believe he was telling the truth. But if he was, what had Stonefish done to him?

They were master manipulators, blackmailing people to do their bidding.

Had they done something to Lee or his family?

She breathed through the throbbing pain in her ankle, her thoughts clearing for the first time since she'd been captured. She glanced up at him. "Truce."

Though it was still dark, she could see the outline of his face. He stared at her for a long moment. "No more games? No more trying to escape?"

Nice of him to think she could escape with her twisted ankle. "No, but you have to share everything you've got with me."

It took a long minute before he said, "All right." He crouched down and touched her ankle.

She hissed, trying to pull it away, but he held firm.

"I'm checking how bad it is." He prodded it, and she forced herself not to kick him with her good foot.

"Are you a doctor now?" she snarked.

"I learnt some first aid when I was in the army."

She stilled. This was the first bit of information he'd volunteered. "Which army?"

"Singapore."

She shook her head. "There's no record of you in the Singapore army."

He let go of her foot and held out a hand to help her up. "Checking up on me?"

"Of course." She shifted to use her good foot and then clasped his hand and let him haul her to her feet. He was remarkably strong.

"My real surname is Kwong."

"How much of what you told me was the truth?"

"As much as I could." He moved his shoulder under her arm so she could use him as a crutch. The closeness was unexpected. How could he possibly still smell so good when he'd been living out here for months? He should stink, but there was a hint of eucalyptus and salt.

She inhaled again. Trees and ocean.

"I've got an instant icepack back at camp," he said. "We'll patch you up, get some sleep, and in the morning, I'll take you to my main camp. It's where I've got the information you'll want."

This time she would use him the way he'd used her and perhaps she could bring Stonefish down. "All right. Let's go."

Chapter 4

Lee prodded the lump on his head and winced. This is what he got for letting his emotions get in the way. Before Nhiari his focus had been absolute. His one goal was to end Stonefish. Now, things were… murkier.

He'd considered letting Nhiari go when she'd tried to sneak out last night. It would have been easier than having to be on his guard all the time, and the ranges were so extensive she wouldn't have caught him, but he hadn't been able to.

Some part of him wanted to prove himself to her. To show her he wasn't all bad. A delusional part of him was trying to convince himself they could have a future together when all this was over.

So he hadn't played any games, letting her think she'd got away before catching up with her. He'd come right out and spoken to her.

He hadn't expected to be pelted with a rock for his troubles.

Nhiari still slept, and that in itself was a miracle. He hadn't put much faith in her request for a truce. Probably wouldn't for a long time yet, but the fact she slept showed she trusted him to some degree. Or was regrouping.

After administering first aid to her ankle the night before, he'd convinced her to take his mattress and pillow and she slept curled on her side facing him. In her sleep her expression was calm. There were no furrows on her forehead or a downturn to her mouth. She seemed peaceful. Beautiful. Almost angelic.

He smiled. That would change when she woke, and he almost didn't want to wake her, but they needed to reach the next camp before too many people were about. He didn't want some random good Samaritan reporting they'd heard or seen a motorbike in the ranges that morning.

The sun's rays were a smudge above the ranges and bushes were getting more shape and colour.

He moved over to Nhiari but stayed standing a few steps away so as not to startle her. "Nhiari, it's time to wake up."

She snorted and her eyes scrunched but didn't open.

Cute.

"Wake up, sleepy head, or I might have to tie you up and leave you behind."

That got her eyes open, but she blinked sleepily, gazing up at him. The morning they'd woken together, a smile had crossed her face and she'd stretched lazily, wishing him good morning.

Today however, her brain slowly ground into action as she shifted away and sat up, her stare now wary and unsure. She flinched as she put weight on her ankle and the rest of the sleepiness vanished in the pain.

"Careful." He held out a hand to stop her from getting up. "You sprained your ankle, remember?"

She didn't respond but took the protein bar he handed her. He moved away, giving her space and time to wake properly. Was she always this slow in the morning, or was it because of the lack of sleep the night before?

He wished he had more experience of her waking in the mornings.

Lee cleared his throat and ate his own protein bar while she reviewed her surroundings and then prodded her ankle.

He joined her. The cold pack had brought the swelling down and compression and elevation overnight had helped. "How does it feel?"

"Not as bad as last night."

Good. "Keep it strapped at least until we get to the main camp."

"Is that where we're going?"

"Yeah." He'd already packed most of his gear, and when Nhiari shifted to a nearby rock, he packed her bed.

"How far is it?"

"Not far." He couldn't help himself. Giving her too many exact details may come back to haunt him. She tucked her food wrapper into her pocket and struggled to her feet.

He hurried over to help her, and she let him, pressing her soft body into his side.

He ignored the pleasure coursing through him. This could all be an act. "Can you carry the small backpack?"

Nhiari nodded and slipped it on. He grabbed the heavier one and paused at the slope down. It had been hard climbing up it last night with Nhiari's ankle unable to take any weight. "Maybe I should carry you down."

She glared at him. "I can make it on my own."

No, she couldn't. He glanced around, looking for a branch she could use as a crutch, but there was nothing suitable. "You'll need to lean on me."

Nhiari pursed her lips, examining the slope, and tugged on her braid. Finally she said, "Fine."

He slid his hand around her warm, lower back and

her fingers brushed his neck, sending tingles down his spine, as she moved her arm around his shoulders. Slowly they made their way down the decline to where they'd left the motorbike yesterday. He uncovered it and then swapped packs with Nhiari, putting the day pack on his front so that Nhiari could sit behind him on the bike.

She didn't cling, which was disappointing, but if she had grown up riding motorbikes, it wasn't surprising. Her hands gripped the underneath of the seat behind her, not even touching him.

He rode slower than he normally would, conscious of the extra passenger, not wanting a sudden jolt to unbalance her and for her to fall off. The journey took almost thirty minutes and the sun was well and truly above the horizon, but on this side of the ranges, there weren't any cars about yet.

He pulled into the small cave where he left his motorbike and switched off the engine. Nhiari was off the back almost before he'd stopped but grabbed onto the seat for balance as if she'd forgotten about her sprained ankle.

"Give me the pack." He'd decided not to leave anything behind in the bolt hole. People would search for Nhiari until she could call off the search and he wanted nothing they could stumble upon.

He hefted the pack onto his back and helped her to the entrance. "Wait here." He didn't wait to see if she obeyed him. She wouldn't get far with her ankle. Quickly he brushed out the tyre tracks, hiding their presence.

Nhiari perched like a sentinel on top of a rock at the entrance to the small cave. Stunning.

"It's a short hike in." Nothing he could do about that. "I can carry you, or you can use me as a crutch like we've been doing."

She shook her head, scanning the ground. "Pass me that." She pointed to a thick stick, which would be long enough to be used as a crutch.

He ignored the hurt at her not wanting to touch him. "Do you promise not to hit me with it?"

Her lips twitched in a smile, and his heart leapt in response. "Yes, I promise."

He handed it to her, and she ripped off the side branches to make her crutch.

Though he missed having Nhiari's body close to him, she seemed far happier with the stick, cautiously making her way over the terrain.

Lee took the lead through the bottom of the canyon. This pass had exits on both the west and east side of the ranges, as well as a canyon running south for a distance. Plenty of escape options should he be discovered.

Nhiari didn't speak as they walked, but as they reached a trickier section her grimaces of pain spoke volumes.

"Let me help." He stepped closer and she held up her hand.

"I can manage."

Her autonomy meant a lot to her. He scowled, but continued until she whimpered in pain and he couldn't stand it any longer.

"Either you let me help you as a crutch, or I carry you."

"How much further?"

"About the same distance as we've come."

She panted and he handed her a water bottle.

Nhiari gulped the liquid down and scanned the terrain. "All right."

He didn't smile, or show any signs of his elation in case she changed her mind. Instead he tucked the bottle back in his pack and slid his arm around her waist.

"Let's go."

It didn't matter that she didn't want to be near him. What mattered was they had a tentative truce which could hopefully blossom into a partnership to take down Stonefish.

After half an hour Nhiari came to a halt. "Where the hell is your camp?"

He smiled. "About another hundred metres." He pointed ahead to where the morning sun shadowed the rock.

She squinted, looked at him with suspicion and then moved towards it. He helped her over the last section, which had larger boulders. It had been hard navigating it in his four-wheel-drive. Finally they ducked into the shade of the cave.

Nhiari scanned the area, and nothing on her face gave away how she was feeling.

Lee tried to see it the way she would, ignoring the nerves which cared about her opinion. His one-room tent was set up at the back where it was out of any breeze that might blow this way. It was also the flattest area of the cave and while one door faced the front of the cave, the other faced the tunnel leading into the ranges. A small camp fire was set underneath a fissure in the rock which allowed the smoke to escape, and his four-wheel drive faced outwards, allowing him a quick getaway if needed.

What she didn't see was the car and the tunnel both had bug-out survival packs in them in case he was caught unaware. "It's not much, but it's home for now."

"It'll do." She sighed as she sat in his camp chair, which was next to the unlit fire.

Lee hesitated. This cave was larger than the one the boys had been in. "Will you be OK here? It's not too enclosed?"

Her eyes showed their appreciation. "It's bigger than a double garage. I'll be fine."

Good. He didn't want to have to move, but he would have.

He shifted a larger rock so she could elevate her ankle on it and then went to the fridge in the back of his car and got out two bottles of cold water.

He handed her one and she raised her eyebrows, impressed. "You really have everything you need. How do you keep it running?"

"Solar blanket." He pointed to the cord running out of the cave. Over his two months here, he'd never seen another person in this area, so he kept it uncovered.

"How do you restock?"

He pressed his lips together. She wouldn't like his answer.

"I thought you were going to share information with me," Nhiari said when he didn't speak.

He shifted closer and sat on a rock. "I will tell you, but I need you to promise me you won't take any action against them."

"For aiding a known criminal," Nhiari clarified.

Lee nodded.

"I can't guarantee that."

"You'll want to when you discover who it was."

Her stare was hard. "Georgie was helping you all this time?"

Georgie was the obvious answer. "No."

She sat back, thinking things through. Finally she asked, "Who then?"

"Your word she won't be mentioned in any of this." It was his one non-negotiable.

"I'll do as much as I can."

"No, your word, Nhiari. I can't risk her."

Hurt flickered across her face. "You want me to protect your girlfriend?"

"No!" Her hurt gave him hope she still might care for him. "I don't have a girlfriend. But this person means a lot to me."

She studied him for a long moment. "All right."

"Thank you." He took a breath. "Lindsay has been helping me."

Nhiari frowned for a split second and then sat straight. "Lindsay from the supermarket?"

"Yes."

"Why would she help you?" Her incredulity was clear. "She knew you were wanted by the police. There's no way Lindsay would break the law and go against Dot." Her voice rose and with it was defiance, as if she couldn't be wrong.

He hated to disappoint her again, but he wouldn't lie to her. It was time to tell her the truth. "Because of who my father is."

This time he saw all of her questions, but she simply said, "Start explaining."

He appreciated her attempts to control the conversation, to take back some of the power by not deigning to ask the questions. "Do you know much about Lindsay's past?"

Nhiari shook her head. "She's owned the supermarket since we were kids. Dot worked there from the time she was old enough to work. Never married, never had any kids." Her eyes widened. "Dot said she had one true love, but he couldn't marry her because he had family obligations."

Lee nodded. "That man was my father."

***

Nhiari gave herself a moment to absorb the information. Lindsay had been a constant in her life since she was young, and she'd given Dot hope and love when Dot had had none from her own family.

There was no way either of them would want Lindsay to end up in gaol.

But Dot would feel so betrayed by the woman she considered a surrogate mother.

Had Stonefish manipulated Lindsay like they'd manipulated so many other people? "Can you prove it?"

He pulled out a folder from his bag and handed her three photos. "These are my father and me."

The first showed a man in his twenties holding a toddler. Both had similar features to the man sitting across from her; same small nose, dark, rounded eyes, and a grin that was full of life and fun. She couldn't help smiling back.

The second photo was of both of them older; Lee was in his late teens and dressed in a military uniform and his father had grey in his hair. The smiles had faded. Both expressions were serious.

She glanced at him.

"Singapore has compulsory military service. That was just before I went in."

The last photo was much more recent. Both were dressed in suits. Lee looked much as he did now, and the suit fitted him to sexy perfection, showing his lean figure. His father's hair was grey and thinning and he'd aged significantly in the ten or so years since the previous photo had been taken.

"Tess's sister's wedding last year," Lee said.

That made sense. Tess was Ed Stokes' partner, and she'd been on the run from Stonefish earlier in the year. Lee had first become a suspect after Tess had recognised him at the Ridge, and then they'd realised they'd both been at the same wedding.

"I brought the photos to show Lindsay, so she knew I spoke the truth about who I was."

Nhiari passed the photos back. "Your father came

back at the beginning of the year and promised Lindsay he was leaving his wife and coming back to her." He'd broken her heart a second time when he hadn't returned.

Pain crossed Lee's face. "That was his plan. He told me when he returned to Singapore about how he'd fallen in love when he'd been backpacking through Australia. How he'd wanted to marry her and stay in Australia, but his parents had already arranged his marriage to my mother. He would bring great shame to both families if he was to refuse. The two families had been doing business together for generations."

"Stonefish," Nhiari breathed as everything clicked into place.

Lee nodded. "Father married my mother, and I was born a few years later."

"You've been part of Stonefish Enterprises since you were born?" He had to be high on the ladder if his father had married into the company.

"I knew nothing about the shady parts growing up. Dad worked a lot and Mother spent most of her time socialising and shopping. I was raised by a nanny, though Dad made as much time for me as he could. We'd do things just the two of us and he always encouraged me to try new things, wanted me to do well at school." He picked up a rock from the ground and rubbed the dust off it.

"What was your dad's role at Stonefish?"

"He headed the shipping side of the business. Paid people to look the other way when certain containers came into the harbour."

He might have been the person who had threatened Tess's family.

"Dad didn't want me to be involved. He encouraged my photography and suggested I could make a career of it." Lee sighed. "But Mother heard and they had a massive fight. She said my only destiny was to take over the family business. She made me swear I would do it."

How could any mother want her child to live a life of crime? "Did she know the truth?"

"I don't know. I don't think so. Dad never spoke about work at home."

"So, what did your dad do?"

"He waited until she went away for the weekend and told me the truth about Stonefish. He explained the history and said it wasn't a life he wanted for me. He had tried to escape when he went backpacking in Australia but hadn't been able to."

The wistful smile on his face tugged at Nhiari's heart. "How old were you?"

"Sixteen. It was just before I had to register for compulsory service. He knew the only way for me to escape Stonefish was to sign up for longer service. So that's what we planned."

A child still. "What did your mother and the other members of Stonefish do?"

"Mother was furious and wouldn't speak to either of us for almost a year. Uncle Lucas congratulated me on my service."

Lucas. It was the first time he'd mentioned that name. She didn't react, just waited for him to continue.

"I managed two rotations in the army before my mother put her foot down. She demanded it was time I learnt the family business." He sighed. "I had no excuse. I started learning the legitimate business."

Nhiari would love to arrest his mother for her involvement in this.

"Dad wanted to get us both out before I did anything illegal. He started building a case against the company, looking over the history to find different angles so we could both walk away without gaol time." Lee smiled. "My ancestor was a pearl diver on the

Retribution when it sank in Retribution Bay."

Nhiari's eyes widened. Everything came back to the damned ship sinking in the 1870s. The start of settlement in this area. She tried to remember what Tess had told her about the event. She had also been related to a pearl diver on the Retribution, but not part of Stonefish. "There were three pearl divers, weren't there?"

"Yes. Tess's ancestor, my father's ancestor and my mother's ancestor." His thumb rubbed the back of the stone. "Tess's ancestor went her own way, but the other two pooled the money they got from their portion of the treasure they found to start a shipping business out of Singapore."

The start of Stonefish Enterprises over a hundred and fifty years ago.

"When Dad was going through the old history, he discovered a journal written in Dutch. He had it translated and found it was from another ship that went down in Retribution Bay a hundred years before the Retribution did."

"The ship that was recently discovered?" There was a team from the maritime museum coming to document it this week.

He nodded. "It was the captain's journal and talked of more treasure he'd buried on the island. Dad thought if he could find it, we could both leave and start a new life somewhere else. He could come back for Lindsay, and I could do whatever I wanted."

Didn't they have enough money from their work with Stonefish? It all sounded a little too naïve for what she knew about the company. No way would they just let them go.

But the mention of treasure sparked a memory. Jordan had been kidnapped after allegedly taking a gold doubloon to school. She'd forgotten about it in her rush to find the boys. Chances were high the Stokes had already found the treasure. It was probably one more thing they had kept from the police. She would have words with her brother and their friends when this was all over.

"That's when Dad returned here to search and discovered Lindsay was still here."

All very romantic. Not at all like the cut-throat organisation she'd dealt with most of the year. "What happened?" Lindsay was very much still in Retribution Bay.

Lee stood and prowled around the space, circling the cave without saying a word.

Nhiari watched him, recognising the emotion of his movement though he was very contained, his steps measured, no arms waving.

He sat back down. "Stonefish murdered my father."

Nhiari's heart jolted not just at the news, but at the deathly cold way he spoke. She was momentarily speechless before her manners kicked in. "I'm sorry."

Lee glared at her. "Not as sorry as Stonefish will be."

Chapter 5

Lee fought back the anger and grief. He hadn't spoken about his father's murder to anyone except Lindsay before.

"How did they do it?" Nhiari's question moved him out of his anger. She didn't question his assertion but wanted details. She used her police voice and the no-nonsense tone helped to calm him further.

"Made it look like suicide—an overdose."

The note had been an excellent forgery, but the one thing they had missed was the way his father had always placed a full stop at the end of his signature.

"Mother ignored my request for a second opinion or an autopsy. Said it was shameful that my father was such a coward and I should stop looking for excuses." Stonefish had enough connections to ensure no one examined the body.

Nhiari raised her eyebrows, the only way she questioned him.

"He didn't take his own life. We spoke every day. Dad was determined to get back to Lindsay. He had so much Stonefish evidence on his computer."

Nhiari squeezed his hand in sympathy and her touch

soothed him. He smiled and turned his hand upwards so he could hold hers, but she pulled away.

Disappointment filled him. "Lucas told me if I continued my questioning, I would be as disappointing as my father. Mother agreed." He could read between the lines. It was a threat.

His own uncle had threatened his life.

So he'd bowed, apologised for his father's weakness and left.

Any remaining love for his mother had died that day. She hadn't seemed sad or scared, or worried, but perhaps she didn't know what Stonefish did. The women of the family weren't expected to work.

But Lee vowed he would avenge his father.

"Did your father share his evidence with you?"

"He refused to." No matter how much he'd wanted to help. "Said it was safer that way. Perhaps he was right and I would be dead if he had."

"Did you ever see it afterwards?"

He tossed the stone in the air and caught it. "No. I searched for his computer the night after he died. Went through his office while Mother was at her brother's place. It was gone, and the safe was empty. I couldn't find any traces of the captain's journal either, but he had given me a copy of the English translation." His muscles tightened and the stress from that day returned.

"So what happened next?" Nhiari's methodical questions calmed him a little.

He exhaled. "Mother and Lucas said it was time for me to take over Dad's position at the company. Lucas sat me down and explained the other side of the business. I was still hoping to avoid being involved, so I showed him the journal translation."

Nhiari frowned. "Why?"

"Because Lucas wants anything rare. He's already flown into space, he bought the most expensive place in

Singapore, he has so many cars he has to garage some of them on a separate property." He swatted a fly away. "Mother's the same. It adds to their status, gives them power and prestige to have things others don't. I knew Lucas would view the treasure as something he was owed." He was a hard-line businessman and a spoilt brat. Perhaps that was why Stonefish was so successful—Lucas didn't take no for an answer.

"Why?"

Lee almost smiled at Nhiari's digging. Trying to get to the bottom of it, trying to understand his dysfunctional family. "His identity is wrapped up in his history. He's proud about coming from pearl divers to being the most influential dynasty in Singapore. He thought his ancestors had been robbed of the rest of the treasure."

"So you brought this trouble to my town?" Nhiari's tone was mild, but her stare spoke of death.

He pressed his lips together. "I'm sorry. I thought Lucas would just send me to find the treasure, but after Bill and Beth refused to sell the Ridge to him, he expanded the business to the north. Saw it as a punishment for the town. He would take what no one would give him."

"I'm surprise Lucas trusted you."

"He didn't. Not at first. I was meant to be eyes and ears only. My mission was to find the treasure," he said. "But my goal even then was to end Stonefish. I made a lot of contacts during my years in the army. Some of those contacts went on to other roles and one of them, an Australian soldier, was an expert in tech. He went through my father's online presence looking for anywhere he might have stashed the files but found nothing." Lee stood and went into the tunnel behind the tent, retrieving the thick envelope he'd stashed there. He passed it to Nhiari. "When I introduced myself to Lindsay, she gave me this."

Nhiari opened the envelope and scanned the contents. Her eyes widened. "Are these your father's notes?" She traced his father's signature, tapping on the full stop.

"Yes. He mailed them to Lindsay with instructions not to open them, but to give them to me if I ever showed up at her door."

"That was risky, wasn't it?"

"No one knew who she was except for me." But he'd been stunned when he'd introduced himself to Lindsay and she'd flung her arms around him, hugging him and dragging him inside for a cup of tea. Then she'd produced the envelope and had said she would help Lee however she could. She'd won his undying loyalty that day as she'd shared stories of his father, and he had told her about his childhood.

Nhiari looked up. "All of this didn't help?"

"All the passwords had changed, and the rest, while useful, wasn't enough actual evidence to prove Lucas was behind it all."

"When did you become more than eyes and ears?"

He hesitated. "Clark gave me a couple of tests—pulling down the windmill at the Ridge and killing the sheep." Nhiari scowled and he continued. "The people he was blackmailing didn't have the skills, and he wanted me to get my hands dirty. But it was after I shot Tan Lewis that I proved myself to them." He had no qualms about shooting Tan. He'd threatened someone who was practically the Stokes's family, and he'd quickly realised the Stokes were decent people. They didn't deserve what had happened to them.

Lucas had thought he showed good initiative, particularly as Tan had brought police attention to Stonefish's more illicit dealings.

"Will you tell me everything from the beginning?"

Nhiari leaned forward a little, her eyes wide and beseeching.

He was a sucker for her eyes.

"From when you arrived at Retribution Bay," she continued.

The quiet question, not a demand, not in her police tone, surprised him, but it could also be her way of manipulating him. If only she knew he would tell her everything, if it wouldn't put her in danger. "It's a long story."

She smiled. "We've got plenty of time."

The whole truth would come out soon. "All right." He shifted to a more comfortable position. "When Bill and Beth refused to sell, Lucas ordered me to set up camp at the Ridge and find out whatever I could about the Stokes. He figured there had to be something he could blackmail them with." Lee shrugged. "It suited me. I could monitor things, and search for the treasure while pretending to be a landscape photographer. The Stokes had no problem with me exploring the property."

Nhiari scowled. "Who told Taylor to cut the brakes of Bill and Beth's car?"

Lee's gut clenched. "As far as I know, no one did." He had to clarify. "By that stage, Clark had arrived in Retribution Bay to set up the animal smuggling."

"Clark is Lucas's son?" Nhiari confirmed.

"Yes. When he demanded to know the information I had gathered, I mentioned Georgie had invited Bill and Beth to go swimming with the whale sharks."

"Who ran them off the road?"

"Clark." He closed his eyes briefly, remembering the rolled car, Bill and Beth inside it. His stomach clenched. Such a loss. "I left the Ridge not long after they did with the pretence I was going to take photos on the coast, but I was going to show Clark some areas to set up his animal traps. I came across the accident. Bill and Beth had died instantly, but Clark was at the scene making sure." Lee had wanted to kill the man right then, particularly when he'd smiled and said how pleased his father would be that he'd got rid of them.

Nhiari's gaze darkened with anger.

He held up a hand. "If they'd been alive, I would have done what I could to save them, I promise." He hoped she believed that much of him. "I told Clark to follow me and we hid the car in the ranges. It's still there. I can take you to it."

"You let him get away with murder and set up the animal smuggling?" Her anger showed in her clenched hands.

She would hate him for that alone. "I didn't have enough information on Stonefish by that stage. I took some photos of his car at the scene and then later after he was gone, but that was the start."

He continued, speaking about Lara's kidnapping. "You questioned me afterwards." It was the first time they had met. He'd seen her at Bill and Beth's funeral, but it had been Dot who had questioned him after their accident. He'd been enticed by Nhiari's buxom body and then enthralled with her intelligent mind. Lee hadn't had to act the bumbling fool, because he'd been so enamoured he'd almost forgotten his cover. He'd wanted to see her again.

"Did you orchestrate running into me in town the week after?" Nhiari asked.

He shifted on the hard rock. "Yes. I needed to find out whether you suspected me and how much you knew about Stonefish." He sighed as her expression shuttered. "But our date was the best night I've ever had. That wasn't faked."

"You played the awkward photographer. That isn't who you are."

"It is," Lee retorted. Or it least it would have been if his father had got his way. "It's just not all of who I am, who I've had to become."

She waved her hand as if shooing away a pesky conversation she didn't want to have. "What about when Tess arrived? Did you know who she was?"

"Yes. Tan sent me her photo, and I was told to keep an eye out for her. I knew she could send Tan to gaol, so I kept her whereabouts a secret, figuring they wouldn't think to look at the Ridge for her." He snorted. "Then Salvatore turned up and blew my cover. The man was an imbecile." It still grated on Lee, but he'd had to deal with it.

"And you shot Tan?"

"I had to. Ed had delusions of being a hero, and I was worried Tan would shoot Tess before Brandon got into position." He'd been trained to kill, but Ed would have agonised over taking a life.

"You mentioned it made Lucas trust you?"

"Yes. Tan was getting sloppy, hiring men like Salvatore, who couldn't be trusted. He also failed to buy the Ridge and was bringing attention to Stonefish, so it worked well. I protected Tess, and Tan was out of the picture."

"Where did you go?"

"Here." Lee gestured to his camp. "I had to stay to help Clark and search for the treasure." He shook his head. "Clark was getting ahead of himself, doing too much at once with the animal smuggling, drugs and gun smuggling."

She tapped her knee and glared at him. "Did you bring Dot's brother, Mark into it?"

***

Nhiari held her breath, waiting for Lee to answer her question. She had so many emotions swirling around and she didn't have time to sort through them yet, but somehow involving Dot's brother in his schemes seemed like a line in the sand.

Lee winced. "No, that was Clark. He thought it was hilarious to hire the brother of the sergeant-in-charge in Retribution Bay. I thought it was too risky."

She exhaled, though she wouldn't question why she felt so much relief. She shifted and bumped her ankle. The pain made her wince.

Lee stood. "Let me get another icepack and some painkillers."

She pressed her lips together, ignoring the rush of pleasure from him taking care of her.

He handed her the tablets and a bottle of water, then wrapped an instant icepack with a tea towel before gently pressing it against her swollen and bruised ankle.

She hissed, but the coolness did feel good. It took her a moment to realise he was still cradling her foot in his hands.

Her face heated. "Thanks. It's fine now." She bent forward to better balance the icepack so he didn't need to hold her foot and he shifted back giving her the space she desperately needed. She cleared her throat, not remembering what they'd been talking about.

"What kind of businessman is Lucas?"

"I never saw much of Lucas as a businessman. Growing up he was the uncle who only paid attention to me when he was telling me off or making fun of me. He liked his fancy things, and appearances were important to him, so I always had to watch what I wore and what I said in front of him."

It couldn't have been a great way to grow up. "And since you've been here?"

"Focused," Lee answered. "He wants to know all the details, but be involved in none of it."

That seemed strange. Surely he would give

instructions to ensure things didn't go wrong. Instead of asking, she changed tack. "So then Matt and Georgie came across the smuggling."

Lee nodded.

"What about Declan? Who involved him?"

He stared at her. "I did. We needed people on the ground to help. It wasn't difficult. Declan was tired of his job and wanted out."

"How did you know?"

"I went into Parks and Wildlife to get permission to go to areas off the main trails so I could take photographs. That way if people saw me poking around, they would know who I was, and that I had permission. I invited Declan out to dinner to thank him, and he was envious of my freedom. He was an easy mark. All he had to do initially was look the other way."

Initially. Right. "And afterwards?"

"His first paycheck was an excellent motivator. After that he started recruiting for us, getting friends to run interference if the police were getting too close."

Nhiari went on alert. "Which friends?"

Lee hesitated. "You can't share it with Dot. Not yet."

"Am I allowed to contact Dot?" she countered.

Lee nodded. "She has people looking for you. We need her to call off the search."

This was her chance to catch Lee. Nhiari and Dot had come up with a code back at the police academy, which they could use if either of them had been taken against their will. She could lead Dot to where they were.

She glanced at Lee, who was studying her.

But did she want to? Lee was filling in information they didn't know. Nothing so far that helped the case, but it filled in the blanks. What she needed was new information. "Tell me the names."

"Will you keep it quiet until I say you can tell others?"

She didn't like making promises to him. "As long as I don't think my friends and colleagues are in danger."

Was that approval in his gaze? "Kristy and Steven Hamilton."

Nhiari frowned. They were as close to a power couple as you could get in the small town. Kristy volunteered on different committees and Steven worked at the council, but they'd been having marital difficulties this year. Her eyes widened. "Those fights were faked?"

Lee nodded in approval. "Whenever you were getting too close, they would fight to draw you back to town and switch your attention. They also helped with small things like supplying Kurt with a drone, taking him out to the islands and hiding people when they drew police attention."

Nhiari had never liked Kristy's attitude, but she hadn't thought she would stoop so low as to put children in danger. Particularly because she loved her own so much.

It put a whole new perspective on the past month.

"Nhiari!" The call was faint, almost inaudible.

She jolted, her head whipping to the front of the cave. Lee strode to look out. "The SES are searching for you at the other end of the canyon."

Their gazes met. Decision time. Lee wasn't holding the gun. She hadn't seen a weapon since they'd arrived. She could get the searchers' attention and be home by lunch. Lee would melt away to another camp and she wouldn't see him until he was ready to be seen.

She glanced at the envelope in front of her.

The file of information still had many pages in it. But staying meant she had to spend who knew how many days with Lee. Could she do that and keep her emotions out of it?

She gritted her teeth. Now wasn't the time to let her feelings get in the way of stopping a crime syndicate. "Let me radio Dot."

"People are monitoring the police radio."

She and Dot suspected someone on their team was working for Stonefish too. "They won't know what I'm saying."

His stare pierced her, and she met it unblinkingly. Finally he nodded and went to his pack to get the radio. The exit was unguarded. It wouldn't take more than four steps to be out in the open and wave to get the searchers' attention.

Nhiari's feet twitched, but she stayed where she was and then switched on the radio. She took a moment to figure out what to say and then pressed the button. "Dot fifteen."

She waited for Dot's reply. "Dot eleven."

She switched the channel to thirteen and waited a moment for Dot to do the same before saying, "Heading to the waterhole at sunset."

"Want me to come with you?" Dot's concern was evident.

Lee watched her, waiting. Trusting she wasn't feeding Dot information.

"No, I need to be alone."

"You coming back tonight?"

Lee shook his head.

"No."

"I'll check the lighthouse is working."

There wasn't anything Nhiari could say to that, so she switched the radio off.

"You want to explain?" Lee asked.

"I told her I was safe and to stop searching. It will probably be a day before she calls off the search if we don't want anyone to be suspicious." But that didn't help them if the searchers found them before that. "Any ideas on how to lead them away?"

"Yeah. Stay here."

He moved to the back of the cave, disappearing into the tunnel.

Nhiari's mouth dropped open. What was he doing? Did he expect she would stay here when there was help right outside? Her heart ached and though the opportunity was there, she didn't shift.

He'd given her the Hamiltons' names, but she still had many more questions.

She wanted to trust him.

Wanted to believe the connection they'd had was more than manipulation, but she didn't have a great track record with men.

She clenched her hands as she remembered Rodney from the police academy. He stuck out the most in a long line of arseholes. She shook the thought away.

From a police point of view, Lee had information she needed. She glanced at the pack. Perhaps she should find her gun while he was gone. It would be good to be prepared, but would it ruin the trust he'd shown her?

Better if she asked for it back.

Another thought occurred to her. Was he running, not trusting she hadn't given their position away to Dot?

There were no more calls from outside and while she waited, she spent the time going through the envelope. Lee returned about twenty minutes later. He blinked as if surprised to still see her here.

"What did you do?"

"Called my contact. He'll radio and say they found traces to the west of the ranges."

"Who's your contact?"

He hesitated before saying, "Martin."

The only Martin she knew was… her mouth dropped open. "Senior Constable Martin Curtis?"

An incline of his head.

Son of a bitch. No wonder they were getting nowhere. Martin was working for the enemy. But the knowledge soothed the part inside her, which was beginning to think she and Dot were being paranoid. "How long?"

"Since the beginning of the year. He was pleased at the opportunity to pull one over Dot."

"Because she was promoted before him." It wasn't a question, but he nodded anyway.

What was it with men with huge, fragile egos? Rodney had been the same back at the academy. Why were they so scared of the female sex? "I look forward to arresting him."

Lee seemed somewhat amused by her statement, but he didn't comment.

Nhiari returned to the conversation. "What about those poachers?"

Lee shook his head. "They were a side business Declan had built for himself. I didn't find out about it until after everything that went down with Penelope and Sam. He should have known better than keeping it going with Sam involved."

"Sam worries you?"

"I know the type of men Sam, Brandon and Sherlock are. They're highly skilled and they're protectors. There was no way they'd be intimidated if one of their own was threatened. The Stokes have shown that repeatedly, and thinking any of them are going to behave differently is dumb."

At least someone from Stonefish realised that, but it appeared as if Lee was the only one who gave them any credit.

"The poachers actually worked for Clark, smuggling weapons."

Nhiari gritted her teeth. "Couldn't Clark just choose one thing?"

Lee chuckled. "Clark was always of the opinion to go big or go home. He took a cut from everything he did. He was an imbecile."

Yes, he was. "Who brought Kurt up here?"

"Lucas. He has dossiers on everyone close to the Stokes, and he found out Kurt was the type of man who would do anything for money. Lucas paid him to cause trouble up here and see if he could force Gretchen to spy on the Stokes for him."

But Gretchen had friends she could rely on.

"I'm assuming you caught Kurt," Lee continued.

"Yes. Just before we came out here." She shut her mouth with a snap, realising she'd offered information he hadn't known for sure. But that led right up to this moment. "What now?"

"Lucas is getting impatient and sloppy. He sent his other son to Retribution Bay to find the treasure."

Nhiari pulled out a notebook. "Name and description?"

Lee smiled with affection. "You don't need to worry about him. He's not much of a threat. He'd much rather be playing video games than spying."

"How well do you know him?" Perhaps it was a silly question as they were cousins, but they might not have spent a lot of time together.

"I've known Andrew since he was born. He's eight years younger than me, but the two of us would hang out at family gatherings, avoiding our parents as much as possible."

That was sad, but at least Lee had someone he could talk to. "Where can I find him?"

"He'll be on Sam's boat for the next couple of

weeks."

Nhiari's mind raced. How? The tour season had ended. Sam had mentioned something about being hired by the marine archaeologists who were studying the new shipwreck. "An archaeologist?"

"First-year student. Lucas made him take the course when the second ship was discovered. Andrew wasn't happy about it. They should have arrived yesterday." He moved over to the car and pulled out a couple of muesli bars, tossing Nhiari one. "Oliver Anderson is running the expedition."

Nhiari's head jerked up to stare at him. "Dot's Oliver Anderson?"

Lee nodded.

Shit. Dot wouldn't take that well. He'd broken her heart. Nhiari stood, wincing as she put pressure on her ankle. "I need to be there for her."

"Dot will manage. Lindsay will make sure of it."

He knew everything that was happening in the town. "Did you warn Lindsay?"

"Yes. Dot will be fine. Oliver was looking forward to seeing her again."

"You've spoken to him?" How was that possible?

"I went down to Perth to meet with Lucas and he asked me to take photographs of the expedition launch dinner. I spoke to him then. Oliver's a nice bloke."

He was, right until he'd broken Dot's heart. "He pretends to be."

"Sometimes we can't help the circumstances that are forced upon us, Nhiari." His intense gaze seared her soul.

She looked away. She couldn't let her guard down. Another thought occurred to her. "Is he working for Stonefish too?"

Lee sat across from her. "No, but Lucas knows about their history. He'll do what he can to manipulate them both, depending on the information Andrew feeds him."

"And you expect me to sit here, knowing all of this, and do nothing to help Dot?" Her hands clenched.

"No, I expect you to sit here, go through all the information with me to see if there's enough for a case, and help devise a plan to draw Lucas out so we can stop him."

She released her fisted hands. That she could get behind. "Let's get to work."

Chapter 6

Lee's muscles relaxed at Nhiari's acceptance. They were finally on the same page. He'd expected her to be gone when he'd left to make the phone call to Martin, but seeing her sitting there, waiting, had given him such a rush of relief. She'd stayed. Her reasons didn't matter right now, only that she was there, and he'd have time to convince her he wasn't the absolute villain she thought he was.

"Before we start, I want to check the searchers have moved on," Lee said. "Do you want to come with me?"

"Where are we going?"

"To the top of the ranges." He put two bottles of water into his daypack, checked he had his phone and a gun, and slung the pack onto his back.

She cocked her head in question but followed him to the back of the cave. He paused. "It's a tight squeeze. Will you be all right with that?"

She studied the gap. "How far is it?"

"About a hundred metres, but you can use the walls to help you climb."

She nodded. "I'll manage."

He moved slower than he normally would,

conscious that climbing around in hot, musty caves took a different level of fitness and Nhiari would be doubly disadvantaged with her ankle.

It took ten minutes to reach the opening. He paused, listening for any further calls from the searchers.

Some birds singing and insects chirping, and in the distance the wash of the waves against the shore. He peered out and scanned the surroundings slowly, looking for movement, shapes or colours which were out of place.

Clear.

He moved further out, scanned again, and then helped Nhiari to sit on a large boulder before retrieving the telescope he had hidden in a nook.

Nhiari gave a low whistle. "That's a pretty techie device."

"Allows me to see what's going on below." He set it up, pointing to the east, and scanned the ranges, taking particular notice of the canyon his camp was in. Some orange-clothed SES workers at the far end, moving their way out of the canyon.

Good.

He adjusted the focus and scanned further, looking towards the bottom of the gulf where the shipwrecks were. He smiled as he spotted Sam's boat anchored off Retribution Island. That meant Andrew was in town.

The telescope picked up people on the island. It was too far away to identify who they were, but he recognised the police boat pulled up to shore. They were picking up rubbish on the island. A blue barrel.

"Good," he murmured.

"What?" Nhiari asked.

"Dot's found the drugs."

"What drugs?"

Lee stepped away and gestured for her to look for herself. "It was another of Clark's side-projects."

"Doesn't Stonefish already have a drug operation set up?"

"They do, but Clark thought it would be another way of getting them in, where he'd get a bigger cut. His boat brought the drugs in with the guns, left the drugs in blue barrels which were submerged in the gulf, and then one of Clark's men would retrieve the drugs and distribute them throughout the north of Australia."

"Was it effective?"

"They had a few drops I knew of. Clark never told me what he'd set up with his men, so I didn't know when to check them to see if the drugs were there."

"Did you randomly check them?"

Lee shook his head. She wouldn't like this next bit. "Martin got Colin involved. Wanted the entire police station working for Stonefish so he could show you and Dot were incompetent. Colin checked them weekly for me and reported back if they were full."

Nhiari closed her eyes. "Colin too?" She sounded weary.

"The kid didn't know what to do. He worshipped Martin, so maybe Martin fed him some kind of line about being undercover. He was always very nervous when he reported back to me."

"And what did you do if they were full?"

"I stored it. I didn't have Clark's contacts, and no one knew what he'd arranged. It's another irritation for Lucas. I've made enquiries and found the chain Clark set up, but Lucas thinks I'm still working on it." He didn't want those drugs to end up on the market.

Nhiari ran a hand through her hair. "Organised Crime will be called up. They'll give Dot help. Is there something we can do from here?"

We. He glanced at her. "Nothing yet. The drugs aren't going anywhere and neither are Colin nor Martin. We have to focus on Lucas." He scanned the rest of the area to make sure no one was near.

"You going to tell me more about him than his name?" Nhiari asked.

Lee packed up the telescope and hid it again. "Yeah. I'll show you everything I have on the company, but there's nothing I can tie directly to Lucas. All of his men are terrified and will take the fall for him. Their families will be killed if they do anything else."

"Aren't you worried about your mother?"

"He won't kill his own sister." Of that Lee was certain.

Nhiari stared at him a moment and then nodded. "All right. Let's go."

***

Nhiari's stomach grumbled and she checked the time. Already past six and they'd barely made a dent in the information they were collating. She was impressed by the quality of data Lee's father had put together, but a lot of it was stuff that would need to be analysed by financial experts.

"I'll make dinner." Lee stretched and went to the back of his car. "I'm low on fresh food, so it'll have to be another MRE." He set his kettle to heat. "How's your ankle? Do you need more pain meds?"

Nhiari rotated her ankle and winced at the dull ache. "It's fine. I'll manage."

He retrieved a bottle of pills and brought them over. "You don't have to be in pain."

She stared at his outstretched hand for a moment before taking the bottle. "Thanks." She shoved down the appreciation and warmth.

"You're welcome." His gentle smile spoke directly to her heart and she cut off the connection, reaching for her water.

"Food won't be long."

He returned to his car and she exhaled. They'd sat side by side all afternoon and his presence was a constant pressure on her mind and body.

He'd been nothing but business-like but it was like his essence had encircled her, caressing her and reminding her of all the hopes she'd had after their first date.

Nhiari limped over to the cave entrance and turned her face to the sea breeze. Cool and constant, bringing a damp, saltiness inland. A welcome reprieve from the musty heat of the cave. Maybe in a couple of days when her foot was better she could convince Lee to go swimming so she could wash off the dirt and grime.

"Dinner's ready." Lee had already cleared space on the table and he placed the two bowls down.

"Thanks." She debated moving her chair so it was on the opposite side of the table, but then he'd know she was bothered by his closeness.

Instead she sat and took a mouthful of the satay chicken. Not the best she'd had, but it was surprisingly good. She'd eat quickly and then get back to work so they didn't have to talk.

"I read that book you recommended," Lee said. "The one with the assassin princess."

Shock and then sadness filled her at the reminder of their date. They'd shared so much and finally she'd found someone who loved reading as much as she did. She raised her eyebrows. "Didn't you say it was too young adult for your tastes?"

"I thought it would be, but it was pretty good."

"That's why I recommended it."

He grinned at her and she shoved another spoonful of the satay into her mouth to stop herself from smiling back.

"I particularly liked the ending with the big reveal on who the Great Khan was."

Excitement bubbled inside her. Hell. How was she supposed to keep her distance when he was talking about one of her favourite books? "You didn't pick it?"

"No." He sipped his water. "Of course then I had to read the prequel and the other two books in the series."

She bit her lip, but couldn't help herself. "Favourite character?"

"Kew, of course."

She waved his choice away. "Doesn't count. Kew's a dragon, she's everyone's favourite."

"Then I would say Shan."

Interesting. "Why?"

"Because despite the lack of control she has over what happens to her, she manages to succeed." He smiled. "Who was yours?"

Shan was her favourite as well, but admitting it felt a little too much like they were bonding. "Checheg."

"The fate of her people resting in her hands. It's a lot of responsibility."

Nhiari nodded.

"What should I read next?"

"There's hardly time to read novels right now." Oh, but she had a list she could give him. She pressed her lips together to stop herself from blurting out recommendations.

"You're right." He collected her empty bowl and cleaned the dishes with some wet wipes.

She ignored the disappointment. It wasn't often she found someone who was well-read. She loved discussing stories with others and getting their opinions.

Nhiari muffled a yawn.

"I tend to schedule my day with the sun," Lee said. "I go to bed when she does."

It made sense to save power, not having to run lights. "Sounds good."

"You can take the tent." He handed her a cup of

white tea.

She sipped and discovered he'd added a half teaspoon of sugar to it, just the way she liked. They'd only had tea together once, the morning after their date.

She closed her eyes against the barrage of emotion. It only made her vulnerable. She hardened herself. "No," she snapped. "It's your bed. I'm fine on the ground."

He studied her for a moment and then nodded. "Whatever you want."

What she wanted was for this to be over, to not have to fight the attraction and the memories of their perfect night together. She didn't want hope to rise again only to be shattered when she had to arrest him.

Leaving the tea on the table, she hobbled over and unrolled the thin mattress and removed the one shoe she still wore.

Then she lay down and closed her eyes. She needed distance and time to rebuild her walls.

Hopefully by the morning she'd be better defended.

***

Nhiari rubbed her hands over her face and then stretched, trying to work out the kinks in her muscles after two nights of sleeping on Lee's thin mattress. He'd offered her the thicker mattress in his tent on the second night as well, but she wasn't willing to sleep in his bed, even if he slept outside the tent. It was far too intimate.

That didn't mean she wasn't ruing her stubbornness now.

"We have to share this with Dot." They'd spent two days combing through Lee's father's notes and comparing them with the information Lee had gathered, and what Nhiari knew. They had filled a notebook and notes were spread everywhere. Lee stood and plugged his laptop into the battery system in his car to charge it.

"If we tip Dot off on who is working for the police, they'll know I've told you, and we're working together."

"She won't tell anyone."

He was quiet a long moment, a furrow on his brow, staring at the ground, an expression she now recognised as his thinking face. "We can tell her someone in her team is working for Stonefish."

"Can I give a name?"

He shook his head. "Not yet. Martin will know I'm working with you. He wanted to know what I'd done with you when I called him the other day."

"Did he seem worried?"

Lee scowled. "No, he was eager to find out if you were dead."

Nhiari flinched. She'd never been close to her colleague, but they'd had a good working relationship. "What did you tell him?"

"I was manipulating you for information and keeping you as a bargaining chip."

Wonderful. "He believed you?"

"Yes. I have a reputation after all."

She didn't know what to think. People had used her in the past, but he'd been open about the information he was sharing. Still, using her as leverage could always be an option down the line if things didn't go his way. They hadn't discussed what would happen when they caught Lucas. They were on opposite sides of the law.

She would need to arrest him when this all came to a head.

Uncertainty shimmered in her stomach. Despite her attempts to keep her defences up, he kept wearing them down. She'd lost count of the times their hands had brushed, or she'd bumped into him after losing her balance. It didn't help that he'd not allowed her to prepare a meal, and it felt as if he was taking care of her. Each night she'd vowed to keep him out, and each day he charmed her with the little things he did.

Stupid.

"I need a break." She pressed her chair back and stood. It had been a long couple of days, and she still wore her police uniform, having refused to wear the clothes Lee had offered her. It seemed too intimate, but now she wished she'd agreed, because she smelled. She climbed the path to the top, her ankle healed enough to put some weight on it now without much pain. At the entrance, she scanned the area out of habit. The search for her had been called off yesterday, but someone might still be around.

She inhaled deeply as she took in the view. Red dirt, grassy shrubs, a few small trees and the endless ocean below her.

No one.

The long ranges had been a constant companion for her whole childhood, always on the horizon somewhere, the turquoise water and reef her friend, even the tiny birds which flitted from bush to bush reminded her of a story from her past. This was home, her land, her place.

The sun headed towards the ocean, ready to end its day's work.

This was why she was working with Lee. She had to make her country safe again. Had to stop Stonefish from hurting her town.

The crunch of rock behind her indicated Lee had joined her. She didn't turn. Instead she watched the few clouds on the horizon change colour to pinks and purples as the sun sank closer to the horizon. The end of another day, and while the picture was coming into focus, there was no clear path how they could put Lucas away for good.

When the sun disappeared below the horizon, Lee spoke. "How about we go for a swim?"

She glanced at him, wishing the sound of his voice wasn't like a caress on her skin. "Is that your way of telling me I smell?"

His lips twitched. "No. I thought we could both do with a break and I always feel better after swimming. I know of a remote spot on the coast."

She nodded. It sounded like heaven, but there was somewhere better than the ocean. A place few people knew about. A place which brought her peace.

Would taking Lee there ruin the place for her?

"Maybe we can get Lindsay to provide some clothes for you at the next drop off," Lee added.

Nhiari glanced at him. "She could get them from my house."

"No. Someone may be watching it. No one knows about my connection with Lindsay and I won't put her in danger."

His loyalty struck a chord with her. "All right."

She followed him back down the tunnel to the cave but lagged behind. Lee could do it in the dark, but she was still learning the path and her ankle slowed her. Nhiari was about ten metres behind when he yelled.

Fear spiked as voices rose over the unmistakable sounds of fighting. Shit. Who had found them?

She hurried forward, peering into the entrance to take stock of the situation. There was still a faint glow from last light, and she spotted Lee grappling with an older man with dark skin. Her mouth dropped open, and she moved forward as her father yelled, "Where is my daughter?"

He had Lee in a head lock and at his words, Lee stopped fighting back.

Nhiari ran forward. "Dad! What are you doing here?" Her heart lodged in her throat, but whether it was fear for Lee or her father, she wasn't certain.

Lee's face was changing colour.

"Nhiari?" Her father glanced at her but didn't loosen his hold, as if confused she was standing there in front of him.

"Let him go, Dad. You're choking him."

"He kidnapped you." But he loosened his grip and Lee sucked in deep breaths.

Lee could get out of the hold and hurt her father, but he didn't. He merely watched her and waited. "Dad, we're working together. Let him go and I'll explain."

Her father studied her a long moment before letting go of Lee and stepping back. Lee rubbed his throat and turned to face his attacker.

"It's nice to meet you, Mr Roe."

Her father grunted. "Explain, Nhiari."

"How did you find me?" Nhiari asked, still not quite believing her father stood in front of her in glorious outrage.

He snorted. "I can follow a track, though he made it difficult, which is why it's taken me so long. What's going on here? If you're all right, why haven't you called your mother? She's frantic."

Nhiari smiled. It was so like him to say it was her mother worrying.

Lee brought over a camp chair and handed him a bottle of water. "Would you like to sit?"

Her father squinted at him with suspicion but took the water and sat.

"Lee did kidnap me, but we've come to an agreement." She hesitated. He knew nothing about Stonefish. "We're working together to stop a group who are doing bad things in Retribution Bay."

"Are you safe with him?"

"Yes," Lee answered. "I won't hurt your daughter, Mr Roe. You have my word."

Her father stared at him for a long moment. "I don't know you. I don't know what your word is worth."

Nhiari appreciated her father's candour. "Lee saved Matt's life a couple of months ago."

Her father raised his eyebrows, but to stop him asking more questions she continued, "I'm sorry I didn't call." She should have, or at least asked Dot to phone them.

"Your mother has been worried out of her mind, and Matt has been too."

Matt knew more of what was going on, so she wasn't as concerned about him. "Truly, Dad. I'm fine. Dot knows I'm safe, which is why she called off the search."

"Why didn't she call us?"

"She's been busy dealing with some issues this group has thrown up," Lee said.

"And who are you in all of this?" Her father demanded. "Why did you take my daughter?"

"Because Nhiari is tenacious and she would have continued searching for me until she found me." He smiled. "Not unlike her father."

He grunted, but his lips curved upwards.

"I've been working for this group, but only to stop them," Lee continued.

Nhiari was surprised he admitted that much.

"You working undercover? You a cop or something?"

"I was military, but this is personal."

"How?"

Nhiari limped over to lean against a rock, enjoying her father giving Lee the third degree. If she was honest, what impressed her the most was that Lee treated his concerns seriously and didn't just brush him off.

"The man in charge murdered my father."

Her father pursed his lips and then nodded. "All right." He glanced at her. "Why are you limping?"

"Twisted it on a rock," she replied. "It's almost healed."

He moved over to her and lowered his voice, shifting so Lee couldn't see his lips. "Are you really OK? Do you have a safe word you need to tell me so that I know you're not being coerced?"

She chuckled. "I'm really fine, Dad. Lee's my best chance to stop these people."

"Do you trust him?"

The question made her blink, but the answer was more surprising. She looked at Lee. "Yes, I do trust him."

Lee's lips quirked up, and he inclined his head a minute amount.

"What do you need me to do?" her father asked, turning back to involve Lee in the conversation.

"Nothing," Lee answered before she could. "If you get involved, you'll put yourself and your family in danger."

"More than Matt and Nhiari are?" he countered.

"They're not interested in Matt anymore," Nhiari said. "And they think Lee is manipulating me. If they find out you're helping us, you put yourself and Mum in danger."

"So I'm meant to leave you here with him and do nothing?" He bristled.

Nhiari put a hand on his shoulder. "You trust me to do my job, just like you always have."

"I don't like it."

"I know." She thought about it. "You could keep an eye out for anyone on our land who shouldn't be. Message me and tell me where and we'll check it out."

"You think they're using our land again like they did with the animal smuggling?"

"They might be."

"But don't approach," Lee said. "If they see you, they may hurt you."

Her father scoffed. "You didn't see me coming."

"No, sir," Lee agreed.

"Do you need any food or water?" Her father turned to Nhiari.

"We're good," Lee answered for her.

When he continued to look at Nhiari, she nodded. "We are, Dad. Do you want a lift home?"

"I won't risk you breaking your cover for me. It's a nice evening for a walk. I'll call your mother and let her know you're safe and she can pick me up away from here."

Nhiari helped him to stand and then hugged him. "Thanks for coming after me, Dad."

"Always." He squeezed her. Then he eyed Lee. "If any harm comes to my daughter, I'm coming after you."

Lee held out his hand. "I would expect you to."

Some kind of man speak went on between the two of them as her father clasped Lee's hand and they both nodded. Nhiari rolled her eyes. She wasn't a child.

Still the little girl of her past would have been thrilled to have two men protecting her. Not that her father hadn't when she was at school. He hadn't known about her troubles.

"How long will this take?" her father asked.

"I'm not sure, Dad. A few more days at least, maybe a couple of weeks."

He scowled but kissed her cheek. "Take care, child."

She walked him to the entrance of the cave and watched him walk away. She smiled, her heart full at the way he moved through the bush without a sound. When the darkness swallowed him, she turned back to the cave. Lee was rubbing his throat. "Did he hurt you?"

"I'll live," Lee answered. "He took me by surprise as I walked out."

"Thank you for not hurting him."

"When I realised he was your father, I couldn't."

She wasn't digging further into that comment. Instead she switched on a light and went over to the table where all their information was spread.

Lee placed the gas cooker on his tailgate and started preparing dinner. From the looks of the food he retrieved, it was something with ramen. "Do you need a hand?"

"No, I've got this. We might need to move tomorrow, though."

"Dad won't tell anyone where we are."

"I need to pick up more food and check in with a couple of people, anyway."

Which reminded Nhiari. "You said I could call Dot."

"Tonight, after she's had time to get home." He didn't look at her as he said it.

"How do you know she's not at home?"

He continued to prepare dinner.

"Lee, what are you hiding from me?" She moved over to him.

He sighed. "There's a tracker on her phone."

"How?" Dot always kept her phone with her.

"Martin sent something to her that allowed it to be installed." He still wasn't looking at her.

Unease crept onto her skin. "And my phone?"

He faced her. "Remember that funny video I messaged you?"

"The cute bulldog puppy one?" It had made her smile and brightened what had been a really shitty day.

"Yeah. Watching it installed the same tracking software on your phone."

"So you've known where I was at all times over the past few months?" Her skin crawled at the idea someone was following her.

"Your location only, not who you were with or what you were doing. It made it easier to arrange for Kristy and Steven Hamilton to distract you."

"Who had access to the data?" she demanded.

"Only me. Martin wanted it, but I refused to give it to him."

Small mercies. The idea of Martin tracking her was unsettling. But why didn't she feel the same way about Lee? She refused to follow that line of questioning. Instead she asked, "So you knew I was coming for the children?"

"Yeah."

"Why didn't you move?"

"Because I wanted Jordan and Cody to go back to their families."

It still made no sense. "Why didn't you leave them before we arrived? You could have left them in the cave, waited from a distance until we found them, and then disappeared."

He dished up the noodles and handed her a bowl. "Because I didn't know if Martin would be with you. It could have been another test by Stonefish. Then Georgie turned up and distracted me before I could leave."

Nhiari stared at the food. He'd been tracking her. For months he'd known exactly where she was if he cared to look.

It felt like such a violation of her privacy.

"So tell me again, why should I trust you?"

Chapter 7

Nhiari's tone was mild, but her eyes sparked fury. Inwardly Lee winced. He should have known his confession wouldn't go down well. Now wasn't a good time to tell her about the other ways he kept track of what was going on in Retribution Bay.

"I'll do whatever it takes to stop Stonefish." He tried to keep the defensiveness out of his tone.

"Including seducing a police officer?" The blunt statement didn't hide the thread of hurt in her voice.

Shit. He stepped forward and she stepped back.

Damn it.

He never had the right words when he really cared. His mother had discouraged him from sharing his feelings. But for Nhiari he'd try. He sat to give her space and stirred his noodles. "I've already admitted I asked you out hoping to get information, but I promise you, that's not how it ended. That night meant a lot to me."

She glared at him and limped to the other side of the cave.

"You told your father you trusted me." He would hold on to that admission.

"I trust you not to kill me," she retorted and glanced over her shoulder at him. "I'm useful to you."

"You're more than that, Nhiari." He hesitated. Telling her the truth would give her the upper hand over him. Was that wise? When this was over, he would be behind bars. Perhaps it was better for her if she still saw him as a villain.

"What was that night for you, Lee?" It was a quiet request which demanded the truth.

His heart ached, and he answered the plea before he could think better of it. "A revelation." It sounded trite and Nhiari's snort made it clear she thought so too. "I've not had a lot of practice putting my feelings into words."

She shifted to face him. "I'm listening."

Those two words resonated with him and all his caution slipped away. He didn't want to be the villain. Not with her. This might be the only chance she gave him. "We met at the brewery and I remember walking in, telling myself I was only there for the information you could provide." He shook his head, amused at how stupid he'd been. "It was a gorgeous night, the perfect temperature and a clear sky with so many stars above. Some low, chill music was playing, and I spotted you sitting at a table, the fairy lights above you and you were stunning. The brown top that made your eyes deepen like pools of chocolate and those jeans…" Like they'd been painted on.

Nhiari lowered herself onto a rock on the other side of the cave.

"You wore a manta ray necklace that drew my eye right to your chest."

"So you found me attractive." Her statement was unimpressed.

Lee shook his head as panic threatened to take control. "No, I found you beautiful, stunning…" He couldn't find the right word. "Perfection."

She flinched and shoved a mouthful of the noodles in her mouth, chewing quickly as if she wanted to end this conversation. He hurried on. "Then we started chatting, and it was as if we were two old friends getting together after not seeing each other for a while. We just clicked. I know you felt it too. There were no awkward silences, and we had a lot in common."

She stared at him. "You still brought up my work."

He nodded. "It was a struggle. I felt awful doing it, but I still needed to stop Stonefish." It had been the first time he'd questioned whether what he was doing was the right thing.

"So you slept with me."

Irritation bubbled through him. Why wasn't she hearing what he said? "I didn't sleep with you for information," he snapped. "I slept with you because I never wanted anything more in my whole life. You might not have realised it, but you captured me that night. From that moment, there was no way I could hurt you or anyone you cared about." Idiot. He was saying too much. He was giving her control over him. Did she understand?

He couldn't read the emotion on her face. She exhaled, but her mask didn't shift. "I didn't realise I was that good at sex." She finished the last mouthful of her noodles. "You promised me a swim. Let's go." She placed her bowl on the rock next to her and hobbled out of the cave.

Lee rubbed the ache in his chest. He'd hurt her just like so many other men in her life. She'd whispered her past pains to him in the dark after they'd made love.

The boy who'd dumped her after she'd given him her virginity. The taunts and teasing about her body when she'd matured faster than others. The man at the academy who had made her life hell after she'd turned down his advances.

Hindsight was a bitch. Lee shouldn't have spoken about how beautiful she was. He should have talked about the connection between them, the way he'd felt no one had ever listened to him before, the feeling he'd found his missing piece. He should have told her about his desire to hunt down those who had hurt her and make them sorry.

With a sigh, he grabbed a towel and a change of clothes for them both and followed her out of the cave and into the night.

***

Nhiari's ankle was nothing compared to the ache in her heart as she made her way down the slope to the motorbike. She would have preferred to take the four-wheel drive, but she had a desperate need to go to her waterhole and settle the emotions swirling around her. The motorbike would get them there.

She got on, glancing behind her as Lee said, "I'll steer."

She shook her head. "I know a better place for swimming."

He hesitated and she felt his doubt. Would he trust her?

Almost before she'd finished the thought, he said, "All right." He slid on behind her and placed his arms around her waist.

She closed her eyes as his warmth seeped into her. This was far closer than she wanted to get to him right now. She swallowed hard even though he kept his hands still.

She turned the key and the roar of the engine helped to clear her mind. On auto-pilot, she headed south.

He spoke about caring for her, but he'd started with her body. As if realising his mistake, he'd tried to regroup and mention the connection he'd felt, but they were just words he spoke hoping to seduce her.

He wouldn't sway her with his declarations of being caught, no matter how much her heart had yearned when he spoke those words.

Talk was next to impossible over the noise of the engine. It was a short trip, covering the couple of kilometres to the creek which flowed through the canyon.

The only person she'd brought here was Dot. Few people knew about it as there was no four-wheel track in and no hiking trails. The waterhole only contained water at certain times of the year, but the massive storm they'd had a few weeks ago would have filled it.

The silence seeped into her and so did her first wave of doubt. This was a bad idea. She'd always run here when she'd needed peace, but now Lee would be one of her memories.

Foolish.

Perhaps she should turn around and head to the beach. Before she could suggest it, Lee was dismounting.

Though she knew she would regret this, she set down the stand and got off the bike.

It was easy to see in the moonlight, and she picked out the rocky path that led to the water. She didn't speak, knowing Lee would follow her. Carefully she picked her way across the rocks and around a bend where her waterhole stretched between the canyon in all its glory.

Lee's sharp intake of breath was satisfying. He hadn't found her place in his exploration of the ranges.

The water was a still hole in the darkness, with the moonlight glistening off one edge. She inhaled deeply and allowed the air to soothe her aching heart.

Here she would find the strength to harden her heart

against Lee and put Stonefish away for good.

She sat and pulled off her boots and socks, then hesitated. She hadn't considered what she would swim in. Her clothes needed a wash, and while the fresh water would remove the smell, there was nothing like the feel of the water on her skin.

She loved skinny-dipping. She glanced at him. Though it was night, there was enough light to make out facial expressions and bodies.

Though perhaps this was her opportunity to play him like he was trying to play her. Show him his words meant nothing to her.

"I brought you a shirt to swim in." He held it out to her.

What was worse—wearing a shirt which smelled like him, or being naked in front of him?

He'd already seen her naked. But wearing his shirt seemed so much more intimate. The brush of the fabric against her skin, being surrounded by his scent, every breath reminding her of their night together.

No. She couldn't do it.

"I'll manage." She turned her back to him and unbuttoned her shirt, leaving it on the rocks before taking off her pants as well. Dressed in her underwear, she slid into the water.

She closed her eyes as the cool water washed over her.

Bliss.

It had been days since so much water had touched her skin. Nhiari swam a few strokes underwater before surfacing and brushing the strands of hair which had escaped her braid out of her face. She kept her shoulders underwater, watching as Lee stripped out of his pants and shoes and changed into a pair of swimming shorts.

She was too far away to see the definition, but she

knew from experience that his body was hard and lean. Nhiari had asked him about it. The bashful photographer didn't seem to be the type to work out at the gym, but he'd said he had to be fit to hike the locations to get the photos he wanted.

It made enough sense, and she hadn't complained. Now she knew it was from his time in the military.

Her fingers untied her hair and then untangled the braid, letting the water run through it and wash it. Then she rubbed her skin, removing the dirt and dust as Lee slipped into the water.

Perfection.

Her thighs tightened. It was only attraction. A physical reaction beyond her control. What she could control was whether she would act on it, and in this case it was a resounding no.

"Feeling better?" Lee asked.

"Yes." She wouldn't lie, but neither would she gush about how amazing the cool water felt against her skin. The less she shared with him, the less he could manipulate her.

He ducked under the surface and then brushed the water back from his hair, the rest of it cascading down his skin.

Nhiari looked away and scanned the area. The water level was high. Much of the runoff from the storm collected here and had had time to settle to form the large waterhole. It would shrink through summer sometimes to almost nothing, before the rains would fill it again.

This was what she was fighting to protect.

"This place is beautiful." Behind her Lee splashed, probably washing himself as well.

"It's not always this full." Did he realise it was her special place she'd told him about during their night together?

Before she'd discovered Lee was working for Stonefish, she'd imagined bringing him here, swimming with him. In her daydreams, they'd camped nearby and she'd shown him places he could photograph and they'd spend their nights making love.

She had fallen just as hard as he claimed to have, but her trust regarding men was non-existent. She wished she could talk to Dot about it.

How was Dot coping with having her ex back in town? Dot had completely fallen apart when Oliver had chosen a job overseas instead of staying with her. Nhiari had been desperately worried, but she hadn't understood the depth of Dot's feelings until Lee had betrayed her.

Instead of collapsing, Nhiari had vowed vengeance. But only a couple of days with him and her conviction was fading.

"Have you started taking lessons from your mum?" Lee asked.

She squeezed her eyes closed and gritted her teeth. She'd hoped he'd forgotten everything she'd told him that night.

"You wanted to learn basket weaving, right?"

He knew he was. Nhiari had felt so comfortable with him she'd told him her regrets. She'd never embraced her indigenous heritage because she'd been teased mercilessly at school. She'd refused to listen to the lessons from her mother about gathering food and basket weaving, not wanting to acknowledge that aspect of who she was. Her mother had been disappointed but hadn't pushed.

Now she was older, she wished she knew more of her heritage. The Bayungu had a joint agreement with Parks and Wildlife to manage the land here and while Nhiari protected the people, she wanted to know more about protecting the land as well.

She couldn't ignore him. "Mum's been teaching me, but I haven't had a lot of free time lately." She swam back to where she'd left her clothes and dragged them into the water to wash.

"Are you enjoying it?"

The information couldn't be useful to Stonefish. "Yes."

"I'm glad. You sounded so sad when you told me about it."

Her heart squeezed. "Don't," she beseeched.

"Don't what?" His question was calm.

"Don't pretend you care."

"It's not a pretence, Nhiari."

"When this is done, I have to arrest you, Lee." Which would leave her in the same position as when she'd learnt of his deception. Heart-broken.

"Both of the people I killed were in the defence of another person."

"And what about the rest of it?" Nhiari demanded. "The drugs, the enlisting people for Stonefish, killing the Stokes' sheep."

"It's all part of stopping them. Will the case I've built against Stonefish work in my favour?"

She didn't know, but he had a good point. She shoved away the hope. This could all be part of his manipulations again. And she wasn't ready to forgive him.

Lee shifted close enough to touch her but kept his hands by his side. "When I started this, I saw nothing past avenging my father. I didn't care what happened to me. But my focus shifted after that night with you. I realised there was something I wanted more—you. I've done everything since then to protect you and those you care about."

His words were seductive, a temptation she desperately wanted to accept. She longed to reach out and touch him, to hold him in her arms again.

He didn't move any closer, waiting for her response to his words. His patience made her want him even more.

"Lee…" She didn't have the words, didn't know what she wanted to do. Her heart screamed to forgive him, and her head reminded her of all the ways Stonefish had manipulated people in the past. "I can't. Not yet."

Lee nodded. "I'm here when you're ready."

Those words. They shouldn't mean so much. Having someone there to wait for her, who wanted her enough to wait until she was ready. She couldn't trust them yet. Not with how she'd been let down by him and others in the past.

"We should get back. I need to call Dot." She waded to the shore, enjoying the cool night air on her wet skin.

Lee hurried ahead over the rocks and handed her a towel, which she used to dry herself, unable to resist inhaling his scent. After she'd spent some time drying her long hair, she wrapped the towel around herself. Lee held out the T-shirt and shorts he'd offered her before the swim.

She hesitated. It made no sense to put on her wet police uniform, especially not with how refreshed she felt. With a sigh, she took the dry clothes and dressed, using the towel to shield her as she removed her wet underwear. Folding everything and wrapping her wet clothes in the towel, she placed them in the backpack Lee held out to her.

They didn't speak on the short ride back to the cave and once inside, Lee handed Nhiari her phone. "You'll get better reception up the top."

She hesitated. He was giving her the freedom of speaking to Dot without him listening. "Do you want to come too? She might have questions I can't answer."

He gave that small smile of his and gestured for her to lead the way.

What did she need to tell Dot? Some of the information she couldn't share yet, but the biggest thing was to make sure she understood Nhiari was fine. The last thing they needed was for Matt to turn up looking for her as well.

The number rang briefly before Dot answered. "Nhiari." Dot's concern came out in a whoosh of her name.

Nhiari switched on the speaker so Lee could hear. "I'm fine. I'm working on something with Lee, but no one can know."

"It's a dark night."

Nhiari smiled at the code. "But the stars are shining."

Dot's exhalation was loud in Nhiari's ear. "You went willingly with him?"

Nhiari laughed and exchanged a smile with Lee. "I wouldn't say that, but it's fine." They had little time, in case someone from Stonefish was tracing her call. "I think someone on our team is working with Stonefish."

"Yeah. I spoke with the Stokes last night and they filled in some blanks. I'm collating the information now."

That could be useful. "Can you send it to me? I can't keep my phone on for long in case it gets tracked, but we should share information." Or at least as much as she could share.

"Yeah. Is there somewhere I can drop a hard copy?"

"Hang on." She placed her hand over the speaker. "Can we head closer to town tomorrow?"

"I've arranged a supply drop near the lighthouse."

Perfect. "How about at the lighthouse?"

"I'll watch the sunrise tomorrow."

Which meant it would be there nice and early. "All

right. We're close, Dot. It won't take long."

"Take care—oh, and call your parents. Matt says they're frantic."

Nhiari smiled. "Will do." Dot didn't need to know her father had already found them. She hung up.

"Shouldn't you have asked her where she would leave it?" Lee asked.

"No need. We used to leave each other notes when we were kids. It was our special message place."

"You and Dot are close."

It wasn't so much a question as a statement which asked for her to provide more information. Nhiari's warning system buzzed. Did it matter if he knew the details of their relationship? He knew enough to know she would protect Dot with her life, so anything else she shared was a sign she was opening up. If this was manipulation, perhaps she could play too.

"She's been my best friend since pre-primary. We'd hang out at school together and as much as we could after school, but it was difficult with me living so far out of town." Neither of their parents liked them spending too much time chatting on the phone, and they didn't have mobile reception at Nhiari's house. That's why they used to leave each other letters at the lighthouse. "When I got older, I'd take the motorbike and meet her at the lighthouse. There was a track which ran all the way along the ranges. Or sometimes her brother would pick me up and take us both to the beach to swim."

"You mentioned Dot stuck up for you," Lee said.

There were a couple of kids who would make fun of her because of her indigenous heritage. Her clothes were always well-worn, and it was when her parents were involved with getting recognition that the land they lived on was Bayungu land.

Some people felt threatened by it, as if the Bayungu

were going to steal their houses, not recognising the irony of that was exactly what the British had done to all the native people of Australia. Those people's children parroted their parents' ugly words to Nhiari. Matt had been younger and by the time he was old enough to understand, things had settled.

But Nhiari remembered the slurs and vitriol that had spewed from the older children. It was why she'd refused to learn about her culture, not wanting to be any more different than she already was.

"We were a team," Nhiari said. "She had parents who were indifferent to their children, and I had the town kids who were cruel. We supported each other."

She stared up at the night sky, finding the familiar constellations. "The emu is dark tonight."

"Don't you mean bright?" Lee asked.

"No, it comprises the dark areas of the night sky, not the stars." She pointed it out to him.

"Oh, that's right. Ed mentioned something about it to me when he took me stargazing."

A reminder the Stokes had welcomed him in as a friend before they had discovered his allegiance. How would they react to him now? Georgie was pro Lee, but how the others felt was an unknown. "Did he tell you the story that goes with it?"

"No."

Nhiari closed her eyes, bringing back the words of her mother. "Many groups have a story about the emu in the sky. Ours tells us when the right time is for us to take different foods from the land." She explained further.

"I imagine you can see a dozen things around us we can eat," Lee said.

Nhiari frowned. "Not as much as I would like to."

When all the mess with Stonefish was done, she would learn.

She scanned the sky and inhaled, breathing in the night air. Dark and peaceful. It would be easy to pretend there was nothing beyond this moment and the rest of the world didn't exist. Especially if she ignored the fact Lee was a wanted criminal.

But there it was.

The truth surrounded her, and she couldn't ignore it.

She stood. "We should get some sleep." She didn't wait for his comment and made her way slowly through the tunnel back to their camp site. Nhiari yawned and eyed the bedroll she'd been sleeping on. Her whole body protested at the thought of sleeping there again tonight.

She wandered over and pulled back the bedding, sitting down and taking off her shoes. She still wore Lee's clothes and didn't want to put her uniform back on until it was dry. It was a few more minutes before Lee joined her. She suspected he had other phone calls to make. At least he hadn't asked for her phone back, though she checked to make sure she'd switched it off.

"Nhiari, why don't you sleep in the tent tonight? The mattress in there is far more comfortable."

She glanced through the open flap. It was tempting.

"I'll sleep out here."

Was it fair? There was plenty of room in the tent for them both and he had a double mattress. But either of them might snuggle into the other during the night and that would be very difficult to extricate herself from. It was too much of a risk, too much of a temptation which would have her forgetting what she needed to do. "I'll be fine. Good night."

She lay down and shut her eyes. Lee sighed and got himself ready for bed.

Nhiari's heart ached. No, this was for her own good.

She stared into the darkness, hoping for sleep.

Chapter 8

Lee watched Nhiari sleep, which would probably be considered kind of creepy under the circumstances, but he couldn't help himself. He didn't want to wake her. The dark circles under her eyes and her constant yawning during the previous days told him she wasn't sleeping very well. The bedroll was hellishly uncomfortable and only good for a night or two if there was no other option.

But she refused to use his bed so what could he do?

He checked the time. Dot should have left the information at the lighthouse by now, and he didn't want to leave it too long in case someone else found it. He'd also arranged for Steven to leave food and clothes for them and he had to get to them before the fresh food went off. He made Nhiari a coffee and despite the noise he'd made, she still slept.

Carefully he approached her. She had the sheet flung back and lay there in just his T-shirt and gym shorts, her dark hair splayed out around her because she hadn't tied it back after they'd gone swimming.

Stunning.

Her wearing his clothes felt like a commitment,

though he knew it wasn't.

He braced himself. "Nhi, it's time to wake up."

She grumbled and opened her eyes.

He offered her the mug. "I made you a coffee. We need to get going before too many people are around."

She blinked at him and sat, brushing her long hair out of the way. It had tangled during the night, and he itched to run his hands through it and comb it, like he had the morning after their date.

Nhiari reached for the coffee. "Thank you."

He smiled. "You're welcome." He left her to wake up and fetched a comb from the tent. It would take some finesse to get all the knots out of her waist-length hair.

Lee held up the comb. "Shall I comb your hair while you drink your coffee?"

"I can do it myself."

"Yeah, but we need to get moving. You can enjoy the coffee while I deal with the knots."

She stared at him a long moment and he read the surprise and want on her face. Still he waited until she nodded. "Please. I'll drink the coffee as fast as I can."

He appreciated someone who understood the time constraints.

He sat behind her, wincing at the hardness of the bedroll, and teased out the knots. Her hair was thick but glossy, and he was careful not to pull too hard. He didn't want to hurt her.

She sat silently, drinking her coffee, and he couldn't see her expression.

He didn't speak, didn't want to risk saying the wrong thing and her pulling away, but he took his time, allowing himself that one luxury. When he was done, he moved away.

"Thank you." She handed him her mug and then braided her hair, her fingers moving so fast he couldn't quite make out how she was doing it. But in very little time, her hair was tied back and she was putting on her shoes.

He needed to get his things sorted.

"Are we riding or driving in?" Nhiari asked.

"Driving," he replied.

"You don't think that's risky?"

"The only one likely to pull us over is Pierre," Lee pointed out.

Nhiari sighed. "Fair enough." She frowned, looking at the car. "You have a different number plate."

He nodded, impressed she'd noticed. "I took the ones from Clark's car."

He drove out of the cave, turning east to move further into the canyon.

"There's a trail along the ranges to the west," Nhiari said.

"I need to pick up something else this way," Lee told her.

She didn't ask him what, which must have taken some effort. Lee gritted his teeth, wanting her to interact with him, to ask him questions. He'd thought they'd reached at least an understanding last night. She'd taken him to her secret waterhole rather than going to the beach. He'd hoped it meant she trusted him.

But no. It seemed for every step forward he gained, she took at least a half step back.

It was a bumpy trip over rocks and shrubs along the bottom of the canyon. When they reached the eastern side, he turned north and followed a barely-there track to where a ranger road was.

From there it was less difficult, and he increased his speed. The road wound up the ranges and in about ten minutes, they were at the top. He pulled up next to a hut and got out. "Won't be long."

He scanned the surroundings, but there was nothing out of the ordinary. The hut was unlocked, and he prised the door open, making sure it was empty before gathering the four bags which had been left behind in a large esky. He shut the door behind him and placed the bags into the back of the four-wheel drive, checking everything he needed was inside. A few of the cold items he placed straight into his fridge. Hopefully this would be the last time he had to ask for food deliveries.

Then he retrieved a hose and went around the back of the hut where there was a rainwater tank. He attached the connection and filled the water tank he had installed in the four-wheel drive.

Nhiari got out. "So that's how you do it."

He smiled. "The tank was getting empty, but the recent storm topped it up. It's been a good source of fresh water as long as I use purification tablets."

"Few people would use it."

He shook his head. "Only the rangers, and most of the time, they carry enough with them."

He packed up and drove towards the lighthouse. There was another path he could take to the other side of the ranges, which would get them to the lighthouse without many people seeing them.

When he turned west again, Nhiari said, "You really know these ranges."

He glanced at her. "Declan shared maps with me, which showed all the ranger trails. It was a real help in finding routes and knowing the areas to avoid, so I wasn't seen."

"I'll add it to his list of crimes."

The slight wryness in her voice made him smile. His knowledge of the ranges was a distinct advantage to them at the moment.

"Who left the bags?" she asked.

"Steven. He picked them up from Lindsay's

supermarket yesterday and brought them out this morning."

"Did you send him a list?"

"No. He thinks I told Lindsay I was a friend of his and camping in the area." Steven didn't question it. He wasn't the smartest man, but he knew how to keep his mouth shut.

"I also heard from Andrew yesterday," Lee continued.

"How?"

"He has my number. He left a message, and I called him back after you spoke with Dot."

"What did he say?"

"The police found one of the drug barrels. He also said Dot and another woman dropped two journals off at the maritime archaeologist's house last night. It identified the ship they were researching and spoke about the treasure." Which confirmed the Stokes had found the treasure Lucas wanted.

"Andrew told his father. I'm expecting a phone call today." He was a little concerned Lucas hadn't called him last night. "I also got a call from one of Clark's men. He's in town and wanted to know if there was any work."

"What did you tell him?

"That I'd be in touch in a couple of days. He might prove useful in some way."

He parked in the small hollow a couple of hundred metres behind the lighthouse. A tour bus was heading down the slope away from the car park and no other cars or people were in the area. Lee followed Nhiari up to the lighthouse where she went straight to a metal box and crouched down, feeling inside. "Gotcha!" She grinned as she pulled a thick, yellow, A4 envelope out of the box. Opening it, she flicked through a few of the documents. "It's all here."

Her smile washed over him and hope filled him for the first time in a long time. His heart skipped a beat. Was it possible for him to stop Stonefish, and have Nhiari as well?

Nhiari scanned a document and her expression darkened. "You have got to be kidding me!" She read some more and then swore, pacing away from him and then back, her eyes flashing with anger.

"What's wrong?"

"They sent Rodney fucking Taylor to head the drug investigation up here."

He waited for her to explain who Rodney was to her.

She stalked to the car. "Let's go. The sooner we can put this together and show Rodney as a complete imbecile, the better."

Lee pressed his lips together. He'd never heard such contempt from Nhiari. Who was this man?

He drove back to camp while Nhiari pored through the documentation. After a few kilometres, his curiosity got the better of him. "Who's Rodney?"

Her eyes were death lasers. "Only the bastard who made the police academy a complete nightmare for me."

His protective instinct kicked in. "The one who'd constantly undermined you?" She had told him a little about the man but hadn't mentioned a name.

"Yeah. He'd blame me for mistakes he made and would do things to make tasks harder for Dot and me."

"Because you were female?"

She snorted. "Partially. Mostly because I refused to go out with him." She shook her head, obviously reliving the moment. "He approached me on the first day and said he'd never seen such an attractive black woman."

Lee gritted his teeth as she continued.

"Told me he could help me get through the course and that I could study at his place. There was a lot he could teach me." She glanced at him. "He said it at the initial get-to-know-you session and half the cohort heard him."

He clenched the steering wheel. "What did you do?"

"I told him I'd met plenty of misogynistic arseholes like him, and I'd choose a lifetime alone over a night with him." She grinned. "Those around us laughed, and he stormed off. I guess I hurt his little ego because he did everything he could to get me thrown out of the academy." Nhiari read another page. "Dot's not sure if he's working for Stonefish."

Lee hoped so. He'd love to see the bastard in gaol. "I don't know the name. I'll try to find out."

Nhiari flicked through more notes. "Here. Dot mentions visiting the archaeologists last night. The Stokes told her about their ancestor, who was on the Retribution when the ship sank in the gulf. The ancestor discovered the treasure from the Dutch captain's journal but hid her portion of it for later."

"Which the Stokes found." Lee waited.

Nhiari glanced at him but didn't comment.

He hadn't yet shown her the long-range drone he had which he used to keep track of what was happening in the area. He'd seen the Stokes dig up the treasure after a recent storm and then heard them discussing it through the bugs he'd left in their lounge room and kitchen.

Nhiari continued to go through the documents Dot had put together. She made a few noises as she read, and he was curious to see how much of a case Dot had built.

He'd just backed the four-wheel drive into the cave when his satellite phone rang. He stiffened. "This will be Lucas. You need to be quiet."

She nodded and he answered the phone.

"They've found the journal," Lucas said. His refined tone spoke of years of privilege and reminded Lee of his mother.

He cringed, not needing to ask who 'they' were. The Stokes were all Lucas ever spoke about. "We suspected as much," Lee replied.

"Well now we have confirmation. Andrew said the policewoman and that girl who witnessed the murder dropped them at the researchers' house last night."

"Them?" Lee asked. He wasn't certain Lucas knew Andrew was feeding him information.

"The Stokes's ancestor wrote a journal too. She was on the Retribution."

"Can you get me a copy?"

"Just sent it. Andrew scanned it this morning while the others went to watch the sunrise."

"I'll go through it now," Lee replied.

"What are you doing with the other cop?"

Lee glanced at Nhiari. What could he say? He lowered his voice as if trying to stop her from overhearing. "I'm using her for information."

Nhiari flinched.

"What do you mean?" Lucas demanded.

"She knows what the police know, which will be useful in putting them off our scent."

"Why would she help you?"

He gave her a helpless look, begging her to understand that he wasn't telling the truth. "Because I seduced her a few months ago. It wasn't difficult to rekindle the relationship. Decent men are hard to find in Retribution Bay."

"So you didn't kidnap her?" Lucas didn't sound convinced.

"She arrested me, but it wasn't difficult to escape the cuffs and overpower her. I convinced her she'd be better off working with me."

Nhiari's expression went hard, but Lucas's next words captured Lee's attention.

"I'm coming to Retribution Bay."

"When?"

"Soon. Andrew heard Oliver talking with the boat owner. It won't be long before they share details of the treasure with him. They'll want to do the right thing and ensure the treasure is returned to the state."

"Do you need a place to stay?" No way Lucas would lower himself to camping, but Lee wanted to know where he was.

"I'll make my own arrangements. I expect you to know where the treasure is being kept by the time I arrive." He hung up.

Lee made sure the phone was disconnected before he spoke. "I'm lying to him, not to you."

She ignored the comment and strode to the table. "We need to go through everything Dot sent us. This might be our only chance to arrest Lucas while he's in Australia."

"Nhiari, I swear—"

She held up a hand. "That isn't what's important right now. We have to stop Stonefish." She sat down, focusing on the envelope Dot had sent them.

Lee bit his tongue to stop himself from rambling on, begging her to believe him, telling her Stonefish wasn't what was important. He rocked back on his heels.

Shit.

At some stage over the past couple of days, stopping Stonefish had lost its all-encompassing importance.

Now Nhiari took centre stage.

He was in so much trouble.

Chapter 9

Nhiari linked Dot's material with the other information, not daring to look in Lee's direction. The plea in his voice pulled at her heartstrings but they'd plucked the wrong note before. He could easily play both her and Lucas. He lied so convincingly.

Finally Lee moved over to the car to unpack the groceries and she let out a small sigh of relief.

She needed space from him.

The best thing would be not to let her guard down and to focus on the case.

"I got you these." Lee held out a reusable shopping bag.

Nhiari glanced at the bag and then at him but didn't take it.

He placed it on the table in front of her. "I thought you might like something else to wear." He walked away.

Nhiari peered into the bag. Inside were a couple of T-shirts and shorts, and a six-pack of cheap cotton underwear. She stared after him. There was no reason for him to get her clothes. How was she supposed to stay impartial when he did things like this? "Wouldn't

Steven think it odd you were buying women's clothing from the supermarket?"

He turned. "I asked Lindsay to pack them amongst the food so it wasn't obvious."

"Thank you."

His smile was sweet. "You're welcome. Do you want to freshen up? Now that I've refilled the water, we have enough for a quick shower. It won't be hot, but you'll be able to wash the dust off."

It sounded like bliss and she wasn't stubborn enough to say no. "Yes, please."

He erected the simple shower set up, which included a modesty screen and a hand-held shower head, while Nhiari tried to concentrate on the notes in front of her.

He was doing an excellent job trying to get her to relax her guard. But he was also well-trained.

"It's ready when you are."

Nhiari took the new clothes with her and had a quick, cold, but refreshing wash. By the time she had dressed, Lee had made them both another coffee and was sitting at the table, going through Dot's notes.

Suspicion hit her. Had he wanted her out of the way so he could go through Dot's notes by himself and hide anything relevant?

She should have considered that.

As she sipped the coffee, she surreptitiously went through the notes to see if there was anything missing.

"I haven't removed anything," Lee said.

So much for being subtle.

She ignored his comment and got to work.

***

Night was falling by the time Nhiari was satisfied she'd collated all the information and had a decent timeline. Dot had sent her a couple of text messages during the day; one to tell her she'd found a hideout on one of the islands, and the other to say she'd arrested Colin for drug-smuggling. The police would have possession of all the drugs by now, which was one less thing to worry about.

Dot was also gathering evidence on Kristy and Steven Hamilton, and would soon have enough to arrest them as well.

Nhiari stood and stretched, groaning as the kinks in her muscles made themselves known. "Are we missing anything?"

"Just Martin," Lee answered. "He's the last of Stonefish's influence in Retribution Bay."

"Can I tell Dot about him?"

"I want to find out when Lucas is coming to town first. I don't want him to think it's too risky to come."

She wished she wasn't supposed to be missing. Normally she'd ring all the accommodation in town and ask if he'd checked in, but she couldn't do that without gossip spreading. "Would he stay with the Hamiltons?"

"No. He doesn't like to get too close to those who are working for him. They don't know who he is."

"So what do we do?"

"I'll call Andrew and see what he knows."

"They're staying out on the boat. He might not have reception."

"He's got a satellite phone." Lee retrieved his phone and made the call, again putting it on speaker.

Lee had done that with Lucas as well.

"How much longer do I have to be on this stupid boat?" The whine was unmistakably petulant.

Lee rolled his eyes. "Not too much longer. We almost have what we need. Has there been any further mention of treasure?"

"No. Oliver and that cop are stuck on the boat until the tide rises. They were fetching the drug barrels but have been trapped by a coral atoll because of the low tide."

Nhiari winced. Dot wouldn't like being stuck alone with Oliver.

"Have they got all the barrels?"

"I don't know. I've been diving all afternoon."

"All right. I'll send someone out to collect them. You're sure Dot is stuck there?"

"That's what she radioed to the boat."

"Good work. Let me know if anything changes." Lee paused. "Have you heard from your dad?"

"Yeah, I saw him yesterday before they decided we had to stay on the boat overnight."

Nhiari perked up and Lee asked, "He's in town?"

"Staying at a motel."

"Do you know which one?"

"The one as you drive into town."

Lee glanced at Nhiari, and she nodded. She knew which one he meant.

"That's great. You all right there? Does anyone suspect you?" Lee's genuine concern came through.

Was he worried about Andrew's safety?

"No. They're all too interested in the shipwreck. Can't I go home?"

"Not yet. Just a few more days. Call me if you run into any trouble."

After he hung up, Nhiari said, "He'll be safe on the tour boat. Sam and Sherlock will make sure no one is hurt."

Lee sighed. "Andrew has no experience in this kind of thing. He's likely to say the wrong thing and get himself in trouble. He doesn't understand the seriousness of what he's involved in."

"Surely as Lucas's son, it affords him some protection."

Lee laughed. "I killed Lucas's oldest son and barely got a rap over the knuckles. Lucas is only concerned about the business and making money. Clark threatened that through his actions, so he was fair game. Lucas has always seen Andrew as a disappointment, so he wouldn't be overly concerned if he was killed either, though his wife would be devastated."

What a horrible way to live. Nhiari couldn't imagine having no one she cared about, or being used like that. "Do you want to track Lucas down?"

Lee shook his head. "If Lucas wanted me to know he was in town, he would have said so. He's up to something. Probably wants to get to the treasure before me. His trust doesn't last long."

Nhiari itched to arrest Lucas, but they had no definitive proof he was involved in all of this. They needed concrete evidence.

"I'm calling Steven," Lee said. "I need to act as if I'm still working for Stonefish and, based on what Andrew told me, we don't know whether Dot has got all the drugs. I'll send him to check the remaining barrels."

"There's still Sam and Sherlock. They'll try to stop him."

He shrugged. "Steven should be stealthy. If he gets caught, it means one more person is out of the picture and Stonefish has less hold on Retribution Bay."

Nhiari liked the sound of that.

It didn't take long for Lee to make the phone call. "It's late," Steven complained. "Can't it wait until the morning?"

"No," Lee replied.

"But I won't be able to pull them up by myself."

Lee's eyes widened. "I'll get someone to meet you at the southern boat ramp in thirty minutes." He hung up and dialled another number.

Who was he calling? He was supposed to have shared all his information with her already.

"Joseph, I need you to make a pickup." Lee gave him the details before hanging up.

"Who was that?"

"Joseph was the guy I told you about who used to work with Clark."

"So the two of them are going to check whether Dot has retrieved all the barrels?"

He nodded. "I suspect she has, so this will give her another avenue to follow. The barrels are close enough together that Dot should be able to see the boat, even if she can't stop them."

It wasn't a terrible plan, and her brain was too tired to think of how to make it better. "All right."

She walked to the front of the cave and stared at the night. The sea breeze funnelled through the canyon, shaking all the leaves, but it also kept the temperature down. It had been a long few days, and she wanted a decent night's sleep so she could think clearly.

Could she trust Lee?

He seemed so sincere, and yet he'd also seemed convincing speaking to Lucas and the others as well.

Perhaps he was only in it for himself and everyone was fodder to be used.

"Are you all right, Nhi?" Lee's voice was right behind her, but she hadn't heard him approach.

She closed her eyes and stopped herself from stepping back so she was closer to him. "I'm tired."

"Sleep in the tent tonight. With Lucas in town, this will end soon, and you'll need all your wits about you."

He was right. Professionally she had to ignore how she felt about sleeping in his bed and get some decent rest. "OK."

He shifted closer and she felt the heat from him. She braced herself, but he didn't touch her.

"I know you're finding this difficult. I wish there was another way we could do this."

So did she.

All she wanted was to step back into his arms, to forget about Stonefish and the lies, and pretend for a night they were just two people who found each other attractive. He'd been an amazing lover.

But perhaps she didn't have to trust him to experience that again. She turned to face him. He stayed where he was, gazing at her.

If she could trust him, he would be a rock for her. She knew that without a doubt. She ached for that. "Can we forget about everything for tonight?" She gave into her urge and stepped closer, sliding her arms around his waist. "Can we pretend nothing exists outside this cave?"

His eyes widened, but he pulled her close. "We can do whatever you want."

Good. She tilted her head and pressed her lips to his.

Warm and tasting of the coffee they'd consumed all day. She nipped little kisses over his lips and he groaned but let her lead.

Finally she deepened the kiss, teasing his mouth open and his restraint broke. He hauled her closer still and took control, drawing a moan from her.

She broke this kiss. "How strong is your air mattress?"

"Very strong." He pulled her over to the tent and paused outside. "Are you sure, Nhi?"

No, she wasn't, but right now she didn't care. She didn't want to think of the future, she just wanted to be in the now. "Yes."

The first time they'd had sex had been slow with Lee worshipping her body. She didn't want that now, wanted nothing that would make her feel anything emotionally. It had to be just physical.

Nhiari stripped off her T-shirt and shorts, but Lee stopped her as she reached for her bra. "Let me."

In one snap, her bra loosened, and she shrugged it off. Then his hands were finally touching her. He kissed her deeply as his thumb teased her nipple. "You're so beautiful."

She squeezed her eyes closed, not letting his words get to her. "Shush," she said. "I don't want your words."

She kissed him hard.

Chapter 10

Lee stilled at her words, the stab of pain piercing his heart. He breathed through it, trying to see it from Nhiari's point of view. She didn't know whether she could trust him, but she wanted to feel good. He didn't need words to show her he cared for her. He could show her with his body.

Nhiari lifted his shirt, and he helped her to take it off, while he backed her towards the tent. He knelt before her to unlace her shoes and it took little time to rid her of her footwear. Then slowly, from his position on his knees, he dragged off her underwear.

Stunning.

Behind him the lamplight illuminated Nhiari perfectly. Her dark skin glistened and her head was thrown back as his hands caressed her luscious bottom.

A goddess unveiled.

Lee pulled her towards him and his lips touched her nub. He licked, tasting her sweetness and her moan was music to his ears. He took his time, licking slowly, holding her steady against him. She trembled as his fingers dipped between her legs and her wetness covered them.

"Lee, I…"

His name on her lips gave him a rush. He slid his fingers inside her and whatever she was going to say was lost as she groaned.

She trembled again.

He pulled away. "Lie down, Nhi."

As she did as he ordered, he removed his shoes and pants, stopping short of his underwear. He had no protection nearby. It was over by the car, but if he left her now, would she change her mind? His whole body throbbed with desire. Perhaps this was how he could show her how much he cared.

He left his underwear on as he followed her onto the bed. She reached for him and pulled him close, kissing him.

He ran a hand down her side, loving the softness of her skin, and then cupped her breast, running his thumb over her dark nipple. She arched into him. "I need you inside of me."

In reply, he sucked her nipple into his mouth and used his tongue to tease. She whimpered and pressed into him. "Don't tease."

He moved to her other nipple and licked it, sliding his hand down her body to touch her core.

"Now Lee," she demanded, thrusting her hips towards him.

"Let me worship you, Nhiari," he murmured against her neck as he nibbled his way back to her mouth.

"No. Just sex."

He smiled as he kissed her long and deep. This wasn't just sex. This was him telling her how much he loved her.

When he kissed his way back down towards her breasts, she thrust her hips towards him and he brushed the sensitive nerve endings between her legs.

"I need you now." He couldn't ignore her

desperation bordering on frustration. He didn't want to upset her.

Lee slid down her body and focused on pleasing her, licking her slowly while his fingers set up a rhythm inside her.

"I want you inside me," she moaned.

He grinned. "I am." He wiggled his fingers. "Protection is too far away."

Her eyes widened for a moment and he rubbed a spot which sent her head flinging back and her hips arching forward.

A deity.

He concentrated on her pleasure, and her muscles clenched around him as her orgasm hit her. She cried his name and his mind took a snapshot of this moment to remember forever.

***

As she relaxed and sighed in satisfaction, Lee moved up the bed to lie next to her, gathering her into his arms. To his surprise, she didn't resist and instead curled into him. His heart swelled.

He brushed a kiss against her hair and held her.

She shifted and her hand moved down his chest to the bulge still in his underpants. His muscles tensed and he couldn't stop his groan as she rubbed him. He was so aroused, it wouldn't take much to set him off.

"Where are the condoms?"

He kissed her. "I'm fine. I want you to be satisfied."

"Only once?" She grinned. "I said I wanted you inside me." She straddled him and her wetness rubbed against his groin.

He was a goner.

"Med kit."

"How very military of you." She stalked over to the back of his car in all her naked glory, and it took her little time to find the foil-wrapped square and return with it. She placed it next to him on the bed and then dragged his underwear from him.

The seductress had come out to play. Her braid shifted to cover one breast as she knelt on the mattress and stroked his throbbing muscle. He clenched his teeth, fighting for some semblance of control. "Nhi, the condom."

"Now, now. Fair's fair. You didn't give me what I wanted straight away." She kept her dark gaze on him as she lowered her head and took him into her mouth.

Holy hell. Lee couldn't stop his thrust as her warm, wet mouth surrounded him. He closed his eyes, knowing if he watched her suck him, it would be the end of him. He did the eighteen times table in his head while sensations flooded his body. A corner of his brain celebrated the knowledge that she cared for him. If this had been just about sex, she could have easily used his body without giving him extra pleasure.

When he was close, he opened his eyes and grabbed the condom. Nhiari plucked it from him and rolled it on.

She hovered above him. "Now?"

He nodded. "Now."

She sheathed him and their moans mingled as their bodies became one. He clenched her hips as she rode him, slowly at first, before moving faster and faster.

This time, when her orgasm hit, it took him over the edge. He yelled her name as they came together, his heart completely hers.

***

Nhiari lay sated on the bed as Lee cleaned up. She couldn't regret what they had done, but instead of being the simple physical release she'd hoped for, it had stirred up too many emotions.

Sticky, warm, and potentially heart-breaking emotions.

Lee switched off the light, and the mattress dipped as he rejoined her and pulled her into his arms. She went willingly, lying her head against his chest as they cuddled.

Nhiari couldn't lie to herself any longer. She cared for him far more than she wanted to. If this was all a game to him, then she'd been played, and he was the victor. But right now, in this moment, she could pretend that it was real, and it could be enough. The morning would come soon enough and with it, the responsibilities and realities of her job.

Neither of them said anything. She'd told Lee she didn't want words, and it was true. They would only bind her tighter to him, make it more difficult to break free when she eventually had to arrest him.

Besides, what could they say to each other? They wouldn't have a future together.

If only they had met under different circumstances.

She closed her eyes as his hand moved lazily along her side, soothing her. If only she could freeze this moment in time.

Reality sucked like that.

His words came back to her. He'd killed protecting others. How much would that balance his other crimes? Lee was cooperating with the police. Could she arrange a deal?

If it wasn't Rodney leading Organised Crime, and if she knew for sure Stonefish didn't have someone in the division, she would make enquiries. But even that was too much risk. No one could know they were working together, no one except Dot and her father.

Rodney was again helping to make her life miserable.

Though there was one other person she knew who worked in Organised Crime. She had spent little time with him since the academy, but there was no way he would be involved with Stonefish. He'd become a police officer to stop these kinds of people. His family had been caught up with bikie gangs when he was younger.

Lee kissed her head. "Sweet dreams, Nhi."

"You too," she whispered. She stared into the darkness, hoping her friend could help.

***

Nhiari was still lying awake several hours later when Lee's satellite phone rang. He jerked awake and reached for it in one swift movement. "Hello." There was no hint in his voice that he'd been woken from a deep sleep.

Nhiari sat up and reached for her phone. Almost midnight.

"Andrew, calm down," Lee said.

What had happened on the boat? Last she'd heard, Dot and Oliver had been going after the drugs. Had someone been hurt?

She collected her clothes, dressing while Lee listened to what Andrew said. Lee sat on the bed, a sheet covering his modesty. "Get him to take you straight to the treasure."

Nhiari spun towards Lee. Who was he talking about? Had Andrew kidnapped someone?

"You can't hurt him," Lee continued and then paused, nodding to something Andrew said. "Yeah, we'll get you straight out of town afterwards." Another pause. "I know you don't want to do this, but your father has been waiting a long time." He was silent again. "Did Oliver say exactly where the treasure was? Then no, I can't help until we have that information. Call me when you know." Lee rolled his eyes. "Then meet me at the base of the ranges. I told you where the track was… yeah, I'll be watching." Lee sighed. "It will be fine, Andrew. Just be careful." He waited another moment and then hung up.

Nhiari sat back on the mattress fully dressed. "What's going on?"

"Dot's gone after Steven and Joseph. They were late getting out there and the tide had risen enough for Dot to give chase. She left Oliver on the boat and Andrew overheard Sam and Sherlock talking to him about the treasure."

Nhiari pursed her lips. Neither man would have divulged the location to Oliver. It put the Stokes at risk and Brandon Stokes was like a brother to them. "What exactly did Andrew hear?"

"That they've already found the treasure."

It wasn't much. Stonefish already suspected that. It was why Jordan and Cody had been kidnapped. "Does he know where it's being kept?"

Lee smirked at her, but she ignored him. No point denying it now. "No. Lucas told Andrew to kidnap Oliver tomorrow."

Nhiari frowned. "How? They're on a boat in the middle of nowhere."

"Kristy is going to pick them up. All Andrew has to do is get Oliver away from the others while they're diving."

It might work if visibility was low. No one would suspect Andrew. "Then what?"

"He'll find out where the treasure is and fetch it. Andrew's freaking out because he doesn't want to go to gaol if he's caught. He wants to make sure there's somewhere he can run to afterwards."

"And you suggested here."

"Yeah."

"What's Lucas doing in all of this?"

"He'll come in when they have the treasure."

Which meant they were very close to stopping him. If he had received stolen goods and was arrested, those who were afraid of him might start talking. "Good." Oliver shouldn't be in any real danger. Kristy Hamilton wasn't someone who knew one end of a gun from another and wouldn't want to get her hands dirty. Andrew didn't want to get in trouble with the law. "What time are they planning this?"

"During the first dive. Should be early morning."

"I need to call Dot."

"No. She'll have her hands full with Steven and Joseph tonight. If she knows about it beforehand, Martin will be suspicious and know we're working together."

"Does it matter?" Nhiari asked. "We're so close."

"Lucas might leave if he thinks we're on to him."

She gritted her teeth. The idea of Oliver in potential danger didn't sit well with her. She'd liked him until he'd broken Dot's heart. "So what do we do?"

He lay back down. "We go back to sleep. Lucas hasn't called, so he doesn't want my help."

"But Andrew called you."

"Yeah, but he doesn't know Andrew has my number." He patted the bed. "We need to get some rest, Nhi. The next couple of days are going to be hectic."

She hesitated. They'd been here doing nothing but going over information for days now. She wanted to act, wanted to ignore what had happened between her and Lee.

But her steps brought her closer to the bed. This could all be over in a matter of days. She'd take what she could get with Lee. She kept her clothes on as she lay down next to him and he gathered her into his arms.

And this time she fell straight asleep.

***

When Lee woke it was bright outside. He'd overslept. Nhiari was snuggled into him and he took a second to appreciate the moment. Last night had been more than he'd dared hope for. No matter what happened from here, he'd had another night with her.

He shifted and she stirred but drifted back to sleep. She hadn't been sleeping well, and he hated to see the shadows under her eyes darken.

Quietly he dressed and moved outside the tent to think through his plan of action. Andrew hadn't heard where the treasure was being kept, which was a worry. Oliver might not know, which meant he would be useless to Lucas. Oliver would be as good as dead if Lucas was there.

He glanced at Nhiari. She didn't need to know that little piece of information. He didn't want her anywhere near Lucas. But leaving her behind would be a betrayal he wouldn't come back from.

He grabbed the satellite phone and climbed through the tunnel to the lookout at the top of the range. Clear skies and no wind yet, but that wouldn't last long. He set up the telescope and peered out at the gulf, picking up the tour boat anchored near Retribution Island. From here he saw people moving about, but not any details of who they were.

As he watched, three people climbed into the tender and were taken a short distance away from the main boat, where two divers entered the water. A little further away, a silver dinghy was set up for fishing.

That had to be Kristy.

The other divers jumped into the water and he turned his attention to the dinghy. It took about ten minutes before there was movement. Three people emerged from the water and eventually climbed onto the boat.

"There you are."

He turned to find Nhiari behind him, holding two mugs of coffee. She handed him one.

His heart warmed. "I didn't want to wake you." He sipped the coffee and gestured to the telescope. "It looks as if they've just picked up Oliver."

Nhiari adjusted the telescope as the dinghy sped across the water towards the southern boat ramp. "Will Andrew call?"

"I don't know. He won't have a phone on him, but Kristy might."

"So we just wait?"

"Nothing else we can do." Actually, there was something. "When was the last time you checked your phone?"

She frowned, thinking about it. "Yesterday morning, I think. The battery's at about twenty percent."

"Might be worth switching it on, and the police radio." He wanted to know what was going on.

"I'll fetch them." She left her mug on a rock and went back to camp.

His stomach clenched. He'd been a fool. He could see that now as clear as day. When his father had died he'd been so overcome with grief and the need for revenge he hadn't thought about what he would do after Lucas was in gaol. Had he known he was going to meet Nhiari, he would have done things differently.

But it was too late now.

He'd made his bed and it would be empty and cold.

He scanned the rest of the area. A couple of cars drove out of Retribution Bay towing caravans, but it was otherwise quiet.

Too quiet.

Lucas was nearby and yet he hadn't told Lee he was here. That made him nervous. What did he have planned?

He had heard nothing from Steven or Joseph either. Had Dot caught them last night?

As if on cue, his phone rang. "Joseph, what can I do for you?"

"They're on to us." His voice was low, and it trembled.

"Who are?" Lee was careful to keep his voice cold and disinterested.

"The police. Martin sent me a message to say they were going to pick up Steven. He'll tell the cops who I am."

Martin was still being the good spy. That was interesting. "Where are you?"

"At the safe house."

He frowned. "Who sent you there?" Someone on Joseph's level shouldn't know about the safe house.

"Martin."

What was the man playing at? He was supposed to run those kinds of things past Lee. Unless Lucas had been in touch and told him differently.

Unease settled over Lee. That instinct right before things went bad. "You should get out of town before they put a roadblock in."

"Where do I go?"

"South. Lose yourself in the city."

"You want me to go to Perth? There are more cops there."

"And more people. Take out as much cash as you can now so you don't have to use your card." The man hadn't considered what he would do if he got caught. Not a full-time criminal then. Where had Clark found him?

Probably in a bar somewhere.

Nhiari returned with her phone and radio and passed him an apple.

"I'm not going to gaol," Joseph declared.

"Then leave now." He hung up, and bit into the apple, bored with lazy men who wanted an easy buck but didn't like the consequences that came with it.

"Who was that?" Nhiari asked.

"Joseph. Dot must have got an ID on them last night, but not caught them."

"What did you tell him?"

"To leave." At her widened eyes, he added, "He won't get far. Dot's likely to spot him on his way out of town, and if she doesn't, I have his details."

"Where is he now?"

"At the safe house. He headed there when he got word Steven was going to be arrested."

She held out her phone. "Dot sent me this last night."

It was a photo of him at the launch dinner for the shipwreck expedition. Oliver must have taken it. He screwed up his nose. "Lucas required me there. We hadn't seen each other since the beginning of the year and he wanted to ascertain whether I was still loyal."

"How did you avoid getting caught?"

"It was a small, private gathering and I'm an executive at an international shipping company. No one looked twice at me unless it was to wonder why an executive was taking photos."

"Do you really like photography?"

His answer was immediate. "Yeah, I do. It takes focus and patience and I love experimenting with light and filters to bring the landscapes into people's homes." He smiled, though he felt sad. "I'll be forever grateful to my father for bringing photography into my life."

"That's lovely." She smiled back at him.

Nhiari's smile warmed his insides, made him feel as if he was the most important person in the world and made him want to do better.

Her radio crackled. “Dot to base.” They glanced at each other and Nhiari increased the volume.

“Go ahead, Dot,” the answer came.

“Just got word Oliver and Andrew are missing.” Dot replied. “Suspect they were taken by a woman in a silver dinghy called Cersei. Need to check all boat ramps. Heading to you now, so Rodney and Martin can check the northern ones. I’m heading south.”

“Copy. We’ll be ready when you get here.”

Nhiari frowned. “She shouldn’t be going by herself.”

“I guess she doesn’t have a choice. Colin has been arrested, you’re here with me, and Pierre will be needed at the station.”

“I don’t like it. Are you sure Andrew won’t get violent?”

“Positive.” The boy was too soft and lazy to get excited about anything except maybe a video game he was playing. “He hates even killing flies or bugs in the house.”

A few minutes later a black four-wheel drive sped down the road out of Retribution Bay. Lee frowned, focusing on it, trying to see who was inside, but it was too difficult. Was it Joseph, or had Lucas got involved? Over by the southern boat ramp, the dinghy had disappeared from view, the land getting in the way.

The black car sped past the road leading to the boat ramp and Lee exhaled. Oliver should still be safe. Perhaps it was a local heading home.

“There’s Dot.” Nhiari pointed at the police car tearing down the road, lights flashing.

She would reach the boat ramp before Oliver could be taken away.

Lee checked on the black car. It had turned off the main road and was heading towards the ranges to the spot he’d taken the children. Shit. It had to be someone from Stonefish.

But who?

Had Joseph decided he was going to hide instead of going to Perth?

He pointed the telescope in the direction but he still couldn't see the driver. "I have to go."

Nhiari noticed the car and frowned. "Who is it?"

"I don't know, but I need to check."

"What do you need me to do?"

"Stay here. Listen to the radio. Find out what you can about Oliver and the others."

"Will you be all right?"

He nodded, faking confidence. "I'll be back as soon as I can." He hesitated. "Keep watch when you hear me return. If Lucas is with me, you need to run. I can't guarantee your safety."

Her expression hardened. "Be careful." She kissed him hard.

The radio came alive. "I've found the boat and its occupants. Send backup." Dot was at the boat ramp.

"Rodney and Martin are heading to you now."

Lee needed to go. The black car was halfway to the ranges. "Take care." He stole another kiss and then hurried into the tunnel to discover what was in store for him next.

Chapter 11

Nhiari watched Lee leave, her muscles clenching as if they wanted to go after him. Who was she kidding? She hated the idea of him going to face whoever was coming on his own. But he was right. She would be safer here and going with him might endanger their long-term plan.

Nhiari turned her attention back to the southern boat ramp. She couldn't see details, but as she watched, Dot called over the radio, "Require ambulance to southern boat ramp. Man impaled through the chest with a spear." The horror and fear in her voice meant it could only be Oliver.

Nhiari's muscles tightened. What had happened? Neither Andrew nor Kristy were supposed to be violent. Oliver should have been fine. She prayed he would be all right as another police car raced down the road. It would be even more time before an ambulance got there, but at least Dot had backup.

Not far away the motorbike engine roared to life. Lee was leaving. The black car heading towards the ranges was already out of her sight, somewhere behind the ridge.

The police car turned at the boat ramp and further behind them an ambulance was speeding down the road after them.

There wasn't anything she could do from here. Better she prepared herself in case it was Lucas heading to the ranges.

As she walked back into the cave, she hesitated, her gaze resting on the car. She could take it and head for the boat ramp to help Dot.

The desire to flee wasn't there any longer. She wanted to see this through with Lee, desperately hoped there was a way he could avoid prison time.

Perhaps she should call her contact.

Nhiari checked her phone reception. No bars here, but she'd had a couple on top. Perhaps she would even see Lee returning.

She pursed her lips as she grabbed one of Lee's day packs and filled it with water bottles and food. If she had to flee, she would need to go back up the tunnel and from there down the western side of the ranges.

Her police uniform caught her eye. She couldn't leave that here. She stuffed the clothes in the bag and then dressed in the police vest, feeling comfort from the sturdy shield. If it was Lucas, she might need the protection.

Feeling better prepared, she headed back to their lookout, glad her ankle had healed and was only an occasional pain.

More reception from here. No cars on the road, so the ambulance must have reached the boat ramp, but there were no other calls over the radio.

She flicked through her contacts until she came to the one she wanted. Detective Doug Pecherczyk had been a good friend at the academy and had gone into the Organised Crime unit. He would know what bargains they could make. But there was always a chance he would have to run it past someone who could be working for Stonefish. And if Rodney knew she had made the request, he would do everything he could to thwart her.

She scowled and tapped her thumb on the front of her phone. Was it better to let Organised Crime know now they had someone on the inside, or wait until it all came out?

Just call.

She pressed the button and waited as the phone rang. She wasn't even sure what cases he was involved in at the moment. He could be working undercover.

"Nhiari, long time no see."

She smiled at the smooth, familiar tone. He seemed happy to hear from her. "How are things, Doug?"

"Really great. I'm going on leave the week after next and I'm going to propose to my honey."

Her heart lifted. "Congratulations. Who's the lucky man?"

"An artist who paints wall murals. He's so talented."

She grinned at his gushing tone and felt a twinge of envy.

"How are you? Are you ringing to complain about Rodney?" He chuckled.

"How did he get the gig?" she asked.

"He insisted. I wanted to go, but we weren't sure how long this would last and I've had my leave planned for months. How's he been?"

"Dot's been dealing with him," Nhiari said, picking up a small twig and twirling it around.

"So what can I do for you?"

"It's more of a query… something you might not want to mention to anyone I asked."

His tone sharpened. "What's happened?"

There was the alert cop she knew. "Theoretically speaking, if you had someone who was working for a crime syndicate, but then gave evidence to end them, could a plea bargain be arranged for them to avoid gaol time?"

He made a low sound, displeased but considering. "It would depend on what illegal activities they carried out and how much they helped to put them away."

She squeezed her eyes closed. "Let's say they killed a couple of people, but those deaths protected innocent civilians."

"That's specific, Nhiari. What's going on?"

She closed her eyes. Could she trust him? She switched the topic. "Dot isn't sure whether she can trust Rodney or whether he might be working for the syndicate we're trying to stop."

He whistled. "That's quite an allegation."

"I know. Maybe Rodney is just being his usual charming self and the things he's hiding are because he dislikes us so much."

"You two must bring out the worst in him. He's one of our best and most people like him."

She couldn't imagine it. She shook the image of a popular Rodney out of her head and asked, "How much do you know about what is going on?"

"Not a lot. They keep it as need to know and I've been working on my own cases."

Right. "We have a couple of officers at the station who Stonefish has got to and with Rodney being Rodney, we don't have a lot of options."

"You can trust me, Nhiari. I still owe you one."

She smiled at the memory and then exhaled. He was her only option. "I've been working with someone from Stonefish. We almost have enough evidence to arrest the man in charge and stop the entire company, but when it's all over I don't want this person to go to gaol."

"Do they deserve to?"

Could she answer that neutrally? "He's done things that aren't great, but his goal has always been to stop Stonefish."

"Why? Are you sure he's not spinning you a tale?" It was a fair question and not one asked with a condescending tone.

"They killed his father."

"Have you proof?"

The question made her stop. She hadn't thought about getting proof. Hadn't been in a position to get it. "No."

"What's his name?"

She clenched her teeth. No, she couldn't do it. Not until Lucas was behind bars. "I can't, Doug."

"I can do a check on him. Find out what he's been involved in. Make sure he's not lying to you."

"Stonefish have people everywhere," she answered. "All it would need is for the information to go across the wrong person's desk and he'd be dead."

"Fine. Tell me when you can. I'll do a little digging on this side into the investigation. The others who went up to Retribution Bay with Rodney are back in the office, and one of them is a mate. I'll chat to him."

Relief filled her. "Thank you. I owe you one."

"No, we'll be even. I'll call you when I know more."

Nhiari hung up. In the distance, an ambulance raced down the road from the southern boat ramp and headed into town. Oliver was on his way to hospital and the speed suggested he was still alive.

Closer to her came the sound of the motorbike. Lee was on his way back.

Her muscles tightened. But was he alone?

***

Lee clenched the handlebars of the motorbike as he bumped over the uneven ground towards the cave where he'd kidnapped Nhiari. Who would be there when he arrived?

Joseph he could easily get rid of, but Lucas would be more of a challenge. And Lucas would be furious that Andrew had been caught.

He pulled up, not bothering to cover the bike in case he needed a quick escape. He unclipped the strap over his gun, checked again it was loaded, then he slipped through the back of the cave and used touch along the rock wall to navigate to the area where he'd kept the boys. As the tunnel lightened, he gave himself enough time for his eyes to adjust as he slipped the gun into his hand. Pressing against the wall, he peered into the cave, his muscles tense.

Joseph prowled the length of the cave, muttering under his breath. Medium height, short brown hair, wearing jeans and a T-shirt with a cartoon character on the front. Everything about the man screamed average. Lee gave himself a second for the tension to release and to check Joseph had no discernible weapons before he tucked his gun back into its holster and stepped out. "Didn't I tell you to leave town?"

Joseph spun, eyes wide, and crouched to a fighter's stance, bracing himself for an attack.

Lee didn't move. He stood, arms crossed, and put all of his disdain into his glare.

Joseph straightened, but didn't relax. "Lee. The cops were after me. I saw the flashing lights behind me."

"So you decided the best idea would be to lead them straight to me?" Lee's voice was ice cold.

The man flinched, glancing behind as if expecting the police to burst into the cave behind him. "I knew you could hide me."

Joseph was a simpleton.

"The police aren't after you," Lee told him. "There was an incident at the boat ramp. They stopped there."

Joseph exhaled.

It was tempting to tie him up and leave him until everything was resolved, but Lee would have to make sure he was fed and it was too much of a hassle. With brains like his, he wouldn't be hard to find.

Lee stalked forward. "Leave." He kept the smile to himself as Joseph hurried back, keeping his eyes on Lee. "Do what I told you and disappear. You've got a couple of hours' grace before the police will even remember you exist. Use it wisely."

Lee had backed him outside the cave now and the dark car was parked haphazardly in the bush. No way was he helping get it out if Joseph got himself bogged.

"Thanks, Lee." His hand fumbled on the handle, but he jerked the door open and leapt inside. In a roar of the engine and a cloud of dust, Joseph disappeared from view.

Lee stepped back to avoid the dust and made note of the licence plate number. He could only be thankful that Clark had hired stupid people looking for a quick buck rather than doing his research and finding people who would do a good job.

His satellite phone rang, and he unclipped it from his belt. "Yes."

"Have you got eyes on what's happening at the boat ramp?" Lucas asked.

Shit. "Not at this second." He strode back into the cave and down the tunnel which led to his motorbike.

"Why not?"

"Because Joseph paid me a visit. He panicked and thought the police were after him."

"They are."

"Yes, but not at this moment. He was driving out of town when the police were heading for the boat ramp. He thought they were after him, so he decided his best course of action was to lead them to me." Lee let his displeasure through.

"I never should have involved Clark," Lucas said.

Lee raised his eyebrows. It was the closest he'd ever heard Lucas come to admitting he'd made a mistake. "The last I heard was Dot calling for backup and Martin and Rodney were on their way."

"You heard that?" Lucas sounded surprise.

"Police radio," Lee answered, not wanting to remind Lucas that Nhiari was with him. He slid through the narrow section of the tunnel and then continued. "Can we trust Andrew to keep his mouth shut?"

"How do you know Andrew is there?"

Shit. "He called me. Told me he had a lead on the treasure."

Lucas made a growl of displeasure. "If he doesn't keep his mouth shut, Martin knows what to do."

Lee's gut clenched. Lucas would kill his own son. Someone who had done nothing but try to live up to his father's expectations. He pushed aside the fear. "Do we know where the Stokes are keeping the treasure?"

"It has to be on the property," Lucas said. "There's been no word of it appearing at the museum or anywhere else."

"The property is a quarter of a million acres."

"I know!" Lucas spat. "Have you got anything out of that cop yet?"

Lee reached the motorbike and straddled it but didn't start it. "She's close to telling me. I think another day and I'll know everything. Where do you want me to take it when I have it?"

Would he admit he was in town?

"I want to be there. I can't rely on anyone to do the job right."

Lee smiled. "All right. Are you still in Australia? I should have the location by tomorrow evening."

"I'll be nearby. Call me when you have it." Lucas

hung up.

Lee clipped the phone back on his belt and then started the bike, heading back to Nhiari. It was time. Andrew would be in gaol tonight, the drug smuggling was over with no one left to carry it out, and he could focus on Lucas.

He had to get Nhiari to tell him where the treasure was so he could set a trap.

As he neared the main cave, he glanced up and spotted Nhiari on top of the cliff. He lifted a hand in acknowledgement and smiled as she waved in return. Soon, this would all be over. He hid the bike and hurried to the cave, but it was still empty. He climbed to the top of the range where Nhiari was watching the road through the telescope. She turned to him.

"Who was it?" she demanded.

"Joseph. Idiot thought Dot was chasing him."

"Where is he now?"

"I sent him on his way, but I have his licence plate number."

"I need to call Dot." The concern on Nhiari's face gave him concern.

"What happened?"

"I think Oliver was injured. An ambulance came to get him. I haven't heard anything else."

"Are the police still at the boat ramp?"

"Yeah. Neither Dot nor Martin's car have left, but the ambulance sped off in a hurry."

Dot could be in danger if Martin was there. "You don't know for sure who is in the ambulance?"

She shook her head. "Nothing on the radio."

He moved forward to look through the telescope. A police car drove back towards the main road. He focused in on it and saw a man behind the wheel. He stepped back. "It's not Dot."

Nhiari looked and swore. "Rodney, but there's no

one in the passenger seat."

"So Martin is still with Dot." There was no way to see whether there was anyone in the back of the paddy wagon. "Would she let Rodney take Andrew and Kristy by himself?"

"Rodney wouldn't have given her a choice," Nhiari said bitterly. "He'll take the glory of bringing in the culprits and leave Martin and Dot to clean up the mess and gather the evidence."

Which Martin would no doubt corrupt.

But hopefully Dot would still be safe. He debated calling Martin, but phone reception was spotty in that area. Still he withdrew his phone as his gaze followed the police vehicle, and he frowned as he spotted another ambulance heading down the road, though not at any great speed. "How many ambulances does Retribution Bay have?"

"One." Nhiari followed his gaze. Her eyes widened. "It's not got its lights on."

"Which means what?" Lee asked, hoping it wasn't what he thought it was.

"Someone's dead."

Chapter 12

Nhiari's heart clenched as the ambulance drove back to the boat ramp. What the hell had happened? Was Dot safe? Her finger itched over the radio, desperately wanting to use it to check in, to make sure her best friend was still alive. But she couldn't. Not without risking Lee.

"I'll call Martin." Lee made the call. He sighed. "Straight to voice mail."

So they had to wait and hope something came over the radio, which would tell them what was going on.

It was interminable. The ambulance moved out of view and about twenty minutes later, it returned and headed back to town.

"We should go. Dot needs my help." Her muscles ached with tension.

Lee placed a hand on her arm. "We can't. If Martin is there, it will break my cover."

"What about if I took your car and said I escaped?" It was difficult to breathe, not knowing the outcome of the incident at the boat ramp.

His expression, though sympathetic, was firm. "Call your brother. He can find out what happened."

Good idea. Dot would expect him to make a nuisance of himself. She braced herself, ready for the anger Matt would direct at her for not contacting him for so long and pulled out her phone.

"Wait." Lee pointed to the road. Dot's police car was driving back to the main road.

Nhiari's heart thumped as she bent down and peered through the telescope. It was difficult to see through the windscreen with the sun glare, but as the car turned, she glimpsed the woman behind the wheel. She exhaled. "It's Dot."

"Anyone else with her?"

"No." She straightened and glanced at Lee. "Martin wasn't in either car." Which meant he had either been arrested or was dead. What the hell had happened? Nhiari waited until the police car reached the part of the road where mobile reception kicked in and dialled Dot, putting it on speaker.

"Sergeant Dot Campbell." Her terse voice was a welcome sound.

"It's Nhiari. What the hell happened? Is Oliver all right? Where's Martin?"

A loud exhalation. "Where are you?"

"Top of the ranges. We saw cars but couldn't see the boat ramp."

"Kristy and Andrew kidnapped Oliver, and Kristy accidentally shot Oliver through the chest with a spear gun," Dot said. "Oliver was in the first ambulance. I don't know how he is." Genuine fear in her tone now. "Before the ambulance arrived, Andrew started telling me everything about his father, said he'd copied files onto his laptop, but then Martin shot him."

"Is he dead?"

"Yeah. Martin then wanted to shoot Oliver, but Rodney killed him."

"So Martin was working for Stonefish." Nhiari

glanced at Lee. His eyes were closed, and both hands were behind his head. Upset about Andrew's death. She stepped closer and slid an arm around his waist. "Are you all right?" She directed the question at Dot, but Lee opened his eyes and shook his head.

"I'm fucking tired. Tell me you've got something to end this."

She glanced at Lee and he nodded.

"Lucas is in town, at the resort as you drive in. He doesn't know we know though. He's playing his cards close to his chest."

"We need Andrew's laptop," Lee said.

"I'll get Sam to find it." Dot sighed. "Can you call him? Tell him Oliver has been found and to return to town."

"Yeah. Take care of yourself and let me know how Oliver is. We'll be in touch." Nhiari hung up.

"We can't risk that laptop," Lee said. "If Rodney is working for Stonefish, we'll never get the information on it."

"They'll all be busy at the station for the next hour or so interviewing Kristy. Can we get to town without anyone seeing us?"

He nodded. "Call Sam. Get him to procure the laptop. We can arrange somewhere to meet."

Nhiari found Sam's satellite phone number and dialled.

"Nhiari, are you all right?"

"Yeah. Dot asked me to call, but don't tell anyone it was me. Oliver's been found. You need to bring the students back to town."

"Is he all right?"

"He was shot with a spear gun. He's been taken to the hospital. That's all I know."

Sam swore. "OK. We'll head back soon. Are you going to meet us?"

"We're still in hiding," she said. "But I need you to find Andrew's laptop for me. I'll be in touch when you get back to the marina. Don't tell anyone you have it."

"Done," Sam said. "I'll see you soon."

Nhiari hung up. "Do you want to call Lucas?"

Lee ran a hand through his hair. "I really thought Andrew would be OK. He shouldn't have blabbed. He knew at least one cop was crooked." Lee sighed, unable to hide the grief in his tone.

She hugged him. "You aren't responsible for other people's actions. You couldn't have known what either of them was going to do."

"Doesn't hurt any less. The kid was lazy, but he was sweet when he was younger."

She felt for him, but right now they needed to focus on the job. "How are we getting into town without Lucas seeing us?" Nhiari asked.

Lee nodded towards the west coast. "We go the long way around."

She waited for him to pack away the telescope and then followed him back to the cave. It would take the boat about half an hour to return, assuming all students were on board and not diving. Another ten minutes for them to disembark and Sherlock to drive them back to the house they'd been renting. Sam could bring the laptop to them. "Let's meet them at the lighthouse."

Lee shook his head. "Not enough escape routes. We don't know whether either of those men will let me go, even if you vouch for me."

That was true. They tended to act first and ask questions later. "What then?"

"We don't know whether Lucas has been told about Andrew. If he knows, he's going to want that laptop. He could demand it from a student."

Nhiari shook her head. "He wouldn't dare get close enough to Sam and Sherlock. They would restrain him."

"But he doesn't know the police are on to him."

"That's still quite the risk to take."

"I honestly don't know anymore." He sounded defeated.

Nhiari pulled him into her arms. "We'll get him. We can use the treasure as a lure. This will all end soon."

He looked into her eyes. "I don't want this to end."

Her heart thumped. He was talking about them. "I know," she said. "Neither do I, but we'll work something out."

"How?"

She couldn't tell him about Doug yet. No point in getting his hopes up as well as hers. Instead she shrugged. "I don't know." She looked around. "Do you want to pack all of this up?"

"No. We may have to come back."

Lee drove them towards town, coming in from the north-west. Before they reached the intersection to turn into town, he pulled into a beach car park. "Call Sam. Get him to meet us at the northern boat ramp."

Nhiari rang Sam's mobile. When he answered, she said, "Are you at the marina?"

"Yeah. Just finished tying up. Sherlock's taking the students back to the house."

"Did you get Andrew's laptop?"

He grunted. "Of course."

His indignation made her smile. "Can you bring it to the northern boat ramp?"

"Yeah, I'll be right there."

She hung up and Lee stepped onto the running board of the car, scanning the road to town with binoculars.

Right. They'd see Sam drive past and could tell whether any other vehicles were with him. It was about ten minutes before they spotted his car. Lee watched for another five minutes until he was satisfied and got back behind the wheel. "Keep watching."

Nhiari scanned the road, but it was quiet. When Lee pulled into the boat ramp, only Sam was there. He leaned against his roo bar, staring out at the ocean as if he was contemplating life.

"You get out, get it and then get back in," Lee said.

"We can trust Sam."

"You can trust him. He's got no reason to trust me."

Nhiari got out and Lee did a U-turn to face the exit as she walked over to Sam. He turned and smiled at her, the wind blowing his longish strawberry-blond hair around his face. "Good to see you, Senior Constable."

She smiled back. "Likewise Sam."

Sam nodded behind her to where Lee waited for her, the engine still running. "You OK?"

"Yeah. You can trust him."

Sam frowned and shifted to get the laptop from the back seat. "You not sticking around?"

"Not yet. There's still a bit to do. Tell Dot I'll get her the information and be in touch later. Have you heard how Oliver is?" She reached for the laptop and he reluctantly gave it to her.

"Still in surgery. We'll go there next. Do you know what happened?"

"No." But it was time they got together and worked through everything. She should be able to convince Lee it was for the best. "We'll be in touch."

Sam stopped her with a hand on her arm. "You're really all right?"

Her heart warmed. "Yes, Sam, but thank you for your concern. I've got this."

He nodded and let go of her arm. "Stay safe."

"You too." She went around Lee's car and got in. Lee nodded acknowledgement at Sam, which the ex-soldier returned. Then he drove off.

"Think he'll follow us?" Lee asked.

"No, but we might need to worry about where Sherlock is." There wasn't enough time for Brandon to get into town.

"Check the lighthouse as we go past."

Nhiari used the binoculars to check the lighthouse car park, but it was empty. Then she scanned the ranges and the other car parks they drove past, but all was clear. Maybe the military men actually trusted her to know what she was doing.

They arrived back at the cave and started the laptop. The password screen stared at them. Nhiari's spirits fell. "Any idea?"

Lee chuckled and typed in a long password. After a moment of processing, the computer opened.

Nhiari raised her eyebrows. "How?"

"I helped him come up with that password when he was about ten. He uses it on everything."

"What is it?"

"Girls Suck Boys Rule as all one word, but the first letter of each word is a capital, the l is an exclamation mark, and the i, o and e are all numbers."

She smiled. "So he was going through a hating girl stage?"

"He'd just had his heart broken by his first crush." The smile faded from his face as he remembered that Andrew was dead. He sighed. "Andrew was an awkward kid and not popular in his class."

She squeezed his hand. "Then let's ensure he didn't die in vain."

She let him go through the computer, checking folders to find the information he said he had on Stonefish. Aside from a bunch of gaming folders, his university studies folder and a lot of porn, there wasn't anything else. Lee sat back.

"He could have saved it in a cloud folder," Nhiari

said.

They went through his internet history and found a couple of links to cloud folders which automatically logged them in when they clicked on them. They hit the jackpot on the last one they opened. Almost a terabyte of data. Lee flicked through folders and whistled. "This looks like backup files of all of Stonefish's financials." He clicked on another folder. "How did he get this stuff?"

"I have a friend who could figure it out." Amani had gone into tech crime after the academy because she was a whiz with computers.

"No. This can't go further."

Nhiari shook her head. "We need to get this to someone who can analyse it." It was over her head.

"I can't risk it yet."

"Lee, this is more than just stopping Lucas. We have to end the entire company and to do that we're going to have to bring in more people to help us." She understood his reluctance. "Dot already spoke to Amani when she found the island hideout. We can trust her."

"We can't get the laptop to her yet."

"We don't have to. The laptop is connected to the internet. She can log in."

He stalked away and paced back and forward. "I can't let Lucas get away with killing my father."

"He won't," Nhiari promised. "We need to come out of hiding." But not so Lucas saw them. There was only one place. "We need to go to Retribution Ridge."

***

Lee's muscles tightened until they ached. Nhiari wanted him to go back and face the people he'd betrayed? She might have forgiven him, but the rest of them wouldn't. He had killed their sheep, spied on them and pretended to be someone he wasn't. Amy had become a friend while he'd camped on their property, and she would never forgive him.

He shook his head. "They want me behind bars."

"Georgie doesn't."

"Georgie's a special case." She never thought badly of anyone.

"Matt will back her up, and so will I."

"You're still outnumbered." There were four Stokes siblings, Sam and Sherlock, plus all their partners. He was way outnumbered.

"Ed and Tess will back you up too."

He'd forgotten they were in town. He'd saved Tess's life, so that had to count for something. Still, "You should go on your own."

He wasn't sure he could forgive himself for treating such kind people the way he'd treated them.

Nhiari stepped closer, ran a hand over his arm. "It's all right. They'll understand, particularly when they find out you weren't involved in their parents' death."

There was one other thing he'd done, something he hadn't even told Nhiari about and would be the ultimate violation. But perhaps he could make it so no one knew about it. The only way he could do that was if he returned to the Ridge.

"When?" he asked.

She smiled at him. "It's going to take Dot at least a day to sort out today's mess. Tomorrow should work."

He nodded. That gave him time to plan, and perhaps he'd get to see the treasure Lucas was so obsessed with.

His phone rang. Shit. That could only be Lucas. Lee hesitated. He had to tell him Andrew was dead. He exhaled and then answered, Nhiari coming closer so she could hear. "Lucas."

"Where's the safe house?"

Lee blinked as his brain tried to catch up. "The safe

house?"

"Yes, in Retribution Bay. Where is it?"

He smiled at the edge of panic in Lucas's voice and told him the address. "Why do you want to know?"

"Because I have someone in need of it. Is it empty?"

"Yes." Lucas still wasn't admitting he was in Retribution Bay. "I have some news you won't like." He kept his tone cool, business-like, knowing Lucas wouldn't go for anything emotional.

"What?"

"Martin killed Andrew."

"I know. Stupid kid was planning to tell the police everything."

Lee raised his eyebrows. The only way Lucas could know was if someone who had been there had told him. The only ones alive were Kristy, Dot and Rodney. With Kristy in gaol and Dot ruled out, that left Rodney. Or the one remaining police officer in Retribution Bay, Pierre. "Then you know Martin is dead as well."

"Yes. You need to find the treasure now so we can get it and leave this town behind us."

We. Lucas was definitely planning to be there.

"I should get eyes on it tomorrow," Lee said. "After I know where it is, we can make arrangements." He glanced at Nhiari who nodded.

"What about the cop with you?"

He chuckled and lowered his voice, his eyes on Nhiari's, hoping she would understand. "She won't be a problem for much longer."

"Good. Call me as soon as you know where it is."

Lee made sure he hung up the phone before he spoke. "We can set a trap for Lucas."

Nhiari nodded. "But that won't end Stonefish," she pointed out. "We need enough evidence to stop the whole company, so we need to send this to Amani."

Of course. She had a bigger picture than he did. He

nodded. “Let’s finish this.”

Chapter 13

The next morning Nhiari woke early. Her stomach swirled as she looked at Lee's sleeping form next to her. He slept peacefully, some hair over his face, but his expression was calm. Today Lee would face up to what he had done. She would have to convince Dot and all of her friends that he didn't deserve to be behind bars, and they needed him to see the rest of this through.

Nhiari might at most have another day with him before that decision was taken out of her hands.

She imprinted the curve of his face, the slight upturn of his mouth, the dark flick of his hair into her memory.

She'd contacted Amani yesterday and given her access to all the information from Andrew's laptop. Amani would sort it out and tell them if they had enough of what they needed to finally stop Stonefish.

This might be the last time she lay next to Lee like this.

Her heart clenched. Though she had told him her friends would be fine, she wasn't certain. He had known about Lara's kidnapping and Darcy might never forgive him.

The temptation to hide here forever was stronger

than she wanted it to be. They had to end Stonefish, stop them ruining so many lives, whether or not it ended their relationship.

She'd spoken to Dot yesterday afternoon and discovered Oliver was alive, and lucky to be so considering his injury. He and Dot had reconciled and Dot had sounded so happy. Nhiari was pleased for her. Oliver was being discharged today and Dot was taking him out to Retribution Ridge to show him the treasure and sort out what to do with it. Nhiari hadn't told Dot that she and Lee would be joining them. They had a few hours before they had to be out at the Ridge.

She would make good use of their final hours together.

She slid a hand down Lee's side, enjoying the warmth of his skin and then lower to brush his morning erection. His eyes popped open, clear and alert, not the least bit sleepy. She smiled. "Good morning. I hope I didn't wake you."

He smiled slowly. "Any time you want to wake me like this is fine by me."

She gripped his length, enjoying the feel of him under her palm. The desire to please him, to show him how much she cared, drove her to shift down the mattress and take him into her mouth.

His quiet curse made her smile, and she teased the tip with her tongue, swirling and licking as he shifted to his back to give her better access. "Nhiari." Her name was part supplication, part moan.

Yes. This man deserved some pleasure, deserved to be shown he was cared for. That she cared for him.

For this short period of their life, they were together, and it may be all they ever had.

This would be a memory she would keep close.

She tightened her grip and worked him up and down, using her mouth to tease and torture. His hips rose, and she swallowed him deeper, loving the groan that tore from his throat.

"Nhiari, let me have you. I want to bury myself inside you." The plea made her glance up, and it was all it took for him to get the upper hand, pull her up his body and flip her onto her back.

She grinned. "Yes, please."

In one slow movement, he was inside of her. She wrapped her legs around him to bring him deeper, and they both groaned as he thrust.

"This," he murmured in her ear as he thrust. "It's only ever been like this with you."

"Yes." She closed her eyes as the sensations built inside her, trying to save this feeling in her memories forever.

"Look at me, Nhiari."

Lee's command made her open her eyes and stare into his beautiful face.

"Come for me." The angle of his thrust was enough to tip her over the edge as her orgasm crashed over her and he yelled his release.

He settled over her, pulling her close, holding her as if she was the most precious thing in the world. They both understood this might be their last time.

She ran a hand down his back, pulling him closer, breathing him in. Her muscles tightened, not wanting to let him go, and it took some effort to release her hold so he could clean up.

"That's one of the nicest ways I've been woken up." He smiled as he handed her some tissues.

"One of?" The grin froze on her face. They hadn't used protection. The shock swept through her. She'd always been so careful, and while she was on the pill, she hadn't taken it in days.

But the thought of having Lee's child wasn't at all disturbing.

Her only concern was the idea it might grow up without a father. Foolish. She really had it bad for him. "I'll keep that in mind." She avoided looking at him as she cleaned herself and had a quick cold shower and dressed in her wrinkled police uniform. Perhaps when they got to the Ridge she could have a proper hot shower.

By the time she was done, Lee had packed the mattress and was dismantling the tent. No matter what happened from here, they weren't returning to the cave.

Nhiari helped him with the tent and then packed the remaining camping equipment while Lee showered. She glanced around the cave. Their little haven was no more. It was time to face reality and the world outside.

She exhaled. They could do this.

Almost mid-morning. Dot should be picking Oliver up from the hospital soon. "I'm going up top to watch for Dot," she called.

"I'll be up there shortly."

She climbed to the top for what was hopefully the last time and set up the telescope. The day was hot, the sun already strong as it heated the land. By mid-afternoon it would be scorching.

At the crunch of footsteps, she turned as Lee arrived next to her. He too had dressed in his cleanest clothes, though they were as wrinkled as hers.

"Any sign of them?" Lee asked as he sat.

"Not yet."

They would wait until Dot drove past before they headed out to the Ridge. They could ensure no one followed her, and also give Dot time to explain Lee's role to the Stokes.

A white four-wheel drive headed south along the road, and Nhiari looked through the telescope. It was full of passengers. "That's Sam and Sherlock." And with them, their partners Penelope and Gretchen, and

Gretchen's son, Jordan.

Georgie would have spent the night with Matt at the Ridge, so that left Dot and Oliver. Another twenty minutes went past before Dot's blue sedan appeared on the road. "That's her." She peered into the telescope for confirmation and saw someone in the passenger seat. Oliver.

Lee broke down the telescope and they carried it back to the car. He took a final glance around the cave to make sure they had missed nothing. "Let's go."

***

Lee hadn't dreaded anything more than he dreaded the upcoming meeting with the Stokes. Nerves thrummed along his skin and tied his insides into knots. While he was almost sure they wouldn't kill him, he had a lot to make up for.

Hopefully the Stokes would accept the package he'd retrieved before joining Nhiari on the ridge top, and help ease his debt.

Nhiari stared out the window next to him, silent.

She was another reason for the dread pitting in his stomach. Arriving at the Ridge would signal the end of their time together. There would be no coming back to their cave. From here on, she was the cop, and he was the felon.

Was it fair of him to tell her how much he loved her, or would it make it harder for her?

He couldn't decide.

"There's a gate up here." Nhiari pointed.

He slowed and pulled over while Nhiari jumped out to open it. They weren't using the main entrance in case Lucas had people watching the Ridge.

After she'd closed the gate behind him, they followed the dirt track past the ridge which gave the station its name and the windmill he'd pulled down, before reaching the sheds.

"Park inside."

He did as he was told. "Did you know there'd be space?"

"Yeah. This is where Bill and Beth used to park their car."

Before it had been wrecked in the crash that had killed them. The guilt was sharp. As he got out, he retrieved the small bag he'd put under the driver's seat.

"What's that?" Nhiari asked.

"A token." Though she looked confused, she didn't question him any further. Appreciation at her trust swept through him.

Several cars were parked outside the farmhouse, including several utes, Dot's blue sedan and Sam's four-wheel drive.

Only two caravans were in the camping area. The car was gone next to one, indicating they had gone out for the day, and there was no one sitting outside the second one. He scanned the area and saw a couple of figures in the distance over by the red dunes behind the farmhouse.

"Ready?" Nhiari asked.

He nodded, though he was anything but ready. They crossed the red dirt between the shed and the house, Lee scanning all directions in case they'd missed someone. The blue heeler on the verandah wagged its tail once in greeting, but otherwise didn't move.

Lee scratched Bennett's head on his way past and then focused on the noise coming from inside the kitchen. Everyone was there.

Nhiari didn't knock, she just walked in, and Lee kept close behind her.

Brandon was by the kitchen sink, Sherlock and Sam were seated at the table, Darcy spoke with his daughter Lara, Ed was over by the laundry and Matt… a hard body shoved into him, slamming him against the wall, an arm against his throat. Matt's angry stare glared at him inches from his face. "Give me one good reason why I shouldn't kick your arse right now," he snarled.

Instant silence. Every person in the room was watching them, but Lee kept his gaze on Nhiari's brother. The pressure against his windpipe hurt, but he rasped, "Because your sister is alive and safe."

"Matt, let go of him." Nhiari tried to press between them, but there was no space.

Lee waited, not giving Matt any reason to punch him, but felt him shaking with rage.

"Matt, he's been helping us," Dot called, but Georgie was the only one who came over to help Nhiari separate them.

"Matt, he saved our lives," Georgie reminded him.

With a curse, Matt stepped back and released him.

Lee took a shallow breath but didn't allow his hand to go to his sore throat. He had expected no less. The others in the room watched him with varying levels of distrust. Lara tucked close to Darcy's side, Jordan stepped protectively in front of her, and his mother, Gretchen, glared at Lee. But it was Amy's steady gaze, full of hurt, which affected him the most.

"I know Lee has done a lot to this family," Nhiari began. "But he's here to help now."

"Did you kill our parents?" Brandon demanded.

He met the man's dark gaze. "No. I had no idea what Clark had planned."

"Clark?" Matt asked. "The man who kidnapped me?"

Lee nodded.

"Why don't we all sit, and Lee and I can bring you up to speed with everything?" Nhiari suggested.

The kitchen table was more than big enough for the eight couples and two children. It was one thing he'd loved about the Stokes and their family. Everyone was welcomed in the kitchen with a cup of tea and something to eat.

He ended up sitting next to Oliver, who was very slow in his movements and Dot hovered next to him as he sat. "I'm fine, Dot," he said.

The look they exchanged spoke of love.

"Are you Lucas Fitton's executive?" Oliver's question drew Lee's attention away from Nhiari.

"Executive?" Amy asked. "I thought you were a photographer."

Yeah, he'd lied a lot to these people. "It's a long story."

"Is it worth hearing?" Darcy asked Nhiari.

She nodded.

"I have a question," Lara said. The ten-year-old straightened from where she sat between Darcy and Faith and stared at him.

He'd always admired her strength. "Go ahead."

"Did you tell Jay to kidnap me?"

Grief filled him at how close she'd come to dying. "No, but I knew he was going to. He was under orders not to hurt you, but I didn't know about the cave flooding in the storm. It's why I came over to the house to help when they were searching for you."

She squinted at him as if trying to ascertain whether he was telling the truth.

"The last thing I wanted was for you to be hurt, Lara."

"How about you tell us exactly what you did?" Ed suggested. "So we don't have to guess."

Lee nodded calmly although his stomach was in knots. He cared what these people thought of him. "I was put into place to spy on you. Lucas Fitton wanted the treasure, and it was my job to find it."

"Who is he?" Faith asked.

"He's the descendant of one of the pearl divers who was on the Retribution when it wrecked off the coast."

Georgie's eyes widened and Tess nodded as if it made sense.

"He's also my uncle." Lee continued to expand on his role in their troubles. He looked Darcy in the eyes when he said, "I slaughtered all of those sheep."

Darcy's jaw clenched. "Why? Why do that and then offer to help us now?"

"I had to kill the sheep to prove to Lucas I was loyal to Stonefish."

"And were you?" Tess asked.

"No. I want to end Stonefish for murdering my father."

***

Nhiari sat next to Lee as he answered questions for over an hour. His ability to stay calm and unemotional impressed her, though it might be to his detriment. She wanted him to show he was sorry for what he'd done. Finally Dot asked, "What did you find on Andrew's laptop?"

"Stonefish's financials," Nhiari answered. "I gave Amani access to it."

Dot nodded, as if satisfied. "She was working on something for me as well. If anyone can make sense of it, she can." Dot glanced at Lee. "Is Rodney working for Stonefish?"

"I suspect so. Lucas didn't tell me, but he knew Martin had killed Andrew."

She scowled and turned to Nhiari. "What's your plan?"

"I'm hoping all the evidence we've gathered in conjunction with the information on Andrew's laptop will be enough to put an end to Stonefish's lines of business. I checked in with Doug."

She felt Lee's gaze whip to her, but she kept her eyes on Dot.

"What did he say?"

"That Rodney insisted on coming up here."

"Maybe we should get Amani to tell Doug what she's found," Dot said.

"I'd trust him more than Rodney," Nhiari agreed.

"Who is Doug?" Lee asked, his tone cold and slightly suspicious.

"A friend from Organised Crime," Nhiari told him, not allowing herself to feel guilty for not telling him. "I called him the other day when you met Joseph."

"He could be working for Stonefish."

Dot shook her head. "When he was a kid, a bikie gang constantly threatened his parents. It's why he became a cop. There's no way he'd work for Stonefish."

"Only problem is, he's going on leave soon," Nhiari told her. "He's going to chat with the other men who came up with Rodney."

"Call him," Dot suggested, passing Nhiari her phone.

Nhiari rose from the table.

"We can't trust anyone," Lee insisted.

She squeezed his hand. "We have to." Stonefish was international, and they didn't have the contacts to end this like they wanted to. She headed into the lounge room to make the phone call and Dot followed her.

"Two calls in one week, Dot. I'm feeling special."

Nhiari smiled at his jovial voice. "It's Nhiari, but Dot is with me." She put the phone on speaker.

"Well same goes. I tried to call you back."

"Yeah, I've been out of range. What did your mate say?"

He chuckled. "I stirred up a hornets' nest with my questions. He wanted to know what I knew and where I'd heard it."

Nhiari winced. “What did you tell him?”

“I couldn’t expose a source,” Doug assured her. “He confided they were organising a full sting across borders but were waiting for all parties to agree on a time. Some of the Singapore team didn’t think they had enough evidence.”

“If I told you I had what looks to be several servers full of information, do you think it would be enough?”

He laughed. “Yeah. Do you want a job in Organised Crime?”

“No thanks.”

“Where’s the information?”

She hesitated. “Safe.” Perhaps she could tell him. Lucas wouldn’t know Sam had given Andrew’s laptop to Lee. They could say the police recovered it.

“Come on, Nhi. Trust someone.”

“The top dog’s son gave himself access to everything in case he needed leverage. I’ve got someone going through the data now to see if it’s legit.”

“I’ll give Amani a call.”

She grinned. She should have realised he’d know there was only one person she or Dot would go to for this kind of thing. “I’ll tell her to expect your call.”

“Before you go,” Doug hurried on. “If your source will give evidence, I hear they might offer a bargain.”

Her heart leapt. “Really?”

“Yeah. People involved with Stonefish have an annoying habit of turning up dead. If there was a witness, it would help.”

“Thanks Doug. I owe you.”

“If this ends Stonefish, you don’t owe me anything.”

She smiled, feeling optimistic for the first time since this began. It put a whole new spin on things. She called Amani and let her know Doug would get in touch. Before she could head back into the kitchen, Dot stopped her.

"You don't want Lee to go to gaol." Her steady gaze wasn't judgemental.

"No," Nhiari admitted.

"Can we trust him?"

Uncertainty filled her. "I don't know."

"But you want to."

"Desperately."

"What happened between you two?"

Nhiari glanced down the corridor, but the others were still in the kitchen. "He kidnapped me and we came to a truce, but he's telling Lucas he's seducing me for information and telling me he cares for me and wants to stop Lucas."

"So you don't know which one to believe."

"No, and trust me, I know how stupid that makes me. Stonefish has a long history of manipulating people."

Dot squeezed her hand. "Don't be so hard on yourself. I wasn't sure whether Oliver was a plant either, but I still fell back in love with him."

Nhiari smiled. "I'm glad, but you two had a history together. Lee admitted he only asked me out to get information."

"Your instincts have always been good, Nhi. What are they telling you now?"

"That he's thoroughly seduced me through his words and I care for him. I want to trust him, but I'm not thinking rationally right now."

"I would say the fact you understand you might be played means you are thinking rationally," Dot countered. "But we'll still be careful and leave some of Doug's details out."

She nodded. "I'm sorry I wasn't here to help you with Rodney and Oliver."

"If you had been, I would have left you to deal with Oliver and wouldn't be back together with him." Dot hugged Nhiari. “But I’m glad you’re back now.”

So was she. They returned to the kitchen.

Lee sat at the end of the table and all the men were watching him, but Georgie and Tess had moved to sit next to him and chat. Both owed their lives to him so it was easy to understand why they were more forgiving.

Lee looked up. “What did he say?”

“Organised Crime are building their case. Doug’s going to contact Amani about Andrew’s laptop information.”

“So this might soon be over?” Darcy asked, looking hopeful.

“Yeah.” She smiled at him.

“Lucas will go to ground if there’s any hint they’re on to him,” Lee said.

“So we need to get to him before he hears.” Nhiari turned to Dot. “He wants the treasure. He’s obsessed by it.”

“We can use that to our advantage. There are a few things you don’t know.” She grinned. “Let me fill you in.”

Chapter 14

Lee relaxed a little after Nhiari and Dot returned to the kitchen. He didn't know what to make of Nhiari contacting her friend without telling him, but he could hardly complain. He was asking her to trust him with little evidence to go on.

Dot studied him. He waited, saying nothing, but hoped Nhiari had put in a good word for him.

"The treasure is going to be moved to Perth on Saturday," Dot said. "Maybe we can set a trap."

"No," Brandon said. "We can't lose it."

"Technically it's not yours to lose," Oliver told him. "But I agree. Its historical value is too high to be used as bait."

"Not to mention the monetary value," Georgie said.

"You have the advantage that Lucas doesn't know exactly where the treasure is," Lee said before they lost track of the point. "Neither do I."

Amy raised her eyebrows. "Really?"

He nodded, pleased she was speaking with him. "I know you have it. I saw you dig it up. I don't know what you did with it."

"How do you know we didn't take it straight to the

authorities?" Ed asked.

"Because I didn't hear about it, and neither did Lucas."

"Are your networks that good?" Tess asked.

"Yes." It wasn't bragging. It was the truth. "Martin would have mentioned it, and even if you hadn't told him, our networks would have heard whispers. No one could keep it quiet for this long." He glanced around the table, noting the way Jordan squirmed in his seat. "Unless their lives depended on it." This close-knit group had surprised even him. If it hadn't been for Jordan taking a coin to school, word wouldn't have spread beyond these walls.

"Can we trust him?" Matt demanded, looking at Nhiari.

"You tell me. You want to tell everyone the truth about what happened when Clark died?"

Matt's anger deflated, and he exchanged a glance with Georgie.

"We all know Georgie didn't shoot Clark," Brandon said. He raised one eyebrow at his sister. "You can't lie for shit."

She smiled, not at all embarrassed. "Clark ordered Lee to shoot us to prove his loyalty to Stonefish. Instead he shot Clark, told me I needed to take the blame short term while he gathered enough evidence to stop Stonefish, and then disappeared into the bush." Georgie squeezed Lee's hand. "He saved both of us."

"That was risky," Faith said. "Clark was Lucas's son. How did you know he wouldn't want you dead?"

"I didn't. But the choice between Clark and Georgie wasn't difficult. She deserves to live."

Matt slid his arms around Georgie as if needing to touch her to reassure himself she was all right. "Damn straight she does."

"Thank you," Ed said as he got up to refill the water

jug then filled Lee's glass.

The atmosphere in the room eased a little. Sherlock and Sam sipped their drinks and Amy got another plate of biscuits from the cupboard.

He'd earned a modicum of respect.

"Is Georgie going to be in trouble for lying?" Brandon asked.

Dot answered. "We can argue against any punishment, particularly if we catch Lucas."

Which brought them right back to the treasure. "He'll want to steal the treasure before it gets to Perth," Lee said. "If possible, he'll take it straight out of the country."

"Private plane?" Sherlock asked.

"I haven't seen his up here, but his boat is in the area."

"There are a lot of places along the coast they could moor and bring the treasure on board," Sam pointed out.

Nhiari cleared her throat. "There are far too many people here for this discussion." Her expression was apologetic as she glanced at all the faces. "The less you know about what is planned, the safer you will be."

A good idea, but, "Before you go…" Lee picked up the bag, which had been lying by his feet.

The military men all stiffened, sharpening their gaze on him and he raised the other hand while he slowly lifted the bag to the table. "Nhiari, do you want to check the contents before you pass it to Darcy?"

She took the bag from him, but the men didn't relax. Lee waited, watched her eyes widen as she looked inside and then rummaged around in the bag. She glanced at him and then said, "There's nothing dangerous inside." She passed the bag to Darcy.

Darcy assessed Lee.

"I can't take back what I did to the station, but it

might help."

Darcy opened the bag. "Holy shit." He withdrew the first wad of bank notes.

Faith gasped as she peered inside. "There's got to be tens of thousands of dollars here."

"Half a million," Lee told her.

Darcy looked up. "Blood money."

Lee shook his head. "That was part of my inheritance from my father. It came from his legitimate investments, not anything he earned from Stonefish."

"Why?" Amy asked.

He hated the distrust on her face. "Because I never wanted to hurt your family the way I did. It was the only way to get Lucas to trust me." He hesitated, not sure how much he should say. "I enjoyed our discussions, Amy. I never wanted to lie to you. I realise money can't make up for the hardship and suffering I've caused, but it can hopefully lighten your financial burdens so you don't lose the Ridge."

"Thank you." Lara picked up a wad of cash. "It will help, won't it, Dad? We won't have to move?"

"Yeah, it will help, pumpkin," Darcy replied.

"If it's legitimate," Matt replied.

"It is," Lee assured him, not that his words had much weight with them. He glanced at Nhiari. "When this is done, I can show you the paper trail."

She squeezed his hand. "Thank you."

"All right, we need to get back to planning," Dot said, "and you need to find somewhere safe to put the cash."

Darcy stood. "Let me know if there's anything I can do to help." He glanced at his daughter and then at Jordan. "Shall we go to the beach?"

Lara looked at Lee, then at Nhiari and finally her dad. "All right."

"The beach sounds perfect," Georgie said.

"I'll make a picnic," Amy added as most of the people at the table stood and went to get ready.

Soon Lee faced the three army men, Dot, Nhiari and Oliver. They shuffled closer together around the table and Lee used the opportunity to remove the listening device he'd planted under the table months ago.

Oliver shifted in his seat, wincing a little. "I can wait in the lounge," he said. "The beach is out for me at the moment."

"Stay," Dot said. "You know how the museum works and whether what we're proposing will work."

"How's the chest?" Lee asked.

"Sore." Oliver placed a hand on his sternum. "Were you responsible for my kidnapping?"

"No, that was Lucas. I didn't know until Andrew called me the night before." His heart panged. He wanted to ask Oliver about Andrew's last minutes, but there would be time later.

"Why didn't you stop it?" Sam asked.

"I wasn't supposed to know," Lee replied. "Lucas didn't tell me he was in town, or what he'd told Andrew."

"Sounds as if he doesn't trust you," Sherlock said.

"His confidence in others is low considering how things have gone over the past year. The business has worked under the radar for generations and it's all surfacing now because of some decisions he made about the treasure and allowing his son to control this part of the business."

"I don't understand why the treasure is such a big deal. The man must have millions." Brandon tapped his hand on the table.

"The company and all his history is built on the idea the original pearl divers overcame their masters. They took their portion of the treasure Reginald found and built the business. They moved away from their poor pasts and became powerful. The knowledge there was more treasure they were cheated out of was enough to make Lucas furious. He is extremely proud of his history and he sees the treasure as rightfully his."

"Seems crazy to me," Sherlock said.

Lee nodded. "Pride is very important to him. He thought it would be easy because he had the captain's journal, but Bill and Beth wouldn't sell the property, no matter how much money he offered them. Not being able to buy what he wanted wasn't a concept he'd ever encountered before. It triggered something in him that made him unreasonable."

"Did you try to stop him?" Brandon asked.

Lee looked him in the eye. "No. I wanted him destroyed."

The others had finished getting ready for the beach and he stopped talking as they passed through the kitchen and out to the cars. When the fly screen door slammed behind the last of them, Nhiari spoke.

"We need to figure out how. Where is the treasure now?"

The others exchanged glances. They didn't trust him yet, which he understood. "I can leave the room while you tell Nhiari."

"Probably best if we talk about when it's going to be moved," Dot said. "The museum will take possession in two days."

That's right, they were taking it to Perth. That was plenty of time to come up with a plan. "Armoured guard?" Even if it was a portion of what Lucas expected, it would be worth millions.

"To a certain extent," Brandon said.

Lee's brain worked through the different options. So few people knew the truth of what had happened. "You three are accompanying it?"

None of the men said anything, and Dot sighed in

exasperation. "We haven't finalised the details yet. Oliver only confirmed the transport before you arrived."

"Road, boat or air?" Lee asked.

Dot glanced at Nhiari again before she finally answered. "Road. Steven Hamilton stole a cannon from the new wreck and the museum wants to add it to their collection."

"So you'll hide the treasure on the transport." A smart idea if few people knew they had found the treasure, but Lucas would examine everything out of the ordinary. "Lucas will know. He's the sponsor for the expedition and is quite within his rights to call the museum for an update. He'll hear the cannon has been found and is being moved on Saturday."

"Which we can use to our advantage," Brandon pointed out.

"What will Lucas do with the information?" Nhiari asked.

A good question. "He'll want to be subtle and not want a fight. If he can detour the truck from the main road, he'll get the treasure and leave Australia."

"There are dozens of airstrips along the coast," Nhiari pointed out. "Plus multiple places where he could meet his boat."

So they had to make sure he knew where to meet the truck.

"Are we going to bring Rodney in on this?" Dot asked.

Nhiari scowled. "Where is he?"

"In town," Dot said. "Going through all the evidence, probably building a case about why I should no longer have a job."

"Does he need to be involved?" Oliver asked.

"Yes," Dot replied. "If I keep this from him, and we can't prove he's working for Stonefish, it's likely to be the nail in my coffin."

"Should we call him out here?" Sam asked.

Nhiari cringed and then relaxed when Dot said, "Let's build a reasonable plan first and then tell him."

"First, I need to talk to Lucas," Lee said.

"Will he tell you his plans?" Nhiari asked.

"He'll have to. There isn't anyone left up here to help him." He waited for that to sink in. He was the last man standing.

"The van will arrive in Retribution Bay tomorrow evening," Dot said. "We'll load the cannon and the treasure first thing Saturday morning and the van will drive until it reaches Perth."

"Two drivers?" Lee asked.

Dot nodded.

"Have you got a map?" Sherlock asked Brandon.

"Yeah, in Dad's office." He left the room and returned with a large map of Western Australia, which he spread across the table. "This is the route they'll take." He traced the Brand Highway.

Lee assessed the map. "We need to mark all the airstrips and roads to the coast."

"There are many unmarked tracks and airstrips on the stations," Nhiari said. "If Lucas has bribed a station owner, he could access tracks we don't know about."

"He wouldn't even need to bribe them," Brandon pointed out. "He could use them with no one being any wiser."

"What's the plane registration?" Dot asked.

Lee rattled off the details. "It needs a long runway. Anything under eight hundred metres would be too short."

"That will rule out a lot of the station airstrips then," Nhiari said. "Most are for small, single-engine planes."

Nhiari and Dot got to work marking options on the map, including petrol stations where the van would stop to refuel. Before they got to Geraldton there were over two dozen. Way too many options for them to cover them all.

"I need to call Lucas," Lee said. "He'll need my help to steal it, so I'll be able to tell you where he'll be waiting."

Nhiari nodded. "Lee needs to see the treasure as well in case Lucas asks questions about it. He may need some kind of proof to show Lucas."

Brandon scowled. "Take him into the lounge and I'll retrieve some."

Fair enough. Nhiari led Lee out of the kitchen. In the hallway he paused at the wall of photos of the Stokes children at various ages from birth to their first day of school, to graduation and the latest one was of Brandon and Amy's wedding.

"I always envied this wall," he said to Nhiari as he followed her into the lounge room. It was a cosy room, with big, soft couches and an average sized television. Nothing like the designer rooms his mother had put together, but far more welcoming.

"Why?"

"Because it represents love," he replied. "The photos aren't professional but show a lifetime of family and support."

"You didn't have family photos in your house?"

"Only if they were professionally taken and matched the decor. Mother isn't sentimental. It was more for appearances."

Nhiari brushed his hand. "I'm sorry."

He shook away her apology. "I was fine. I had a very privileged upbringing."

"You can have all the wealth in the world and still be unhappy."

"Dad made it up to me when he could."

"When did you see the photos?" Nhiari asked

suddenly.

He glanced at her. "What?"

"You said you always envied the wall, but the Stokes don't invite guests down this way."

He winced. "They never locked the house," he said. "I've been in a few times looking for clues to the treasure when Amy went to town and the others were working."

"Did you take anything?"

"Only photos of potential things." He didn't mention what he'd left behind.

She nodded as if satisfied. "Giving them the money was very generous."

"It was the least I could do." One photo he'd taken at Amy and Brandon's wedding had been enlarged and framed, taking a prominent position on one wall. It contained the Stokes children, their partners, and Lara. Though Matt and Georgie hadn't been together then, they stood next to each other and Tess had been a part of the photo too. Lee smiled. He'd done something they appreciated. He could hold on to that.

"Have you had that money with you the whole time?" Nhiari asked.

"Clark smuggled it in for me. He thought it was for bribes. I knew as soon as I met Amy and Beth that I was going to be hurting good people. Prior to that, all I thought of was revenge for my father. I didn't consider what I might have to do to get it."

She slid her hand around his waist. "The money will help. As will stopping Lucas, but it might take time for them to forgive your actions."

Lee knew that. He'd be surprised if they ever forgave him. He glanced at Nhiari. These were her friends. Even if he somehow avoided gaol time, they wouldn't want him in their lives. He hadn't considered that before.

The pit in his stomach grew deeper. He'd let himself hope he'd get leniency for helping the police, but that wasn't the real hurdle now.

He couldn't let Nhiari be ostracised from her friends for his actions.

There really was no future for them.

***

It was about half an hour before Sam fetched them. Nhiari had heard doors open and close throughout the house and a car leaving and return. She suspected they were trying to make it difficult for Lee to know where the treasure was being kept.

They returned to the kitchen, where a backpack sat in the middle of the table. Brandon gestured to it. "Take a look."

Lee opened the bag, and she peered in. Gold and jewels. Nhiari gasped. "It's beautiful." She pulled out a ruby bracelet.

"You haven't seen it yet?" Lee asked.

She glanced at him. "I've been with you all this time, remember?" And the Stokes had only just found the treasure when Jordan and Cody had been kidnapped.

Lee tipped the contents of the bag out on the table, and coins and jewels poured out.

It was impressive, but not that much for the amount of fuss it had caused. "What proportion of the treasure is this?" Nhiari asked.

Brandon stared at Lee for a long moment before he said, "About a tenth."

Lee nodded. "Can I take some photos? Lucas will want proof."

"Put it back in the bag," Nhiari said. "And we should all make sure we're back so we aren't caught in a reflection. We don't know what kind of tech Lucas has available to him."

They did as she suggested, and then Lee took a couple of photos. "I'll send them tonight. He has to believe I'm lying to you."

"Just as long as you aren't," Brandon growled.

"I'm not."

Nhiari felt a twinge of uncertainty. She didn't doubt Lee wanted revenge for his father's death, but there was still a niggle that maybe Lee was lying to both Lucas and her. If that was the case, he might take the treasure for himself to start a new life and avoid gaol time all together.

"Have you got more questions for me?" Lee asked.

"Not at the moment," Dot said.

"Why don't you call Lucas now?" Nhiari suggested. "You can pretend you're going for a walk or something." The sooner they got information, the better, and she wanted to talk to Amani about something.

"I'll need to go by myself in case he has eyes on the Ridge, which means you can't listen to the conversation."

"We need him to be convinced," Sherlock said. "Otherwise this won't work."

"Don't go far," Brandon said.

Lee glanced at Nhiari and she nodded her confirmation. The kitchen fly screen banged shut behind him as he left.

"Nhiari, do you really believe him?" Brandon asked.

She waited until Lee had crossed over to the shed before she spoke. "I want to believe it." She got out her phone. "But I'd be foolish not to take precautions. I'll be back."

She returned to the lounge, where she called Amani. Dot followed her in.

"I haven't gone through the information yet," Amani answered.

"I've got another favour," Nhiari said. "If I send you a video which is embedded with a tracking device, can you extract it and put it in something I can send to someone so their phone is tracked?"

"Maybe. Send it to me so I can look."

Nhiari pressed a few buttons and sent Amani the video Lee had sent her to get access to her phone. "Sent."

"What's your priority?"

"I need it on the phone by Saturday morning."

"Geez, Nhiari. What are you doing to me?"

"I owe you big time," Nhiari assured her.

"Give me a second. I'll see if it's anything obvious."

Dot raised her eyebrows.

"Lee tracked both of our phones," she said. "It's how he knew where we were. If I can get something similar on his phone by Saturday, we can follow him if he can't be trusted." Her gut clenched.

"If that's all you need, I've got something that will work," Amani said. "All you need to do is make sure the person opens the message and it will install on their phone. You'll have real-time tracking."

"What are the legalities?" Dot asked.

"You need court approval," Amani said. "Have you brought Rodney into this yet?"

"No." Nor did Nhiari want to, but she also acknowledged they would have to at some stage. "If he's working with Stonefish and knows we've put it on Lee's phone, then it won't work. Lee could just leave his phone off for the entire time."

"Let me know what you're going to do. I've got to go." Amani hung up.

Nhiari looked at Dot. "What's your gut telling you?"

"That he's a professional and only he knows who he's telling the truth to."

Her phone dinged and she looked down at the

screen.

Use it wisely.

She didn't recognise the number, but she smiled at the photo which accompanied it. Amani had come through for her. She considered what to write and then sent Lee a quick message before she could second-guess herself.

Then she downloaded the tracking app and hid it in a folder on her phone.

She hoped she didn't have to use it.

Chapter 15

The heat took Lee's breath away as he jogged across the yard under the piercing sun to the shade of the sheds. There were no cars parked next to the caravans any longer, though someone could still be inside. He sent a message with images of the treasure and before he had a chance to call Lucas, his phone rang.

"You've found it."

Lucas's chortle made Lee cringe. It reminded him of family dinners when Lucas was making fun of Lee or Lee's father. "Yeah. I don't have long," he said. "The museum knows about it and they're planning to move it on Saturday with the cannon Steven Hamilton brought up from the wreck."

Lucas laughed. "Steven didn't take the cannon. I arranged for it to be dropped there after he got caught."

Lee raised his eyebrows as concern filled him. What contacts did Lucas still have in Retribution Bay? "Did Martin do it?"

"No."

Lee waited, but no more information was forthcoming. "Joseph?"

"No." Lucas was enjoying this game.

"Then it had to be Rodney." It was a stab in the dark, but unless Lucas had an entire team hidden up here, Rodney was the only other option.

"Well done. I was wondering whether you would pick him."

"He shot Martin because he was no longer reliable." It was another guess, but it made sense.

"This whole attempt in Retribution Bay has been a failure. It was time to wrap up loose ends and go back to what we do best." He paused for a second. "Do the Stokes really trust you after everything?"

"Yeah. They trust Nhiari, and she trusts me. Wasn't hard to convince her she's shown me the error of my ways and that I want to help her." He forced out a derisive laugh.

Another chortle. "Well done. I knew you had it in you."

Lee wanted to be sick. Did any of his family have empathy or consideration?

He shook his head. Focus on the end game. "All right. How do you want to play this? The Stokes haven't shown me where the treasure is being kept, and I suspect they are guarding it. Our best chance is hijacking the truck, taking it to Perth."

"They're not flying it down?"

"Cannon is too hard to move," Lee said. "But there are multiple points along the road where we could stop the truck and offload the treasure. Then we get it to your plane or boat."

"You've thought it through," Lucas said, a hint of suspicion in his words.

"It's what you sent me here for. If I hadn't, then I haven't been doing my job. Is your plane nearby?"

"It's within an hour's journey," Lucas said.

"And you got to the safe house all right?"

Silence. Lee waited, not explaining to Lucas.

"Yes. How did you know?"

"Andrew called me, freaked out the night before he died. I reassured him everything was going to plan. He mentioned you were in town."

"Yet you said nothing before now."

"Wasn't my place to question you. You'll tell me what I need to know."

More silence, but Lee could practically hear Lucas's mind ticking over. If Lee had known he was in town, he could have told the police and had him arrested days ago if he wasn't loyal. Would the fact he hadn't been enough to earn Lucas's trust?

"Let me think about options for Saturday. I'll call you back." Lucas hung up.

Lee stood in the shade of the shed and scanned the area. He'd spent time here, sneaking into the storerooms to go through boxes of memorabilia, hoping to find a clue to the treasure. Amy had nearly caught him a couple of times and Tess caught him inside the house on the day of Brandon's wedding, but he'd come up with an excuse that had worked.

His phone beeped with a message from Nhiari. We'll get there. It included a gif of a puppy trying to climb onto a couch and eventually succeeding.

He smiled.

Lee wandered back to the house, tapping on the door frame before letting himself in. Everyone was still sitting at the table.

"What did he say?" Nhiari asked.

"He's considering options. He confirmed he's staying at the safe house and Rodney is involved."

Nhiari swore. "That's going to make things more difficult."

Lee shook his head. "I've told Lucas I've convinced you I'm swapping sides, so anything I do will make sense to Rodney."

Nhiari glanced at Dot. "Where is he?"

"In town. Should I call him?"

The reluctance on Nhiari's face was clear. "I guess so."

"He won't come out to the Ridge," Dot warned.

"Tell him I won't go into town," Lee suggested. "If he's as bad as Nhiari suggests, he will want to see me and the treasure for himself and make his own assessment."

Dot nodded. She made the call and though she didn't have the phone on speaker, Rodney could be clearly heard.

"Where the hell are you?"

Dot rolled her eyes. "I'm out at Retribution Ridge. You'll want to come out here."

"We have a shit-tonne of paperwork to get through and you visited your friends."

"It's related to the case. I have a good idea how we can catch Lucas Fitton."

"He'll have left town by now."

Dot glanced at Lee, and Lee shook his head. No, she shouldn't tell Rodney that snippet of information. "I have what he wants."

"And what is that? He doesn't care about anyone. Both his kids were killed, and he didn't break his stride."

"Several million dollars in treasure," Dot said.

A long silence. "What? How did you come in contact with treasure?"

"It's a long story, which I don't want to discuss over the phone. You need to come out to Retribution Ridge. I'll send you directions."

"I know where it is." A pause. "Do you believe you're in any position to make demands right now, Dot? The brass aren't feeling friendly to you at the moment."

"And whose fault is that?" Dot asked. "I didn't have to bring you into this, but I'm doing you the courtesy. If you don't want to be there when we catch Lucas Fitton, then don't come."

"We?"

"Nhiari and I. She turned up at the Ridge this morning."

"Where the hell has she been?"

Lee stiffened at Rodney's tone. Everything about it put Lee on edge. It was as if Nhiari hadn't been doing her job properly.

"I can't discuss it over the phone, Rodney," Dot replied. "Are you coming or not?"

"I'll be there in an hour." He hung up.

Dot blew out a breath.

"He hasn't changed," Nhiari said.

"No, he hasn't."

Nhiari hugged the sergeant. "I'm sorry you had to deal with him on your own."

"I'm glad you didn't have to."

Lee scowled. It would be a pleasure to bring Rodney down along with Lucas. He hated bullies.

"So how much are we going to tell him?" Sherlock asked.

"We'll show him the treasure and where you found it," Dot replied. "Lucas thinks Lee is double-crossing us, and has seduced Nhiari, so they'll need to hint at that."

Nhiari grimaced. "I can hear his comments already."

"Maybe he won't say anything," Lee said. "If he doesn't want you thinking too hard about our relationship, it's in his best interest to let you continue to be seduced by me." He winked at her, trying to make her feel better, not wanting her to second-guess their relationship.

"If he's playing his part as lead investigator right,

he'll want evidence from you that you've turned," Sherlock said. "Won't he demand information about Stonefish? You'll need to tell him enough to get him off your back, but not too much that will actually threaten Stonefish's set up."

It was going to be a very fine line to tread. "Maybe I can get him to interview me alone," Lee said. "He won't want civilians present, and if his past behaviour is any indication, he won't want Nhiari and Dot present either." And if he could get Rodney in the lounge, the listening device he'd planted months ago would record all of their discussion.

"He'll want to see all the treasure." Nhiari gave a pointed look at the bag on the table. "Do we want him to know where it's kept?"

"No," Dot responded.

Lee got to his feet. "Want me to wait in the lounge again?"

Dot nodded.

He left the room, moving as quickly as he could without arousing suspicion so he could check the bug he'd planted in the lounge before Nhiari followed him in. As he entered the room, he glanced over his shoulder. Nhiari was still talking to the others. Quickly he ran his hand underneath the coffee table. Yeah, it was still there. He sat as Nhiari entered the room.

She played with the tail of her braid, a sure sign she was stressed. "What's wrong?"

Surprise danced across her face. "Nothing."

"You're playing with your hair."

She looked down at her hand as if unaware of what she was doing. She released the braid and sighed. "I don't want to see Rodney's rat-like face again. I don't want to deal with him. He makes me doubt myself and feel deeply insecure."

He pulled her down to the couch with him and

wrapped his arms around her. "You are an excellent police officer," he said.

"Am I?" she said. "Rodney's going to have a field day with our relationship." She pushed him away. "He'll make me feel inferior, he'll question my loyalties and say I have no right to be an officer if I'm so easily manipulated." There was pure misery in her eyes. "And worse yet, he won't be saying anything I haven't already thought myself."

Shit. His stomach twisted in knots. He had made her feel like this and there wasn't anything he could say to help her. "I'm making this extremely difficult for you," he said. "But for what it's worth, this thing between us is real to me." He squeezed her hand. "If I had a choice, I would want to spend my life with you, Nhiari." He hesitated. This might be the last chance he had to be alone with her. He sighed and then said the words that had been in his heart since the night they'd gone on their date. "I love you."

Tears welled in her eyes and she stood, pacing away. "I can't. Not until this is all over."

"I know." As much as it pained him, he understood.

But at least she knew the truth.

***

By the time Bennett barked announcing Rodney's arrival, Nhiari was a bundle of nerves. She left the kitchen where they'd been waiting since Brandon and his friends had fetched the rest of the treasure and stalked down to the lounge to get a hold of herself.

Nhiari shook the nerves out of her arms and exhaled, counting to ten. She could handle anything Rodney threw at her. She had all the way through the police academy where he'd made it his mission to belittle her and make things difficult.

Now she was a senior constable, she'd been working

for over ten years and was damned good at her job.

But the one way he could get to her was through Lee. She doubted herself with him, and it would be an easy attack point. She would have to convince Rodney that she was using Lee, not the other way around.

The thought settled her. She took another breath and returned to the kitchen as Rodney was walking up the steps to the verandah.

Dot raised her eyebrows in question, and Nhiari nodded. She had this.

Dot opened the door. "Thanks for coming out."

Rodney grunted. "You didn't give me a choice." He scanned the room and his eyes widened as he spotted Lee sitting between Sam and Sherlock. "What's he doing here?"

Rodney's puffed up chest and incredulity was convincing. Perhaps Lucas hadn't been in touch with him to say Lee was at the Ridge.

Was everyone in Stonefish playing each other? It didn't seem to be a great way to run a business.

"Nhiari brought him in," Dot said.

Nhiari braced herself as Rodney's gaze fell on her. Her skin prickled at his derisive sneer and the dismissive up and down scan. "Rodney," she acknowledged.

"You've finally come out of hiding?"

Why did it have to be him on this case? She brushed aside the useless thought. "We have information which might be useful to your case."

"Doubtful. Lee's been out of the game since he fled after shooting Tan."

Was Rodney trying to convince them, or was that what he believed?

"I've kept my eye on things," Lee said.

"The Stokes have something Lucas Fitton wants," Dot said, getting to the heart of the matter.

"What's that?"

Brandon opened the backpack in front of him. "This." He tipped the coins and jewels out on the table.

Rodney's eyes bugged out of his head, and Nhiari smiled. Finally, something that shut him up.

"Where did you get it?"

"It was uncovered during the storm," Dot told him. "We believe it was originally on board the ship Oliver has been examining."

"And you were going to keep it?" Rodney asked Brandon.

"No. We've been waiting to figure out what to do with it. We suspected Stonefish wanted it and we weren't sure who to trust. We only told Dot about it today."

That was a lie, but probably for the best. Nhiari and Dot had discovered the Stokes had it on the day Lee had kidnapped her.

"Why would Stonefish want the treasure?" Rodney asked. "They're a billion dollar company."

"Because Lucas's ancestor was on board the Retribution when it sank," Lee said. "They found part of the treasure then, and he set up Stonefish with his cut. He sees the rest of the treasure as his."

Rodney assessed Lee. "Why should we believe you? You're working for him."

Nhiari lifted a hand towards her braid and dropped it again, conscious of not showing her nerves.

"Nhiari offered me a deal if I helped her catch Lucas," Lee lied.

"She doesn't have the authority," Rodney said. "And you're smart enough to know that."

Lee shrugged. "Maybe I was tired of being Lucas's lackey. Nothing I said made any difference and Clark made a complete mess of what I was trying to do here. Everyone I've come across is incompetent. Why should

I let them take me down?"

The nonchalance in his stance, the uncaring tone in his voice, everything pointed towards a man beyond caring any longer. He was so convincing that Nhiari again questioned her feelings.

Why did he have to be such a good actor?

"I need to interview Lee," Rodney said. "I'll take him into the station."

"No," Dot said. "Lucas can't know he's here. You can use the lounge." She gestured down the hallway.

"This is highly irregular," Rodney blustered.

"I didn't need to bring you in on this, Rodney," Dot reminded him. "You do it my way."

"I hope you enjoy your last days as a police officer, Dot," Rodney snarled. "This way," he ordered Lee and stalked down the hall.

Lee glanced at Nhiari. "I see what you mean." He followed Rodney out of the kitchen.

Nhiari exhaled. "What did he mean about it being your last few days?"

"I've been asked to explain everything happening up here and why I haven't trusted Rodney with all my information." She tugged her dark hair. "It's been difficult."

Oliver ran a hand over Dot's back. "I'll speak with whoever's in charge to make sure they know she's been doing her job well."

Nhiari smiled at his defence. "It's good to see you again, Oliver." They hadn't had a chance to talk yet.

"Likewise. It's been too long."

She nodded. "We'll have to catch up when all this is over. I'd love to hear some of your stories." Oliver had worked on shipwreck expeditions all over the world. She had no hard feelings for him. Not if Dot had forgiven him for breaking her heart, which it appeared she had.

"Do we need to listen in?" Brandon asked, nodding towards the lounge.

Nhiari glanced down the hall. "They've closed the door."

"Perhaps we should make our own contingencies while they're gone," Sam suggested. "Depending on what Lucas comes back with." He glanced at Nhiari.

She understood his unspoken message. They needed to make plans in case Lee was double-crossing them. She nodded. "Let's talk."

Chapter 16

Lee walked past Rodney into the lounge room and stood near the coffee table as Rodney clicked the door shut. This man was an unknown. Obnoxious and arrogant from what he'd seen and heard, but with no personal experiences, he wasn't willing to make a firm assessment.

"Sit down," Rodney ordered.

Lee stood, legs apart, hands in his pockets, casual and non-threatening. "I'm fine standing."

Rodney puffed up as if to explode and then relaxed with a smile, his bluster and officiousness gone. "You've turned on Lucas." Smooth and confident.

Interesting. Which was the real man? He had slid into this new personality with no effort.

Lee watched him. Who was Rodney actually working for? "I hear you planted the cannon at Steven's place."

Rodney raised an eyebrow. "Something had to be done with it."

Should he admit to his ignorance? What did he have to lose? "Did you use Lucas's boat to raise it?"

Rodney smirked. "I believe I should ask you the questions."

"Just filling in a couple of blanks. Has Lucas spoken to you about the treasure?"

"You're not planning to double-cross him?"

Not answering the question made Lee think Rodney's surprise when Brandon had opened the backpack had been real. "Do I look stupid to you?"

"It looks as if you have a thing for Nhiari." Some derision slipped into his tone. "She has a way of leading men on."

Lee's skin prickled but he made sure his fingers didn't curl into fists like they wanted to. "In my case, it's the other way around," he said. "She's smitten. I hear she's quite picky about who she dates."

His shot hit its mark, and Rodney scowled. Enough of these games. "Let's get to the point, shall we? Lucas wants the treasure. He's devising a plan to get it. Is his boat in the area?" If it wasn't, there might not be enough time to get it into position.

"There are plenty of places along the coast we can take the treasure, so it doesn't matter where the boat is."

Perhaps he didn't know or was holding his cards close to his chest. Rodney would have the facilities to track it and the plane down.

"So we wait until Lucas tells us what he wants?" Lee asked.

Rodney nodded. "I'll travel with the treasure. What are Dot and Nhiari planning?"

Lee shrugged. "They've talked options but haven't finalised anything. They're waiting for Lucas to tell me his plans."

"And will you tell them the truth?"

He chuckled. "What do you think? We'll all be able to get away from this god-forsaken town."

"How will you escape? The Stokes aren't likely to let you go."

"We'll need eyes on the van at different points of the road. Nhiari and I can take one of those positions, and I can slip away from her easily enough."

Lee's phone rang. He glanced at the screen and then at Rodney. "It's Lucas." He answered, and Rodney strode closer so he could hear. "What's the plan?"

"Coral Bay," Lucas responded. "There's an airstrip. The plane will meet us."

"What time?"

"That's where you come in. I need to know where the truck is at each moment. You'll tell me."

Lee frowned and glanced at Rodney. "Wouldn't Rodney be better at that? He'll be in the truck."

"So will you."

What did he mean? "They won't let me into the truck."

"I'll get Rodney to say he'll transport you to Perth in it," Lucas said.

"That's highly irregular. Do you think they'll go for it?"

"He'll have to make sure they do."

Rodney's lips pressed together.

"Call me when the truck leaves Retribution Bay. Then call again when you turn on to the Coral Bay road. I'll meet you there." Lucas chuckled. "We'll kill any police riding with you and make our escape."

"Except Rodney," Lee clarified.

"As long as he doesn't outlive his usefulness." Lucas hung up.

Well shit. That wasn't good, but Lucas didn't know Rodney was listening in. This could all go badly if Rodney was loyal to the police. Lee would have to watch his back and somehow make sure Nhiari and Dot weren't with the truck.

He cringed. His chances of achieving that were slim. What was Lucas thinking? It wasn't a well thought out plan.

Lee looked at Rodney. This was awkward. "The Coral Bay airstrip is pretty barren. Not a lot of places to hide." He'd investigated a lot of exit and entry options while he'd been up here. "We can tell the others Lucas is planning to take the treasure to the Coral Bay boat ramp," he continued. "That way when we turn off the main road, they won't be suspicious. They can lay an ambush at the boat ramp and we'll turn off early."

"Dot will insist someone rides with the treasure," Rodney said.

"So convince her it should be you," Lee said. "You go with the driver. I'll be in the back. You can insist on that, right?"

Rodney hesitated, which seemed out of character for him. "Nothing I've insisted on has worked with Dot. She's tenacious."

Was that a hint of admiration in his tone?

"Then I'll take care of them while we're in the back of the truck," Lee said. "They won't expect it. I can have them tied up before we arrive, and we can drop them before we get to the airstrip."

He didn't discount the fact Lucas might shoot them out of spite if they were still in the truck when they arrived at the airstrip.

"All right," Rodney answered.

Lee narrowed his eyes. His agreement was too fast. What was Rodney's end game?

He kept his gaze on the man, tension settling into his muscles. "Let's get into the nitty gritty."

***

"We should use Jasmine," Sam said.

Nhiari glanced at him. They'd been discussing various options for almost an hour now, trying to decide where to place people depending on where

Lucas wanted to do the heist. She suspected he'd want to do it close to Retribution Bay because he was there, and there weren't many authorities left. The most obvious place would be around Coral Bay. "Jasmine?"

"The woman who spots whales and sharks for us when we're running tours," Sam said. "She's still in town. She could take her light aircraft up and act as a spotter for Lucas's boat."

"That's assuming he uses the boat, and not his plane," Nhiari pointed out. Still it was a good option and if Rodney was indeed working for Stonefish, they couldn't rely on backup from his department. Though maybe she should call Doug and let him know.

Down the hall a door squeaked open, and a minute later Rodney and Lee walked into the kitchen.

"Lucas rang." Lee didn't look at all frustrated. Nhiari couldn't imagine being forced to spend an hour with Rodney and not wanting to punch something. But then again, Lee was male, and Rodney was working for Stonefish.

Perhaps they should have insisted on listening in.

"What did he say?"

"He wants to take it by boat," Lee said. "I said I could convince you to let me travel in the truck and I'll hijack it and drive to the Coral Bay boat ramp. He'll meet me there."

Nhiari studied him. It was in line with what they had thought, but he wasn't telling her the whole truth.

"How are you going to take the truck?" Dot asked.

"I told him I'll catch the driver and Rodney by surprise," Lee said.

It was a weak plan. "And what are you going to do with whoever else is travelling in the truck?"

"You can't both go," Lee pointed out. "Someone needs to stay in Retribution Bay with Pierre, so at the most, there will be one in the truck."

"Unless we insist on accompanying the treasure," Brandon pointed out. "We did find it."

Nhiari nodded, and while she didn't want civilians involved, it was a sensible option.

"I can arrange for some colleagues to fly up," Rodney said.

Lee shook his head. "Lucas will watch the airport."

"So then they fly to Carnarvon and drive up. He can't possibly watch every entrance."

Interesting that Rodney was still pretending to be loyal. Could they rely on him to do what he said he was going to do?

Not likely.

Brandon brought up a satellite view of the area on his laptop. "This is all sand dunes." He pointed. "We can't stop anyone going to the ramp before the truck arrives because it will make it obvious to Lucas that we're on to him.

"Anyone on the ramp when this goes down will be in danger," Sherlock pointed out.

"Can we get Parks and Wildlife to do some random boat checks?" Dot asked.

"No!" Sam responded. "Penelope is not going anywhere near the boat ramp."

Nhiari understood his panic. Penelope had already survived one run-in with Stonefish. "He's right. Any sign of people in authority would make Lucas nervous. He knows we caught the PAWS Stonefish plants."

"So we need someone on the ground who can clear civilians and people who can stop Lucas," Dot said.

"The boat ramp shouldn't be busy," Nhiari said. "Not at this time of year." She turned to Lee. "Did Lucas confirm he would be on the boat, or do we need to consider he'll get picked up at a different location after the drop?"

"He said he wanted to be part of it, because

everyone else has been incompetent."

That was good.

"We'll need to be close to the ramp," Brandon said. "If we can borrow a small fishing boat, we can be in the area and go onto the ramp when the truck arrives."

Still it would put them at a disadvantage should anything change. They needed a car in the parking bay and people on the ground.

She studied the satellite image. Her parents' place was a few kilometres from Coral Bay. They had a property and there were multiple shortcuts into the small tourist spot, one which passed the airstrip. It was private and they could easily anchor the police boat offshore, ready to give chase.

She studied it further. That's what was bothering her about this whole thing. A boat was far too slow. Even if the police didn't know what Lucas had planned, they could have a plane in the air in less than an hour. If they put a tracker in the bag of treasure, they'd easily follow the boat and call border patrol to pick it up.

The sensible option, considering Lucas had a private plane, was to land at the airstrip, do the transfer and take off again. He could be halfway to Singapore before they could get anyone to help.

There was also the small airstrip on her parents' property in case they spotted the police's presence.

"Nhiari, you all right?" Lee asked.

She nodded. "Just thinking about options." She waved her hand indicating they should continue their discussions. She needed to call her parents anyway to tell them she was all right, and to return the missed call she'd had from them yesterday. They could tell her whether anyone had been scoping out their place recently. It was almost impossible to sneak around in a car with all the dusty tracks.

It took another hour and some phone calls to the

Organised Crime division by Rodney to come up with a plan. Brandon and Lee would be in the truck's rear with the treasure. Lee would be officially under arrest and being transported to Perth for processing. Dot would be on the ground at the boat ramp with a team from Organised Crime, and Sam and Sherlock would be seen with Oliver and his team in the gulf—out of harm's way. They would be available, if necessary, to chase Lucas's boat if it headed north.

Nhiari would stay in Retribution Bay with business as usual. Lee seemed relieved by the plan. Nhiari stood and stretched. "I need to call my parents." She ignored Rodney's grunt. "They'll want to know I'm safe."

She didn't wait for an answer and instead walked outside and around the side to the small patch of grass and shaded trees. She dialled their number and her father answered. "Finally! I didn't think you'd ever call me back."

She smiled, pleased to hear his gruff voice. "Sorry. I've been conserving my phone battery. I'm at the Ridge and I'm safe."

"You still with that Lee man?"

"Yes, he's here. We're hoping this will be all over by the weekend."

"Good. I don't like this business. I don't feel as if I can trust any strangers coming around."

Her interest peaked. "You've had strangers at the property?"

"That's what I was calling you about. Yesterday we had a bloke drive in. Said he was interested in learning about our culture. Was real interested we had our own airstrip and wanted to know how big our community was."

All her senses dinged. "What did he look like?"

"About my height, Asian guy, neat dark hair, wore a suit in this heat."

Could have been Lucas. "Did he look at the airstrip?"

"Just asked how long it was and whether it was regularly maintained. When I asked why he wanted to know, he said he was a tourist operator, thinking of starting custom tours to this area from Singapore. Asked if I was interested in being part of it. Teaching people bush tucker."

Had Lucas lied to Lee about his plans, or was Lee lying to them? "What did you tell him?"

"Well I didn't trust him, but I said I'd be interested to read his official proposal and gave him my email address."

"He might be part of what is happening here," Nhiari told her father. "It might be worth you and Mum coming into town for a few days until this all blows over."

"I'm not letting anyone push me off my land again," her father blustered.

She winced, not surprised by his vehemence. "Will you promise me if anyone comes by on Saturday that you will leave them alone?"

"Not if they're on my land."

She sighed, keeping hold of her patience. "Dad, these people are dangerous. They're likely to shoot you and Mum if you try to stop them."

He was silent a long moment.

She glanced back at the house, but no one was outside. "I'll come out," she said. "Monitor things."

"You think I'll let my daughter put herself in danger and not protect her?"

"Think about Mum," she said. "I can't protect you both and stop the bad guys. I need you to protect her."

He grumbled, but finally said, "Call me when you're coming out."

"I will. And if you see this man again, call me."

She hung up and started making a few plans of her own.

***

Rodney argued hard to take Lee into custody before he left. Perhaps he wanted another chance to talk to him alone and consolidate Stonefish's plan, but Lee was relieved when Nhiari argued it was too much of a risk.

Rodney also wanted to take the treasure into town where it could be kept more securely at the police station. This time it was Brandon who gave a definitive no. He wasn't letting it out of his sight until it got to the museum.

They didn't mention they didn't trust Rodney not to steal it.

Rodney had to think they still believed he was working for the good guys.

So he had left and now they had almost a day to kill before the truck arrived from Perth. The rest of the Stokes had returned from their swim, and Tess and Ed were making dinner.

Faith, Lara and Jordan were seeing to the horses and everyone else was busy doing their own thing. With so many people it seemed almost impossible they weren't tripping over each other, but no one seemed to get in each other's way.

A cohesive family.

Something Lee had never had. The longing was so strong and he pushed it down.

All he got were looks of suspicion.

Which he deserved.

The expression he liked least was on Nhiari's face as she met his eyes. Her uncertainty pained him and he would hurt her again before this was finished, but he couldn't let her get anywhere near Lucas. Lucas wouldn't hesitate to kill anyone who got in his way, particularly when he discovered Lee had been playing him.

Far better that Nhiari hated him and was alive.

During dinner they spoke about the farm and what Lara and Jordan had been doing at school. Both Darcy and Gretchen had decided to keep the children away from school for the next couple of days so they couldn't be used by Stonefish as leverage again.

Instead the Stokes were battening down the hatches, and keeping everyone they loved close at hand. Faith had adjusted any appointments she had booked, and both Georgie and Penelope had arranged to take the day off. Only Sam and Sherlock were heading back to town with Oliver and Dot in order to complete the expedition tomorrow and get the university students out of town.

The university had wanted the students to travel with the cannon since the car they'd driven up in hadn't been repaired yet, but Dot and Oliver had vetoed the idea. Instead they would fly back and Oliver would arrange for the equipment to be taken in the truck.

A much safer option.

Dot and Nhiari had spoken together before Dot had left and when they were done Nhiari turned to Amy. "Is there a room free in the shearers' quarters?"

Amy nodded. "There's a couple."

Nhiari glanced at Lee. "We'll only need one."

Matt shot her a suspicious look. "You can't guard his room on your own."

Lee bit back a smile. He could imagine Matt's reaction if Matt knew they'd slept together. His hand went to his throat, which was a little tender from the earlier attack.

"I can handle it," Nhiari said.

Brandon looked at them both. "Matt, you can help guard the treasure."

He looked as if he was going to argue, but Georgie squeezed his hand. "Nhiari's a big girl. She's been handling Lee all week."

Matt shot Lee a look of disgust and then nodded. "Fine."

He was one person who wouldn't accept Lee into their group if he managed to escape gaol. Lee couldn't come between Nhiari and her family.

Brandon showed him into the bathroom so Lee could have his first proper shower in weeks. Before Brandon left he said, "She trusts you."

Lee nodded.

"I don't."

"Noted." And he was happy Nhiari had so many people around her who would take care of her when he was gone.

As he showered, he noticed a shadow outside the window. Someone was guarding the exit and someone would be guarding the door as well.

After Nhiari had cleaned up, they went to the outbuilding which was built to house shearers at shearing time. The room was small with only a single bed in it and a small sink and wardrobe. Brandon dragged in a second mattress from the room next door, but made no comments. After Brandon left them, Lee gestured to the bed. "You take it."

She shook her head. "I'm on guard duty, remember?"

He glanced at her. "I won't escape."

"I know." Her assertion wasn't convincing.

He wanted to take her in his arms and tell her everything would be all right, but he couldn't. Nothing would be right after Saturday and though he wanted a last night holding her in his arms, he couldn't. Not when he was already lying to her and someone might check on them. They had a game to play.

He lay on the bed, and she turned off the light, but it was a long time before either of them fell asleep.

Chapter 17

The next day was interminable and Nhiari's fatigue didn't help matters. She'd barely slept lying on the mattress in front of the door. She couldn't stop thinking this was the beginning of the end for them.

Nhiari hated the fact she'd sent a tracker to Lee's phone, and she was making plans based on the assumption he would betray her.

That wasn't a healthy relationship in anyone's world.

The only positive was she'd got her period.

Finally Dot received word the truck would be in Retribution Bay by mid-afternoon and they would load the cannon when it arrived. Debate was still raging over when the treasure would be loaded; whether the truck would make a stop at the Ridge on the way back to Perth, or whether the Stokes would take the treasure to town either today or in the morning.

The less time the treasure was unguarded, the better.

Lee was kept out of the discussions, but someone was watching him. Around mid-afternoon, Amy and the other women ganged up on Nhiari and insisted she get some rest and she'd slept for a couple of hours.

When she woke, it was around five o'clock and Dot

called. Nhiari walked outside into the evening heat to answer it. "What's up?"

"We tracked down Lucas's plane in Newman, but it's lodged a flight plan to Carnarvon this afternoon. It should land there soon."

"Getting into position." Like she'd suspected. Did Lee know the truth, or was Lucas keeping him in the dark as well?

"Yeah. Organised Crime have been back and forth all day," Dot said, her exasperation clear. "We need to bring the treasure into town this evening and keep it at the police station overnight. The truck will pick it up in the morning."

"And Lee?"

"He's to be arrested and transported with the treasure to Perth."

Nhiari felt sick even if this was part of the plan. "What support are the Organised Crime division giving in relation to the ambush?"

"They have a team in Coral Bay now. Doug's watching the ramp."

At least they could trust him, but the complete plan didn't ring true. Nhiari strode across the red dirt to the shed, unable to keep still. "It makes no sense. Lucas would be a fool to put the treasure on his boat."

"The team is covering the boat ramp and the airstrip."

She shook her head. "I think they'll land at Mum and Dad's."

"Why?"

She had forgotten to tell Dot about her phone call with her father, so she filled her in.

"It makes sense," Dot said.

"Do you think they'll do it tonight, or wait until tomorrow?" Nhiari asked.

"If Rodney wants to keep his cover, they'll do it

tomorrow."

"He might plan on boarding the plane himself," she pointed out.

"Yeah," Dot agreed. "There's more. I've been told I'm no longer needed on this case. I've been ordered to leave it in Rodney's hands and concentrate on day-to-day matters."

Idiots. But it again pointed towards Rodney working for Stonefish. Her mind whirled as she considered options. "Do you want me to bring Lee into town, or is Rodney coming out?"

"Rodney's coming out for Lee and the treasure. He just left."

"So they could do it now if it's the two of them," Nhiari said. "Where's Lucas's plane?"

"Brandon will insist on accompanying the treasure," Dot pointed out as she tapped some keys. "The plane is in Carnarvon. It wouldn't take more than an hour to refuel and fly to Coral Bay."

Shit. "Lee and Rodney could overwhelm Brandon. Where are Sam and Sherlock?" Her heart thudded as her muscles tightened.

"They're back from the shipwreck and waiting for instructions."

They were the only other people who could be trusted and had the right experience. "Do we want to involve them?"

"We have little choice." Dot sighed. "I told Doug about Rodney and he told me to leave it with him." She made a sound of frustration. "I'm not supposed to be working this case. There are so many unknowns and variables; we don't know how many people Lucas will have with him, or where he's really going. We don't know who to trust."

Nhiari felt for her best friend. "Let's make arrangements in case Lee and Rodney overwhelm

Brandon and take the treasure now. I'll call my parents." How quickly could she get to her parents' place? Not long if she took a motorbike and cut through the station using the track Matt used to visit the Stokes when he was a kid. The only problem was anyone on the road would notice the dust and Lee would know someone was out there. "I could insist on accompanying Rodney, Lee, and Brandon. I need a lift back into town."

"Rodney said you need to stay there, so Lucas doesn't know you're safe."

A good excuse and it would limit what she could do. She had to leave the Ridge after Rodney did. A plan formed.

"Can you send Sherlock and Sam to my parents'? You'll need to stay in town in case they arrive as planned."

"What are you thinking?"

"I'll leave here after Rodney and Lee. When they hit the main road to Coral Bay they shouldn't see any dust from me. I can be at Mum and Dad's before they are… if that's where they go. Between Sam, Sherlock and I, we can stop anything they have planned."

There were a lot of contingencies to consider. Perhaps she was being paranoid.

"I'll get someone in Carnarvon to monitor Lucas's plane. They can call if it takes off again."

"I'll tell Brandon and Lee that Rodney is on his way and call my parents."

"Keep me posted."

Nhiari hung up and strode back to the homestead, finally feeling as if she was helping. "It's time," she said to Lee and Brandon.

"What's happening?" Brandon asked.

"Rodney is coming here," Nhiari said. "He's going to pick up the treasure and Lee. Organised Crime wants the treasure kept at the police station overnight."

Brandon frowned. "How many people are guarding it?"

Nhiari shook her head. "I don't know."

"Do you need me to call Lucas?" Lee asked.

Nhiari shook her head. "He won't believe the Stokes would let you make a phone call now. Rodney will have told him what's going on."

"I'm not letting the treasure out of my sight," Brandon said.

"We'll arrange for you to go too."

"What are you going to do?" Lee asked.

"I have to stay here," she said. "Rodney doesn't want me in town. I'll liaise with Dot, and she'll tell me where she wants me tomorrow when this all goes down."

Lee studied her, and she did her best to keep her expression neutral.

"I need to talk to the others." Brandon left the kitchen to round up his family, who were distributed around the house.

Lee stepped closer. "The only reason to take the treasure into town now is to give Lucas a better chance to get to it."

"I know."

"Where are Sam and Sherlock?"

She shook her head. "Dot hasn't told me what she's got planned."

"Because she thinks you'll tell me," Lee said.

Nhiari shrugged. "Maybe. You haven't heard anything more from Lucas, have you?"

"No." He glanced towards the hallway and then took hold of her hand. "No matter what happens, Nhi, know that what I feel for you is real. I—."

Brandon strode back in. He glanced at their hands and Lee let hers go.

Nhiari ignored the jumble of emotions inside her and focused on what Brandon was saying.

"Darcy and Matt are on their way back. Ed's putting his drone in the air to make sure there's no one else out there."

Nhiari nodded. "Lucas would be foolish to take the treasure from here." Though it was an option they hadn't considered. The Stokes had an airstrip on their property as well.

It would be a short drive to get the treasure there.

Her skin itched with the stress of all the options. At least the plane was still in Carnarvon. Unless he'd hired another one. "I'll check how Ed's doing."

She went outside and spotted him nearby. "See anything?"

He shook his head. "Nothing is moving in the area except Darcy and Matt coming back."

"How far is the range on that thing?"

"A couple of kilometres."

That could be her answer. "I need you to track Rodney when he leaves."

Ed glanced at her. "What are you thinking?"

She checked over her shoulder to make sure they were alone and spotted Lee on the verandah watching her. "There are three ways he can go; into town as planned, towards Coral Bay or towards your airstrip."

Ed's eyes widened. "I hadn't thought of that. No one has used it in a while."

The fewer people who knew about her plan the better, but she would have to trust Ed. "When they leave I'm going to need to borrow the motorbike in case he doesn't choose option one. Can you make sure it's fuelled?"

"Yeah."

"Thanks. Do you know what happened to my clothes, which were washed earlier?"

"I'd guess they're in the laundry."

"Great." She nodded to the drone feed. "Keep an eye out and tell me when Rodney's almost here."

She walked back to the house. "Looks all clear," she said to Lee as she climbed the steps.

"You think Rodney has something else planned," Lee said.

"I don't know what Rodney is doing," she agreed. "So it's best to have contingencies."

"Are you going to tell me?"

"If you need to know." She looked him in the eye, daring him to argue with her. He gave a small nod and followed her back inside. "Have you got what you need?"

Lee would leave his car and all his possessions at the Ridge.

"Yes."

In the laundry she found her police uniform ironed and hung on a coat hanger. Bless the person who'd done it. Her police vest was in Lee's car, as were all of her weapons. Brandon entered the room.

"Can you take Lee outside while we bring the treasure up?"

She nodded. That would give her a chance to get her things. She returned to the kitchen and gestured to Lee. "I need to get some things out of your car."

They went outside into the cooling afternoon air. "What do you need?" Lee asked.

"I want to put my vest back together," she said. "I might need it tomorrow, and I'm not sure where everything ended up."

"You're not going to be at the bust," Lee said, his voice sharp.

"No," she said. "But Stonefish has done the unexpected before, and I'll need it for my day-to-day."

He nodded, though he didn't seem happy about it.

"Lucas said he'd shoot any police."

"I'll warn Dot, but I dare say she's expecting that."

Lee opened the back of his car and got out the pack with her weapons in it. She fetched her vest and put it over the T-shirt she was wearing and loaded the pockets with the items Lee passed her. They worked in silence.

"Nhiari—"

She braced herself.

Lee sighed. "I wish you all the best for the future."

A lump lodged in her throat and she fought back tears in her eyes. This was their last goodbye. His future was uncertain.

Her heart raced as he turned away. Panic gripped her, and she grabbed his arm before she could stop herself. They stared at each other but she couldn't find any words. There was no future for them. Telling him she cared too would only cause them both more pain. Finally she said, "Be careful of Rodney. He might double-cross you the way he did Martin."

Disappointment flitted over his face and he nodded. "I will." He walked away.

Nhiari watched him go, her body straining to follow him.

Ed jogged over to her. "Rodney just drove past. He's in a police car."

She blinked. It was time to focus. "Thanks." She crossed the yard and trotted up the steps. "He's here," Nhiari told Lee and Brandon as she slipped into the laundry to leave her police vest on the bench.

Amy hugged her husband. "You be careful."

He nodded. "I'll be fine, Ames."

"I'll keep an eye on him for you, Amy," Lee said.

Her grateful smile made Nhiari ache. No one would look out for Lee. They'd all be watching him for betrayal.

He'd brought it on himself, but the knowledge didn't bring any comfort. Nhiari wanted to hold him in her arms one last time.

She'd had her chance and hadn't taken it.

Rodney clumped up the steps and Tess opened the door before he knocked. He scanned the room suspiciously. "Dot called you?" He directed the question at Nhiari.

"She said you were coming to arrest Lee and pick up the treasure." She gestured to the table where the bags of treasure had been placed.

"Nice of you to have it organised for me." He strode to Lee. "Lee Kwong, you're under arrest for murder."

Lee held out his hands and Rodney handcuffed him. Nhiari almost warned Rodney the cuffs wouldn't hold Lee, but the words disappeared as she glanced at Lee, who gave her a small smile.

He was remembering it too.

"Brandon will go with you," Nhiari said.

"No, he won't."

"He will," Brandon insisted. "The treasure is mine until the state says otherwise, and where it goes, I go." His smile almost seemed sincere. "So unless you'd prefer to leave the treasure here, I'll go with you. I'd prefer not to ride in the back though."

"I don't have time for this bullshit," Rodney said. "Grab the bags." He pushed Lee towards the door.

Nhiari and several of the others carried the treasure outside, loading it into the back seat of the police vehicle. Lee got in the paddy wagon and Brandon kissed Amy one last time before he got into the front. "I'll see you tomorrow."

Nhiari's gut clenched as they drove away, but the moment the car disappeared from sight she sprang into motion. "Ed, the drone. Darcy, get the motorbike for me." She ran inside and changed, throwing on her police gear. She checked her gun was loaded and then grabbed a Ridge radio before she strode back outside. Darcy had the motorbike ready and Ed jogged over. "They didn't go to our airstrip."

Good. She got on the motorbike. "How far are they from the intersection?"

"Almost there."

She itched to take off, but there would be no rush if they turned right instead of left. Ed showed her the screen, as the police car slowed at the intersection. She couldn't see which direction it was indicating, but it shifted towards the left of the road.

Shit.

She grabbed the throttle, and Ed placed a hand over her arm. "Wait."

The car turned right. Back to town. She exhaled. There was still one other track they could take which would lead them across country towards her parents' place, but it was unlikely. Still she revved the engine. "I need to go."

"Where?" Matt demanded.

"Mum and Dad's," she said. "I want to get them into town. They'll be too close to the action for my liking."

Matt pursed his lips. "That's not all."

"No," she agreed. "But you don't need to know. You should be safe here. The treasure is out of the house, so there's no reason for Lucas to come after you, but still be vigilant. He may decide to be spiteful." She didn't think there were any of his cronies in Retribution Bay to carry out revenge, but it was worth the warning.

Darcy scowled. "We'll keep everyone close to the house for the next few days. Take care of yourself."

Matt thrust a key at her. "Tell Mum and Dad to stay at Georgie's."

She nodded and then twisted the throttle, heading to her parents with a warning she hoped was unnecessary.

***

Lee didn't enjoy being locked in the back of the paddy wagon. He rattled the handcuffs but didn't bother dislodging them. No point letting Rodney know what he could do.

He'd asked whether there had been a change in the plan as Rodney had loaded him into the back, but Rodney said nothing, which made Lee nervous. Had plans changed, or was Rodney double-crossing Lucas and actually undercover for the police? Too many variables.

His phone was tucked in his pocket, but he wasn't certain for how long. It would be confiscated when they arrived at the police station. The police didn't normally keep prisoners overnight in Retribution Bay, so that meant either they were going to make an exception for him, or he and Rodney would take a trip to Carnarvon tonight.

Which would leave the treasure unguarded except for Brandon and perhaps Dot.

His skin crawled. He hated not knowing the whole plan.

He felt every bump along the road back to town, but at least there hadn't been a detour.

What weapons did Brandon have on him? Lee would bet he was armed, but he had seen no evidence.

Rodney would be foolish to under-estimate Brandon, and Rodney—while an arrogant son-of-a-bitch—was no fool.

Focusing on the task at hand soothed Lee and allowed him to block the expression Nhiari had given him as he'd been loaded into the car. Her whole demeanour had changed, and he didn't know whether

Dot had told her something which had changed her feelings for him, or whether she didn't want to show her emotions in front of the others. They probably thought she had Stockholm Syndrome. Matt would.

He exhaled. What did he expect? He'd already accepted they had no future, though she had asked about a plea bargain for him.

The car slowed as they entered the town, and Lee tracked the turns to the police station. The engine stopped and two car doors slammed. Then there was a clunk as the back lock disengaged, and Rodney stood there with a scowl. "Out you get."

Lee climbed out and looked around. They'd taken him to the rear of the police station, where there was a walled yard and the gate they came through was shut. Discouraging anyone from running.

Brandon stood next to the car and waited.

"This way," Rodney said, gesturing for them both to follow him.

"I'll wait here with the treasure." Brandon crossed his arms and stood with his legs apart, daring Rodney to disagree.

Rodney rolled his eyes and pushed Lee on the shoulder. "Let's go."

Lee walked into a room with two doors leading from it. One led into the offices, and the other to a corridor with a cell in it. Dot walked out of her office and raised her eyebrows. "We don't have facilities to keep him here overnight."

"We don't have the time to take him to Carnarvon and we can't leave the treasure unattended either," Rodney replied. "I'll set up a watch."

Dot studied him. "You got someone to agree to that?"

"Of course."

Lee watched the discussion. Rodney was keeping his

cards close to his chest, and Dot was unimpressed. Rodney prodded Lee and indicated down the corridor. "Through there is the cell."

Lee followed his orders, waiting until Dot was out of earshot before saying, "What's going on, Rodney?"

"You'll know when you need to know," Rodney replied. "Lucas has everything under control."

Not good. Had there been a change of plans he was unaware of, or was the heist happening in the morning?

He moved into the cell.

The clang of the door sounded quite final. Rodney smirked as he walked away.

Chapter 18

Nhiari relaxed her hold on the motorbike's handle bars as she bounced over the ground. She'd forgotten she needed to let the bike find its way. The more relaxed she was, the easier the ride.

When she had to stop to open a gate, she radioed the Ridge. "No news?"

"Nothing," Amy answered.

So as far as anyone knew, the police car was still heading into town. Still, she continued towards her parents' place. She needed to get them out of the way in case things centred on their airstrip. No way was she allowing them to become hostages.

It took almost an hour to get there and by then the sun was nearing the horizon. She slowed as she reached the house and spotted Sam's four-wheel-drive.

Good. She had backup.

Her father came out onto the verandah and she waved as she rode the bike into the nearby shed. He met her halfway as she walked back to the house.

"You want to tell me why I've got two military men in my kitchen?"

"They were just in case," Nhiari said, hugging him.

"Come inside and I'll explain everything."

He grunted, but followed her in.

The interior was cool and her mother handed her a glass of ice cold water as she walked into the kitchen. Nhiari sculled the refreshing drink.

She hugged her mother. "How are you?"

"Better for seeing you." She squeezed Nhiari, and Nhiari felt a pinch of guilt for worrying her family so much.

Nhiari nodded at Sam and Sherlock sitting at the table. "Thanks for coming."

"Dot didn't explain why we're here," Sam said.

She sat and gestured for her parents to do the same. "Rodney changed his mind," she said. "He went out to the Ridge just now, arrested Lee, and took the treasure into town with him."

Sam swore and Sherlock said, "You all right with that?"

He wasn't referring to the treasure. Trust him to notice. She pushed down her concern and nodded. "We weren't sure whether they would steal the treasure immediately, so we needed backup in case."

"Why here?" Sam asked.

"Because someone came around yesterday pitching a tourism idea to Mum and Dad and was interested in the airstrip."

Sam nodded.

"This is about the dodgy man?" her father asked.

"Yes." She brought up a photo of Lucas on her phone. "Was this him?"

He nodded.

Her stomach clenched at the thought of Lucas so close to her father. She turned to Sherlock and Sam. "Lucas is flying the treasure out. I suspect he's going to use the airstrip here."

Sherlock pursed his lips. "Might be he wants us to

think that. Why else would he come and look for himself? It would make more sense to sneak in after dark or even just land on the day with no visual."

"How far is the Coral Bay airstrip from here?" Sam asked.

"About five kilometres. Our airstrip is two kilometres in the opposite direction."

"He wants us to split our resources," Sam said.

She nodded. "Rodney should know what's happening, and he still says the heist will happen at the boat ramp," Nhiari said. "His men are in position in Coral Bay."

"It's what… ten kilometres between here and the boat ramp?" Sherlock asked.

"Yes."

"So the truck turns off here with no one the wiser until it doesn't show at the ramp," Sherlock surmised.

"Organised Crime will track the truck," Sam said. "But the plane has time to land, load the treasure and leave before they get here."

"Smart," Sherlock said.

"They're not using my land," her father said.

It was possible to set up an obstacle on the airstrip to force them to land elsewhere, but then Stonefish would know they were on to them.

"Dad, I need you and Mum to go into town tonight," Nhiari said.

"They're not scaring me off my land."

"No," she agreed. "But I need you both to be safe. I'm asking you to trust me and let me do my job. You can stay at Georgie's or go to the Ridge."

"You want us to go now?" her mother asked.

Nhiari nodded. The sooner the better.

"Now wait a minute—" her father blustered.

"Cecil, don't you go arguing," her mother interrupted. "These people are dangerous and we have to trust our daughter knows what she's doing."

"She might need my help."

"We've got your daughter's back, sir," Sam answered. "We're armed and trained for this kind of situation. You and your wife would only be a liability."

He scowled and glanced at Nhiari.

"He's right, Dad. I appreciate your desire to help, but I need to know you're somewhere safe."

"I'll go pack our things." Her mother left the room.

"They might not even come here," Nhiari said, trying to console her father. "The man who came may be trying to spread our resources thinly." She handed him Georgie's key.

He grunted. "Fine."

"Call me when you get there." She walked her parents to the door and watched them drive away and then turned to Sam. "Park your car in the shed so it's out of sight. Then we'll go through our options."

It was going to be a long night.

***

Lee sat on the wooden bench in his cell. There wasn't room to pace in the tiny space and he needed to take stock of the situation. He rubbed his wrists, more out of habit than because he had any pain. He was uncuffed, so that was a win.

Something dug into his thigh and he patted his pocket. His eyebrows rose. His mobile phone. Rodney should have taken it from him.

He checked the corridor. Clear and no sounds coming from either direction. He took out his phone. No messages.

He typed a message to Lucas.

Under arrest. At the police station at RB. What's the plan?

As he waited for a reply, he tested the door. It

clicked open.

Lee frowned. He hadn't noticed Rodney locking it, but this wasn't an accident. What was Rodney planning here? Why hadn't he told Lee what to do?

He cautiously closed the door again in case someone came to check on him. In the distance he heard Brandon and Dot talking in the main office.

I'll let you know. When I send word, bring the treasure.

That wasn't helpful, but he knew better than to ask for more details.

He sat and considered the options. Lucas still wanted the treasure, so at some stage Lee was expected to break out of here.

The heist would happen tonight.

He would have to neutralise Brandon. His gut swirled. From what he could see, a door led from the back area into the offices where Brandon would be with Rodney and the treasure.

With the rear exit leading to a locked car park, the most likely escape route would be straight out the front door.

Sounded like something Lucas would have the balls to do.

He lay on the hard bench and put his hands behind his head. There wasn't much he could do until he got word from Lucas.

He closed his eyes and rested.

***

It was past midnight when Lee's phone finally vibrated.

Meet you outside in 10. Bring the treasure. Tell Rodney it's now.

His heart raced. Right. It had been quiet for the past couple of hours, and he didn't know where anyone was.

He tucked his phone into his back pocket and

pushed the door open. Slowly he moved down the corridor and peered through the window into the office. Brandon sat in a chair facing away from him, talking to Rodney.

Where was Dot? Had she gone home, or was she in her office?

The treasure sat in the middle of the main room, so it wasn't something he could sneak out without Brandon seeing.

Not that Lee expected anything else. Brandon wasn't stupid.

He peered into the room again and took stock. He would have to come into the room at ninety degrees to Brandon, which meant he couldn't sneak up on him. It would have to be fast.

He crouched down under the window and moved to the other side. The corridor came out in another room and on the bench lay a taser gun. Lee turned it on in relief. He could disable Brandon without causing him permanent injury.

Next to them was a set of handcuffs. Lee tucked the cuffs into his back pocket and crept to the door which led into the office. This was when he would find out whose side Rodney was really on.

He listened to the conversation in the room.

"Have you got any stories about Dot and Nhiari from the academy?" Brandon asked.

"We didn't hang out in the same crowd," Rodney replied, a chill in his tone.

Because neither woman would have a bar of him. Lee hated the idea of tasering Brandon, but it was far preferable to knocking him unconscious or shooting him.

Lee exhaled and then stepped into the room, shooting the taser at Brandon. Brandon had time to turn, widened his eyes before the taser hit him in the chest then fell to the ground, jerking.

Rodney whirled, hand on his gun.

"Lucas says it's now," Lee yelled at him as he followed Brandon to the ground, making quick work of handcuffing Brandon to the desk. "Sorry," he murmured. "Amy would kill me if you were hurt."

Brandon glared at him but hadn't quite got control of his muscles yet.

"Catch."

Lee turned as Rodney threw a tie to him, which he used to restrain Brandon's feet. Rodney was already carrying the bags of treasure towards the door.

Lee took Brandon's gun from his shoulder holster and checked it was loaded. He tucked it into his pants and then hefted several of the backpacks.

It would take a couple of trips.

Brandon was already tugging against his restraints. It wouldn't hold him for long.

Lee ran outside as Lucas pulled into the car park in a four-wheel-drive. Rodney threw his bags into the boot and ran inside for the second trip.

Lee followed suit.

Brandon had already broken the ties on his feet and was working on his handcuffs. Shit.

Lee grabbed the last couple of bags. "It's not safe for you to follow," he murmured and ran back outside.

By the time he'd thrown the second load into the back, Brandon was at the door of the police station.

Shit.

Lee slammed the boot shut. Rodney opened the front passenger door and the crack of a gunshot made Lee flinch. His eyes flew to Brandon, who was still in the doorway unharmed.

Rodney staggered back from the car, his hand on his chest, eyes wide in disbelief.

Lucas had shot him.

"Get in, Lee!" Lucas called.

Lee's heart pounded, but he moved on auto-pilot towards the car. Dot raced out of her house behind the police station wearing pyjamas and holding a gun.

No time to help Rodney. Lee leapt into the car and Lucas took off before he'd shut the door.

More gunshots and Lee ducked as the car peeled out of the car park and headed north.

"What was that about?" Lee looked back, his breath coming fast. Dot and Brandon both crouched next to Rodney. They would call an ambulance.

"Rodney was working for Organised Crime."

Lee blinked as he clicked his seat belt on. "Yes. That was his job."

Lucas shook his head. "No. He was double-crossing me. There's a team of Organised Crime men in Coral Bay ready for tomorrow."

Lee frowned. "Why weren't they here to stop us?"

"Because I didn't tell Rodney the entire plan," Lucas said.

That couldn't be right. "But he left me with my phone and the cell unlocked."

"I told him to after he'd fetched you from the Ridge." Lucas looked at him. "Did you think I'd let my nephew rot in gaol?"

Perhaps Lucas didn't suspect him. That was good.

But he was surprised Rodney hadn't split his team and kept some in Retribution Bay. Perhaps people were waiting on the outskirts, heading south.

Except they were heading north, around the peninsula.

"Where are we going? Did you decide to take the boat after all?" There was a boat ramp on this side.

"No. There's a road south this way which will take us to an airstrip."

The Yardie Creek track. They hadn't considered it as

it was four-wheel-drive only and the truck wouldn't have gone that way. "Coral Bay?" Lee asked.

"No. There's a station to the north."

Nhiari's parents. Lee's skin prickled. Her father would investigate anyone on his property. Lucas would shoot him.

Somehow he had to stop that from happening. Could he stop Lucas now before they reached the property?

Not at this speed. It would be too dangerous. He'd have to wait until they slowed on the dirt track.

And hope for the best.

Chapter 19

Nhiari's phone blared, shocking her out of sleep. She answered it without checking who it was, and sat up, already reaching for her vest. "What?"

"Rodney's been shot," Dot said. "Lee and Lucas have the treasure but they've disappeared. Rodney's team outside Retribution Bay haven't seen them heading south, so either they've found a safe house or headed to the boat ramp on the west coast."

"How's Brandon?" She put her police vest over the uniform she'd slept in and strode into the main room where Sherlock had slept. He was already up and waiting for her to fill him in. She put the phone on speaker.

"Lee tasered and restrained him before Rodney and Lee carried the treasure out to Lucas's car. Brandon doesn't know how he got out of the cell. Rodney was getting in the front seat when Lucas shot him. Lee jumped in and they took off."

Nhiari's gut clenched. What game was Lee playing? "Let me see if I can track Lee's phone." She pressed some buttons and said to Sherlock, "Get Sam in here."

Sherlock made the call as the app opened and a dot

appeared on the screen heading south along the western road.

"They're almost at the boat ramp," Nhiari said.

"I'll tell Organised Crime." Dot hung up.

Nhiari stared at the phone, her instinct screaming at her. "They aren't going to the boat ramp."

"There's nowhere else they can go," Sherlock argued. "They wouldn't be stupid enough to hole up in the ranges. Lucas would want to get out of the country."

She shook her head. "There's a track across Yardie Creek which is accessible during low tide. It's rough and nowhere near as fast as the bitumen, but Lucas doesn't know we're tracking Lee's phone. He'll think we'll waste time checking the boat ramp while he gets away."

She opened another app which tracked flights. Sometimes it also showed smaller aircraft. There was no air traffic north of Carnarvon. She called the Carnarvon police station. "I need to know whether a plane is still at the airport." She gave the registration.

"I'll send someone to check," the constable said.

"It's urgent. Call me as soon as you know." She hung up and switched back to the tracking app. The dot had gone past the boat ramp.

"Call Dot," she ordered Sherlock. She paced the living room while she waited for Carnarvon to call her back.

"Went straight to voice mail."

Damn. She tapped out a message telling Dot what was happening.

When she was done, she brainstormed out loud. "If the plane is on its way, they're going to want to time it perfectly. If the plane arrives too early, Rodney's team at Coral Bay will have time to converge."

"That's assuming Rodney left any in place," Sherlock said.

Good point. Rodney was arrogant enough to have pulled them all back to Retribution Bay assuming he'd catch Lucas in town. "It will take at least an hour to drive from Retribution Bay, but Lucas will be slower taking the dirt track. They might beat him here." If they don't waste time chasing him around the peninsula. "Try Dot again." She checked the time. How long did it take to send a car to the airport?

"Nothing." Sherlock pressed another button as Sam strode in.

"What's going on?" Sam asked.

Nhiari held up a hand as Brandon's voice came over Sherlock's phone. "What have you got?"

Sherlock smiled. "You're OK?"

Brandon swore. "Yeah. Bastard got me with a taser."

Sam's eyebrows raised and he moved closer.

"We think they might head here," Sherlock said. "Nhiari's trying to find out whether Lucas's plane is still in Carnarvon."

"The Yardie Creek road," Brandon said, understanding. "It's low tide."

"Does Rodney's team have a four-wheel drive?" Nhiari asked.

"No. Let me get Dot." His voice was more distant as he said, "Dot, I've got Sherlock and Nhiari on the phone."

"What's happening?" Dot demanded.

"I think they're coming here," Nhiari said. "Are any of Organised Crime still in Coral Bay?"

"No," Dot said. "Rodney pulled all of them to Retribution Bay and now they've taken off after Lucas."

"Can you call them back?"

"Rodney wouldn't give me their details, but I'll try Doug."

Hampering them at every move. Getting shot almost served Rodney right. Her phone rang.

"Yes?"

"The plane is gone," her contact said. "Departed just as the team pulled up at the airport."

"Can you track it?"

"Its flight plan was set as Singapore. No passengers. Just the pilot."

With a stop here on the way, no doubt. "Thanks." She hung up. "Plane is on its way."

Dot swore. "Where's Lee?"

She checked the tracker. "Near Yardie Creek." Lucas must be doing about a hundred and fifty kilometres an hour. Dangerous. The road was bumpy and at this time of night dingoes and kangaroos would be out.

She hoped Lee would be all right.

Unless he'd been playing her. Her gut clenched.

"I'm calling Doug," Dot said. "My guess is Rodney didn't give them a full run down of all exits from town. They might not know Lucas can cross Yardie Creek."

Sam went over to the map they'd been examining earlier when they made some contingency plans. He tapped on it. "There's another airstrip here."

Shit. Nhiari strode over. "There's an airstrip at the station north of here." Maybe Lucas turning up here was a red herring. They'd thought the truck would come in from the Coral Bay road, not Yardie Creek, so they hadn't considered that airstrip an option. But this changed everything. The other station had a strip which was closer coming from that direction.

Dot swore. "How long will it take you to get there?"

"It'll be close. We should get there about the same time as Lucas." If Lee was telling the truth and wanted to stop Lucas, he would delay, but if not, it would be tight. "Has Lee got a weapon?"

"Yeah, he took my gun," Brandon said.

The tracker dot still moved towards them. Lee hadn't used the gun to stop Lucas yet, but Lucas was also armed and with Lucas behind the wheel, it would be too dangerous. "We'll head for the airstrip," she said. "They can't pass us because there's only one road. We'll be out of phone range, though. I'll turn my police radio on when we get there."

She had little battery left.

"We'll take the main road in case they get around you," Dot said.

Nhiari hung up. "Let's go." Sam and Sherlock followed her outside and across to the four-wheel drive.

"I'll drive," Sam said, getting into the driver's side.

Nhiari jumped in the passenger seat, with Sherlock behind her. "Turn off the lights."

Sam immediately did as she asked.

"That way."

Sam took off, heading down the track she pointed to. It was only a few nights until the full moon and there was plenty of light to see the track. It also meant Lucas wouldn't see them coming. Light travelled a great distance out here and if they kept the headlights on, Lucas would know they were out here.

And hopefully they'd see Lucas before they were anywhere near him.

"You haven't heard from Lee?" Sam asked.

"No." The fact she hadn't was telling. He could have messaged her before leaving the police station to update her.

She refused to think about it. Right now she had to concentrate on stopping Lucas and retrieving the treasure.

Nhiari directed Sam over the sandy tracks towards the neighbouring station. Their airstrip was north of the house, so the occupants shouldn't be disturbed. She held onto the handle above the door as they bounced over the ground, Sam pushing the vehicle to its limits.

She checked her phone. Lucas was making good

time on the dirt track, though there was potential they would slow down and even get bogged when it turned sandier. She doubted they'd let air out of the tyres.

Bringing up a satellite map on her phone, she zoomed into the airstrip area. The main track had a road leading off to the north of the airstrip and one to the south. She didn't know from which end the plane would land, but it would have to turn around and take off again. Depending on the strength of the wind, they might have to taxi back to the other end before taking off.

Perhaps she should drop one guy halfway along, though she wasn't sure what effect a few bullets in a plane's tyre would have. Their current advantage was in numbers. Lucas and Lee against the three of them. Though the pilot might also be armed and willing to fight.

"There!" Sherlock pointed to a blink of light on the horizon.

Nhiari kept her gaze on the location, and a moment later, the flash of light came again. Definitely headlights bouncing over the dips and mounds of the track. She checked the tracker again. Not far to the airstrip for either of them.

"Any eyes on the plane?" She peered out of her window and twisted to look behind but couldn't see any lights in the sky.

"Could it already be there?" Sam asked.

"We would have seen it fly overhead," Nhiari said. "It won't be flying dark."

"Five o'clock," Sherlock said. "Still about ten clicks away."

It was going to be tight.

Nhiari switched on her radio and contacted Dot. "We've got eyes on the plane." She gave the coordinates.

"On our way," Dot answered.

The car jolted over a nasty bump and Nhiari's head almost hit the roof.

"Sorry." Sam's voice was curt and his grip on the steering wheel tightened.

"What's the plan?" Sherlock said.

"You two go for Lucas and Lee," Sam said. "I'll block the plane."

Good idea. If Sam parked in front of the plane, it couldn't take off.

They were still a couple of kilometres away from the airstrip when the plane flew low overhead, coming in to land from the south. It would stop at the other end, closer to Lucas and Lee.

But they still had to load the treasure, and that would take time.

Sam swore. "Hold on."

Nhiari had only a second to tighten her grip before Sam accelerated again.

***

Lucas's driving impressed Lee. He would have thought his uncle had no idea how to manage a four-wheel drive on a sandy track, but Lucas drove as if he'd been doing it all his life. Perhaps his car collection hadn't just been for show.

He didn't speak and Lee was too confused to ask questions. Why was Lucas rescuing him? It didn't fit with the uncle he knew. At no stage in Lee's life had Lucas done anything that made Lee think he cared for him.

It made Lee nervous.

When they crossed Yardie Creek without issue, Lee pictured the area in his head. There were two stations between here and Coral Bay. Nhiari's parents and the one just south of the ranges. Both had airstrips.

It would make much more sense to land at the northern airstrip, which meant Nhiari's parents would be safe. "Is the plane on the way?"

"Of course. You know where we're going?"

"Yeah, the airstrip on the northern station."

"Very good. I always thought you would be a useful asset to Stonefish. You were far smarter than either of my sons, but your father was so stubborn. If only your mother had more influence over you."

Lee glanced at Lucas as his unease grew. "Mother had her social causes." It was the nicest way he could say she'd never given him a second glance.

"Yes. She was thrilled when you finally fulfilled your family obligations."

Right. He had to be convincing. "If I'd realised how much more challenging it would be compared to the army, I would have joined sooner. Father was… vague about everything that was involved."

"Your father was soft. He didn't like doing what had to be done."

Lee bit his tongue. Was Lucas testing his loyalties? "Why?"

"His heart was never in it. He fell in love with someone before he married my sister."

Lee raised his eyebrows as his heart raced. "Who was she?"

"Someone he met in Australia," Lucas said. "He never told me her name, but he asked me to help convince our parents not to arrange the marriage between him and my sister."

So Lucas had known about Lindsay. That was a worry. "That wouldn't have been the best for the business," he replied.

"Exactly." Lucas nodded as if pleased Lee understood. "The merger between our families was a long time coming. It was the only way to consolidate and bring the company into the twenty-first century."

"Did you tell him?" Lee asked.

"Of course, and when it didn't work, I told both our parents. They set him straight. Your grandparents were humiliated he wanted to back out of the arrangement."

Both his grandparents had been more concerned about the business and appearances than anything else. He'd hated it when they came to visit because he'd always had to be perfect.

"So he married Mother. Did Father ever mention the Australian woman again?"

"No. He was told if he did, they would make sure she was no longer an option."

Lee's blood chilled. They would have killed Lindsay if his father had run away with her. He closed his eyes briefly. His family was horrific.

"We will need to arrange you a marriage when we get back to Singapore," Lucas said.

Lee looked at him, every muscle in his body tensing. He swallowed before he said, "Of course. Did you have anyone in mind?"

"Your mother has a list of appropriate women."

Of course she did. Nhiari would never make his mother's list. And Nhiari was the only one he wanted to marry.

This would soon be over and he wouldn't have to deal with his mother again.

Ahead he noticed the lights of a plane coming towards them. "Plane is almost there."

"Right on time."

Hopefully they would get to the airstrip before the plane landed. He needed to disarm Lucas before the pilot came out, otherwise he'd be outnumbered.

As they came over the final mound and the airstrip stretched out in front of them, the plane touched down. Lucas slowed as the plane reached the end, turned to face back down the runway, and powered down.

Lucas stopped just near the wing and got out. "Let's go."

Now was Lee's chance. He got out, grabbing the gun from his waist band. He strode around to the back of the four-wheel drive and levelled the gun at Lucas. "You're not going anywhere."

Lucas blinked at him. "What are you doing?"

"Stopping you," Lee said. "You killed my father and I'm not letting you escape." His pulsed roared in his ears.

Lucas threw his head back and laughed.

That wasn't the reaction he'd been expecting. Nerves tickled Lee's skin. He said nothing, waiting until Lucas was done, monitoring the plane for the pilot.

"I didn't kill your father," Lucas said when he'd finished laughing.

The engine died, and the noise echoed in the distance.

"He wanted to be free of Stonefish and you wouldn't let him leave." He stepped forward and retrieved one of the extra ties Rodney had thrown him from his pocket.

Lucas shook his head. "It wasn't me."

He was lying. "Then who killed my father?"

"Me." The female voice had Lee turning towards the plane. His mother walked down the steps dressed in a pilot's uniform.

Lee gaped at her and in that split second of inattention, Lucas lunged, grabbing the gun and pointing it at Lee.

Shit.

Lee raised his hands as he stared at his mother, trying to get his head around it. Why was she dressed as a pilot? She couldn't fly. He shook his head. "You killed Dad?"

His mother was a shrewd socialite, but he'd never considered her a killer.

"Of course I did. He wanted to leave me, wanted to risk everything we had built here. He was weak." She shrugged as she moved towards them. "I had high hopes when you joined us, but then things started to go wrong and I questioned whether you were any better than him."

"I told you he was causing all our problems," Lucas said.

Our problems. He felt as if he was on some crazy prank show. This couldn't be right. "How long have you worked for Stonefish?"

Her eyes flashed. "I am Stonefish," she said. "Not that my parents ever acknowledged a woman could run a company better than a man."

What the hell? He glanced at his uncle.

"Surprising, isn't it?" He smiled. "She had a head for it that I didn't. I've taken orders from her since before our parents died. No one knew. Not even your father."

Lee reviewed his life. His mother had always been too busy for him, always out with her friends, coming home with bags of shopping. Or there were the days when she was holed up in bed with some kind of malady and he wasn't allowed to disturb her.

She could have run the company from her room with no one knowing. Lucas made a good figurehead.

Lee had never had a clue.

"Did you kill Clark?" The question was mild and had Lee coming back to the present to see death in Lucas's eyes.

Had Lucas actually cared about his son? He'd put on a convincing front.

If Lee admitted the truth, he would be dead before he took his next breath. In his mind he apologised to Georgie. "I told you, Georgie Stokes killed Clark. He threatened the man she loved."

"Love makes people weak and vulnerable," his mother spat.

The echo of the engine was getting louder. Lee frowned. That wasn't an echo. It was a car engine. Someone was coming.

It had to be Nhiari. No one else could have got here so quickly. Somehow she'd found him. He had to get this done before she arrived, otherwise she'd be in danger.

The others didn't seem to notice.

His mother wasn't holding a weapon, but it didn't mean she was unarmed. And she was cool. Nothing riled her. But he had to try. "Dad loved me."

"Your father was always weak."

Lee clenched his hands, but kept his mouth shut. Lucas stood a metre away in front of the boot of the car, the gun pointed at Lee. If he so much as flinched, he'd be dead.

His mother glanced in the direction of the car noise. "We've got company."

"We need to get out of here," Lucas said. "Help me with the treasure."

"I don't care about the treasure," she answered. "Get in the plane, or I'm leaving without you." She turned and walked up the steps.

Leaving. The person responsible for his father's death was getting away. Lucas grabbed a bag of treasure and hauled it over his shoulder.

Still obsessed. That's what made him weak.

Lee lunged, twisting the gun from his uncle's hand. Lucas hefted the heavy bag, and it slammed into Lee's side, almost taking his breath from him.

Lee stepped back as a car burst onto the far end of the runway and barrelled towards them. It flicked its lights on as the plane engine turned over. Shit. His mother would get away.

He shot Lucas's knee as the man lunged and he fell to the ground with a yell.

Lee raced for the plane steps and was halfway up them when another gunshot cracked and pain exploded in his right shoulder.

He stumbled into the cabin and glanced out the door. Lucas had pulled his gun and was pointing it at Lee. Lee ducked out of the way as another shot cracked and the plastic moulding around him splintered.

The plane shifted and Lee strode to the cockpit. The door was locked, but a bullet saw it open. His mother was pressing the throttle forward as the white four-wheel drive pulled up in front. Nhiari and Sherlock leapt out.

Lee's heart stopped, his eyes widening.

Lucas still had his gun. Nhiari might not see him on the ground, and she wouldn't hear his warning over the engine. He should have killed Lucas before he came after his mother.

Now Nhiari was in danger.

He twisted so he could see out the door of the plane as well, but levelled his weapon at her.

His mother chuckled. "I suspected this might be the case."

Her words brought his focus back to her. "What?"

He flinched at the gunshots from outside and his mother raised the gun he hadn't spotted. "That you were lying about seducing the officer. You're just as weak as your father."

Lee had no words as he processed the gun pointing directly at Nhiari.

"So either you lower your weapon, or I'll kill the woman you love."

***

Sam parked in front of the nose, not giving the plane any space to manoeuvre. Nhiari couldn't hear anything over the roar of the engine as she leapt out of the car with Sherlock.

Nhiari focused on Lucas lying on the ground in front of her, one hand on his knee, his gun raised. Shit. Before she could raise her gun, Sherlock shot twice, and Lucas lay dead on the ground.

Where was Lee?

She looked up into the plane cockpit and saw a female pilot behind the controls. In the glow of lights, she spotted a man standing behind her.

Lee.

Why was Lee in the plane when Lucas was on the ground? Hadn't his goal been to stop Lucas?

Or was this all a lie?

The door to the plane was still open and Sherlock strode around Lucas's car, checking to make sure it was clear.

A quick glance showed a bag of treasure on the ground.

Where was the rest?

As she stepped out from behind the car, there was an explosion of glass and she stumbled as something slammed into her side. She gasped for breath, hand going to the hot bullet in her vest.

She looked up, saw Lee with his gun raised pointed at her.

He'd shot her.

Disbelief filled her as Sam swept around the front of the car, grabbed her arm and dragged her under the cover of the plane.

"Lee…and pilot…inside." She tried to take deep breaths, but the impact and shock of everything made it difficult to inhale. Lee had shot her.

"Are you all right?"

She nodded. "Hit the vest." She'd have the mother of all bruises tomorrow, but it was nothing compared to the pain in her heart.

Sherlock joined them. "They won't be going anywhere with a hole in the windscreen," he yelled.

They. Lee and the female pilot. Her uncertainty vanished. The heartbreak threatened to steal her remaining breath.

"Nhiari." Sam shook her, and she blinked. "You all right?"

She pushed the pain away. She had a job to do. "Yeah," she yelled back.

They moved down the back of the plane so they could hear a little easier and put their heads together.

"Who shot you?" Sherlock asked.

"Lee."

Both men's eyes widened and Sam felt her vest. "He could have aimed for your head."

Meaning what—he hadn't wanted to hurt her? Which meant he was still playing the game. Or she was grasping at straws.

"Two potential exits," Sherlock called. "Windscreen and door."

Of course. "Two vehicles," she added, not allowing herself to hope.

Sam shot out two tyres of Lucas's car. "One." He slipped a fresh magazine into his gun. "Anyone else in the plane?"

"Not that I saw," Nhiari said. But there could be more people in the cabin.

"Do we want them alive?" Sherlock asked.

Sam looked at her.

She nodded. "Yes." Questions still needed to be answered.

"Sherlock, you take the front. We'll take the rear."

He nodded. "I'll get eyes." He moved down the

belly of the plane and Nhiari and Sam took position on either side of the stairs.

Her heart beat in her ears as she gripped the warm gun.

It would be easy for Lee to shoot them as they climbed the stairs into the plane. She would go up first. If he wanted to kill her, he'd aim for her head this time.

She held up her fingers. Three…two…one.

She stormed the plane.

Chapter 20

Lee saw the truth in his mother's eyes. She would kill Nhiari. Only one thing he could do. Lie. He smirked at her. "Let me do the honours."

Her confusion gave him the split second he needed. He prayed as he adjusted his aim and shot Nhiari in the side.

His mother ducked as the shot reverberated and she swore as she spotted the round hole in the cockpit window. Nhiari stared up from the ground, disbelief in her eyes. Hopefully she would understand he'd done it to save her.

Lee pointed the gun at his mother, ignoring the throbbing in his right shoulder and the blood soaking his shirt. "Drop your weapon."

Sam dragged Nhiari under the plane. She was safe.

"You traitor!" His mother raised her gun, and he squeezed the trigger, shooting her in the shoulder.

"Drop it."

The gun clattered to the ground as she slammed her other hand over the wound. "You shot me."

Why was she so surprised? Did she actually think he had any loyalty to the woman who had done nothing aside from giving birth to him?

She had killed the one person who had ever loved him and showed him any support.

He strode forward and flicked off the engines, picking her gun off the floor. "You threatened the woman I love."

Footsteps pounded up behind him and he turned as Nhiari ran up the stairs, gun in hand. She pointed it at him. "Don't move."

He shifted away from his mother, raising his hands as the engine faded. Sam pushed into the cabin behind Nhiari, taking position next to her, pointing his gun at Lee's mother. He glanced around the cabin, obviously satisfied it was empty. "Just two," he said. "We've got them covered."

He must have comms with Sherlock. Maybe Sherlock had Lucas contained.

"Are you all right?" Lee nodded towards Nhiari's side where the bullet was still lodged.

"Slowly put both guns on the ground." She kept her gun pointed at him.

He did as she asked, wincing as the movement pulled on his bullet wound. "The pilot is my mother." He pressed the wound to stem the bleeding. "Lucas reported to her. She killed my father."

Sam swore and Nhiari's aim shifted past him to his mother and then back again, as if not trusting he was telling the truth.

"He shot me," his mother cried. "I need a doctor. I don't know what he's talking about. All I did was fly the plane here like my brother asked me to."

Liar.

"Dispatch, I need an ambulance," Nhiari called into her radio.

He shifted so he could monitor his mother. "If she keeps pressure on the wound, she shouldn't bleed to death." He nodded to the guns on the ground. "One of those is hers. She was going to shoot you."

"You shot me," Nhiari said, her voice dull.

"To get you out of the way and stop her from flying the plane." From his position he could see out of the cockpit where Sherlock had taken position behind the car door, but with his gun pointing at them.

Where was Lucas? Had he run?

"Are you injured?" Sam asked, nodding towards his shoulder.

"Caught a bullet Lucas sent my way."

Nhiari's eyes widened. "We need to get them both medical help." She shoved her gun into her holster and pulled out her handcuffs. "Both of you come out of the cockpit. You first, Lee."

He kicked the guns away from his mother and slowly moved into the cabin. Both Sam and Nhiari moved back to give him space, but not much. He glanced out of the door and saw Lucas lying face down in the dirt.

Dead.

He couldn't bring himself to be sad about it.

"You shot a cop," Sam said, but moved towards the cockpit to cover Lee's mother.

"To save her," Lee reiterated.

"I'm innocent," his mother said, holding one hand up while the other pressed against the wound. She leaned forward as if in pain, but the hand from her wound slid down underneath her seat. The knife blade glinted in the cockpit lights as his mother flung the knife directly at Nhiari.

"Look out!" Lee lunged in front of Nhiari as the blade flew through the air. Shots rang out and his mother jerked as twin bullets hit her body.

Then the knife sank deep into the middle of his chest and pain exploded through him. He hit the ground, his head banging against a chair, bringing with it a wave of nausea. Pain spread throughout his entire chest and he clutched at the knife, fighting to stop the pain from knocking him out.

Where was Nhiari?

She stood above him, horror on her face, but in one piece. Safe. He smiled. "You're OK."

Then he let the pain take over.

***

Everything happened too fast for Nhiari to process. Lee's mother slid off her chair onto the floor as Lee landed with a thud by Nhiari's feet. Sam strode forward to check the woman. "Dead." He gestured for Sherlock to come around.

Nhiari dropped to her knees next to Lee, who had a knife protruding from his chest. Her heart pounded as she pressed her hands against the blade, feeling his warm blood coating her hands. His breathing was shallow.

"What did you do that for?" she demanded. "I'm wearing Kevlar."

His smile became a wince. "Instinct. I couldn't let her hurt you."

Idiot. She didn't know what to think or to say. She pressed her radio. "Stab wound victim. What's the ambulance ETA?"

"Sixty minutes."

Shit. That was far too long.

Sherlock came up the stairs carrying a first aid kit.

"Can either of you fly this thing?" she asked as she moved aside.

"No." Sherlock applied a bandage to the wound, keeping the knife in place.

"Drive him in," Sam said. "I'll guard here until Dot arrives."

Nhiari looked at the two dead bodies. She couldn't leave civilians in charge here and Sherlock had medic training. Lee would be better with him. "No. You two take him. I'll tell the ambulance you'll meet them halfway." She visualised the map they'd studied. "The track to the main road should be through there. You'll go past the main house."

Sam nodded.

She leaned close to Lee as she battled letting the fear take control. "You're going to be all right." Her voice shook.

"I'll make sure of it," he gasped, pain washing over his face.

"I think his lung is punctured," Sherlock said.

"He's been shot too. Right shoulder," Sam told him.

Nhiari helped Lee to his feet, but he leaned against Sam as he climbed down the stairs. Sherlock brought the car close to the door. Sam lay the backseats down to make a larger area for Lee to lie down in and Sherlock climbed in beside him.

Nhiari bit her lip and clasped her hands together. She desperately wanted to go with him, to figure out the truth. She wanted to tell him she loved him, but the words stayed unspoken. Instead she stood where she was while Sam climbed into the driver's seat and they drove away.

She moved over to Lucas and checked his vitals, though she was certain Sherlock would have already done so.

Dead.

Good. She radioed dispatch to inform the ambulance Lee was on his way to them.

She had two dead people on her hands and if Lee was to be believed, they were in control of Stonefish. This could all be over.

She almost tripped over the backpack full of

treasure. With a sigh, she picked up both bags and put them back into Lucas's four-wheel drive.

All of this was over a few bags of riches.

And everyone who wanted it was dead. The only person alive who might know the truth as to whose side Lee was on was Rodney.

She wanted to be sick. Chances were high, Lee would go to gaol after he'd been patched up. Rodney was unsympathetic.

All the stress and agony of the past few months rolled over her. She stumbled to the stairs of the plane, sank down and cried.

***

Rodney's team arrived about an hour after Dot and Brandon and had taken over the scene. It gave Nhiari plenty of time to get herself together.

One of them strode over to her as others set up the lighting, and she managed a smile through her exhaustion. "Doug! It's so great to see you."

"I couldn't let the two of you have all the fun." He hugged her and she winced from her bruises. "How did you come to be here?"

She told him about Lucas speaking with her father and her waiting in position in case Stonefish used that airstrip.

"Why didn't you tell Rodney?" Doug demanded.

She stiffened at his tone. "Because he was working for Stonefish."

He swore. "You could have told me."

"I thought you were going on leave."

He sighed. "Damn it. This whole case has been a mess."

"How's Rodney?"

Doug raised his eyebrows at her. "This wasn't all his fault. Last I heard, they were taking him into the operating theatre, but he'd be fine."

Together they watched Doug's team load the treasure into the back of a police car. "I don't think Stonefish has anyone left who will go after it, but there are plenty of civilians who would," Nhiari said. "You need to be careful with it."

"Your friend Brandon has already told me he'll be guarding it. We'll fly it to Perth in the morning."

She sighed. Good. Someone else could deal with it.

Doug pulled out a notebook. "So tell me everything that happened."

"This will take a while." She took a deep breath and began.

***

The sun was rising before Nhiari climbed into the police car next to Dot. She would kill for a coffee, but she was driving because Dot looked as if she was about to drop. Brandon was staying with the treasure.

"Any news from Sam?" Dot asked.

"Yeah. Lee was transferred to the ambulance and after some surgery, he's recovering well in hospital. Sam and Sherlock are standing guard since Lee is technically still under arrest."

"Do you think it's over?" Dot asked.

Nhiari slowed over a hump. "We still need to work out Lee's role in all of this."

"I can't believe he shot you."

She clenched her hands on the steering wheel. "He said it was to protect me from his mother."

"I guess if he wanted to kill you, he would have aimed at your head."

Nhiari scowled. "That's what Sam said."

"You know what I mean," Dot insisted. "He's got skills. He wouldn't miss his target at that distance."

She was right, not that it made her feel any better.

"What are you going to do about Lee?"

She closed her eyes briefly. "I don't know."

Dot squeezed her leg. "I understand. I didn't know whether I could trust Oliver."

"At least you had a history with him. Lee admitted that first date was so he could get information out of me."

"It would be easier if there was someone who could vouch for him," Dot agreed.

Nhiari glanced at her. Should she mention Lindsay? Though she could have been manipulated too.

"What is it?" Dot asked, sitting straighter. "What haven't you told me?"

Nhiari grimaced. "Sometimes I wish you weren't so observant."

"Don't avoid the question."

She exhaled. "You won't like it."

"Tell me." Dot's voice was icy, the fatigue gone from it.

Crap. "Lee's father was the man Lindsay fell in love with." Nhiari spoke quickly. "The one who broke her heart. He returned at the beginning of the year and left again, promising to return, but he was killed by Lucas." She pressed her lips together. "No, I guess his wife killed him if Lee is to be believed."

"Lindsay knew Lee was his son?" Dot asked.

"Yes. Lee visited her when he first arrived. She's been helping him while he's been on the run."

Dot swore. "She said nothing to me."

"She trusted him." Though love could make people see only what they wanted to see.

"Then let's pay Lindsay a visit now." Dot's tone was grim, and Nhiari almost felt sorry for Lindsay.

***

When they pulled into Lindsay's drive, she was just

about to get into her car. She turned, walking over to them. "You're up early today," she said. "I was just on my way to work."

"We haven't been to bed," Dot said. "And this isn't a social call."

Lindsay examined Dot's face and then glanced at Nhiari. She sighed. "Come in." The older woman went into the kitchen and switched on the coffee machine. "What is this all about?"

Nhiari spoke, knowing this was already difficult for Dot. "Lee Kwong."

Lindsay nodded as she measured ground coffee. "I thought it might be."

"Why didn't you tell me you were helping him?" Dot demanded. "You knew how exhausted I was. You knew I needed a break in the case."

Lindsay set the machine running and turned to her. "Because I believed Lee was trying to help you stop them."

"He shot and killed two men!"

"Both of whom would have shot innocent people," Lindsay pointed out. "He saved lives by taking some."

Dot's face turned red and before she could speak, Nhiari said, "Sit down and tell us how you met him." She went to the coffee machine and finished pouring the drinks, putting one on the kitchen table for Dot, who was still standing with a look of utter betrayal on her face.

"He knocked on my door," Lindsay began. The story which followed mirrored what Lee had told Nhiari. "After he shot Tan, he came to me in the middle of the night to ask for food. I agreed to provide him with care packages regularly so he could continue working to stop Stonefish."

"Why did you think he was telling you the truth?" Nhiari asked. It was the question she needed to resolve.

"Because he had the same tell as his father." She smiled sadly. "I knew my Julian would have come back to me if he could."

Nhiari said nothing. What could she say? This woman had lost the man she'd loved not once, but twice.

"What will happen to Lee now?" Lindsay asked.

Nhiari glanced at Dot. It was a question she also wanted answered.

"He was injured last night," Dot said. "We'll need to question him again and then it's up to Organised Crime how they will prosecute him."

Rodney would throw the book at him. Nhiari paused. No. Rodney might be under arrest himself, which meant there might be a chance.

But did she want a chance with Lee? He had shot her.

Lindsay placed her hand over Nhiari's. "You can trust Lee. I could tell how much he cared for you when he called me to organise your clothes. He has such a big heart. Don't throw it away." She sighed. "I would do anything to have his father back again. We never got the life we wanted."

Lee wasn't his father.

Dot got to her feet. "We need to get going." She hesitated, then hugged Lindsay. "You should have told me everything, but I understand why you didn't."

Lindsay nodded. "I'm sorry."

Nhiari followed Dot to the door.

"Can I visit Lee in the hospital?" Lindsay asked.

"I'll need to check with Organised Crime," Dot said. "I'll call you."

Nhiari drove to the police station. Only Pierre's car was in the car park. Dot sighed. "I'll fill him in and then I'm getting some sleep. Make sure you do as well, and we'll reconvene at midday."

"All right." She hadn't had a minute to herself. Should she go home? After a week away, her pot plant was probably dead and she couldn't remember if she'd done her breakfast dishes the morning the boys had been kidnapped. She rubbed her eyes. A lifetime ago.

Or should she visit Lee?

Lindsay's words came back to her. This might be the only time she got alone with Lee, and she wanted to sort a few things out. She turned towards the hospital and drove through the town.

A few residents were walking their dogs, but it was still early. Being the weekend, no kids were off to school, but there were a couple riding bicycles and a father was already down at the park with his young kids.

Such normal life.

She'd had none of that in the past week. She wasn't sure whether she would ever feel normal again.

The hospital car park was empty, and she parked close to the door, walking through to reception.

"Nhiari!" the receptionist, Tracy exclaimed. "It's so good to see you. I heard you were lost in the ranges. Are you all right? Do you need to be checked by the doctor?"

Nhiari smiled at the enthusiasm from Georgie's friend. "I'm fine. I'm here to see the patient who was brought in last night. Lee Kwong."

Tracy nodded. "Just down the hall to the left." She buzzed the door open for Nhiari. "Sam and Sherlock haven't left since Lee got out of surgery. It must be nice to have such good friends."

Nhiari didn't correct her. She followed the directions and stood outside the room for a minute. A murmur of voices came from inside, but with the door closed she couldn't make out the words.

Taking a deep breath, she stepped inside. It was a two-bed room. Sam and Sherlock sat on either side of

Lee's bed and in the one next to him lay Rodney.

Shit. She'd forgotten about him. She was far too tired to deal with Rodney today, and she definitely didn't want to have the conversation she needed to have with Lee in front of him.

"Nhiari." Lee's cautious smile made everyone turn and look at her. Lee looked good for someone who had been stabbed and shot. His colouring was normal, and he wore a blue patient robe.

Machines beeped and everything was white and sterile.

"Finally!" Rodney said. "Someone who can get me out of here. These two wouldn't let me leave."

Sam and Sherlock both smirked.

Nhiari's feet twitched, and she almost walked out. She braced herself. "The last I heard you were under arrest." He looked far worse than Lee. His face was pale, he had IV tubes in him and he lay with his bed only a little raised so he could see around the room easier.

"You didn't catch Lucas?" Rodney demanded.

She glanced at Sam.

"We didn't tell him anything."

That was helpful. She could figure out what Rodney knew. She drew out a notebook. "Why don't you two go home?" she said to Sam and Sherlock. "Get some rest. I'll take over here."

"Have you slept?" Lee asked, shifting to a more upright position with a wince.

"I'm fine." She shooed Sam and Sherlock out of the room and then studied the two men who were left. One who she had hated with all her being while at the academy, and one she loved but couldn't trust.

She couldn't question Rodney with Lee present, even if the two heads of Stonefish were no longer in the picture.

"You need to tell me what happened," Rodney blustered. "I am lead on this case."

"You were caught helping a suspect escape and helping Lucas steal the treasure," Nhiari said. "I don't have to tell you anything." She did, however, want to know what was happening with him. "How injured are you?"

"I'll live."

Shame. She called the station and Dot answered. "Shouldn't you be in bed by now?" Nhiari asked.

"Just filling in Pierre on what happened."

"Are Organised Crime there?"

"Yeah. Doug's about to come to the hospital to check on Rodney and Lee."

"Rodney and Lee are sharing a room."

"Oh. Doug will sort it out. He'll be there soon."

Nhiari hung up.

"What's going on?" Rodney demanded.

Still an arsehole even though he was lying in hospital with a gunshot wound. "Doug is on his way over." At Lee's questioning look, she added, "One of the Organised Crime team."

He nodded his thanks.

She studied him. She couldn't quite believe he'd leapt in front of a knife for her. Especially as she'd been wearing her bullet-proof vest. She wanted to hold his hand and tell him how foolish it was, to ask what the doctor had said and what happened to them from here.

But anything personal would have to wait until she had him alone.

Which might never happen if Organised Crime took over.

Perhaps Doug could organise it for her.

"About time," Rodney said. "What took them so long?"

Nhiari didn't answer. This man deserved none of her

time. He'd betrayed his role as a police officer by working with Stonefish, and he'd almost destroyed her chance of becoming a police officer at the academy.

A nurse walked in. "Good morning!" She went over to Lee and did his observations before asking, "How's your pain?"

"Manageable."

She nodded and turned to Rodney to do the same. Nhiari brushed her hand over Lee's foot while Rodney was distracted and Lee smiled.

When the nurse was done, Doug walked in with another plain clothes detective who he introduced as Karen.

"Did you get things sorted out there?"

He nodded. "I still need to ask the two who were with you some questions."

"I sent Sam and Sherlock home to bed, but they'll be available when you want them."

"Great." He turned to the nurse. "Do you have a spare room so we can separate these two?"

She shook her head. "We're full, but the doctor was talking about discharging Mr Kwong this morning."

"We can talk in front of Lee," Rodney said. "The man's been working against Stonefish from the beginning."

Nhiari jolted. "What? You believe him?" She pinched herself to make sure she hadn't drifted into a daydream.

Rodney directed his answer at Doug. "Lee's highly competent. He could have taken over the operations here when they were failing and fixed everything without breaking a sweat. Instead he helped it crumble."

She gaped at him, trying to reconcile this man speaking calmly in front of her with the arsehole she knew him to be. Was this his personality with

Organised Crime? "Why didn't you tell Lucas?"

"Because it suited me. I was working undercover at Stonefish. I've been building a case against them for years."

She raised her eyebrows. "You weren't crooked?" She shouldn't feel so disappointed.

"No."

Nhiari glanced at Doug. "Can you confirm?"

Rodney chuckled as Doug nodded. "You don't trust me, do you?"

"No. Not after what you did to me at the academy."

He sobered. "I'm sorry. I was young and stupid."

Who was this man? "Whatever drugs they're giving you for the pain must be pretty good."

"I'm serious, Nhiari." He glanced at Doug and Karen and then sighed. "Something happened to me after the academy that made me realise what an arsehole I'd been. I've changed, but I knew when I came up here, neither you nor Dot would trust me no matter how I behaved, so I reverted to the man you knew."

She couldn't believe what she was hearing. She stepped away, bumping into Lee's bed, and glanced at Doug again.

"It's true, Nhiari. He's not really an arsehole."

"There's nothing I can do to make up for what I did to you at the academy. I took my hurt at your rejection out on you and Dot, and it wasn't fair."

"You almost got me kicked off the force."

"I'm glad I failed. You're an excellent officer. You got through to Lee when none of us could."

She wasn't touching that comment. This was too much on top of everything that had happened.

"Why did Lucas shoot you?" Doug asked and Nhiari was glad about the change of subject.

"He must have suspected me," Rodney replied.

"He did," Lee spoke. "Lucas knew the Organised

Crime team was up here. I guess he spotted them when he was scoping out the area."

"Where was he staying?" Nhiari asked.

"There's a safe house in town." He gave the address and Karen made a phone call, telling their team to check it out.

"You didn't tell Lucas about the team?" Doug asked Lee.

"I didn't know. I think trust was low for all parties," Lee said, glancing at Nhiari. "Rodney didn't tell me what was going on with Stonefish or the police. He didn't even tell me he'd not locked my cell."

"That's because Lucas wouldn't tell me what he had planned," Rodney explained. "I half expected you to escape out the back, but I was hoping he wanted the treasure badly enough to take it."

"The treasure was his obsession," Lee said. "He wasn't leaving it behind."

"What happened?" Rodney asked.

Nhiari moved to a seat further away from both beds and sat. Before Lee spoke, Doug came over to her. "You know all of this. Why don't you get some rest? I'll call you later and fill you in." He lowered his voice. "I'll make sure you two have a chance to talk."

She glanced at Lee. "All right. Thanks."

She couldn't think rationally now anyway.

Without another word, she walked out of the hospital.

Chapter 21

Lee vowed it wouldn't be the last time he saw Nhiari as she walked out of the room. Somehow he would figure out a way for them to talk, even if they arrested him and were planning to gaol him for life.

"What happened last night?" Detective Doug Pecherczyk asked.

"Rodney arrested me." Lee glanced at Rodney. He was still having difficulty believing the man had been working for the police all along and wasn't a crooked cop. "He brought me into town from Retribution Ridge and threw me into a gaol cell," he continued. Lee explained everything that had happened until he arrived at the hospital.

By the time he finished, he'd drained his water jug and fatigue clouded his brain. The doctor walked in and glanced at everyone in the room. Doug introduced himself and the other detective, Karen.

"Are you discharging Lee?"

"Possibly." The doctor picked up Lee's chart, glancing through it. "How are you feeling?"

"Sore," Lee admitted. "But it's nothing I can't handle."

"Good." He turned to Doug. "I'll get the nurses to organise his discharge papers. If he's being remanded in custody, there are some things you'll need to know."

Doug nodded. "I'll sort it out."

Lee watched the detective. He was nicer than Rodney and didn't have the attitude. Lee wasn't certain he believed Rodney's statement that he'd gone back to 'old' Rodney as part of his cover, but at least Doug seemed to be on Nhiari's side.

"I'll need to take your passport," Doug said.

Why? Wasn't he going straight to Carnarvon gaol? "It's in my backpack out at the Ridge."

"I've asked Darcy Stokes to bring your things into town," Doug continued. "We'll need you to sign your statement and be available for more questions as needed."

Lee frowned. "Am I not under arrest?"

"Nhiari contacted me several days ago to ask about clemency for you. With the information Rodney's been feeding us and your willingness to cooperate with the police, it has been decided your sentence will be suspended indefinitely. You helped us stop Stonefish."

Lee stared at him, not comprehending it. "I'm free to go?"

"To a certain extent. Consider it a type of parole. We'll need your passport, and for you to check in regularly until we can clean up the rest of Stonefish's operation." Doug smiled. "We're bound to have more questions as we go through the files Andrew extracted for us."

Lee closed his eyes as the disbelief made him dizzy. This was more than he had ever hoped for.

"Your mother's and your uncle's bodies are at the hospital," Doug continued. "They will be released to family in a few days if you would like to arrange what you would like done with them."

"I'll give you my aunt's details. She can decide." He didn't care, but his aunt would want Lucas's body back in Singapore. She'd lost her whole family in only a few months.

"Karen will take you back to the police station to finalise things when you get your discharge papers."

Lee nodded. His heart pounded with the anticipation which came just before the first dip of a rollercoaster.

He wasn't going to gaol.

His life stretched out in front of him, myriad paths for him to choose.

There was only one path he wanted to follow.

***

A couple of hours later, he stood with Dot at the police station entrance.

"What are you going to do now?" she asked.

There were so many people he needed to contact, but only one he wanted to speak with. "Find Nhiari."

Dot smiled. "She's at home. Good luck."

"Thank you." He walked over to his car where Darcy, Ed, and Matt waited. They'd driven his car with his things into town. He didn't blame them for hanging around to find out what had happened. There was a lot Lee had to make up for, but right now, he wanted to see the woman he loved.

"They let you go," Darcy said.

"I'm on parole," he answered, sizing up the man. "There's nothing I can do to make up for what Stonefish did to you and your family," he began. "For what I did to your family. I would have stopped Clark if I'd known what he had planned. Your parents were kind people."

"You killed Clark and prevented the deaths of more of my family." Darcy looked him right in the eyes. "For that, I thank you."

"You killed Tan and saved Tess," Ed said, holding out his hand. "You have my eternal gratitude."

Lee shook it and turned to the scowling Matt, who shifted next to him. "You lied to my sister."

"I protected Nhiari as much as I could."

Matt gave a reluctant nod. "Pretty stupid to jump in front of the knife."

Lee raised an eyebrow. "Instinct. If I recall, you stepped in front of the woman you love too."

Matt's eyes widened, and he whistled. "Shit."

Lee smiled. Finally he had found a way to shut Matt up.

Darcy cleared his throat. "It might take some of us time before we can forgive you completely."

"I understand." He was being more than generous.

"However our women are very forgiving. They've invited you to dinner tomorrow night at the Ridge."

Lee stared at him.

Ed chuckled. "Tess said she and Georgie would drag you there. They have questions." The love in his voice was clear.

Darcy handed over the car keys. "You'd better be there. Dinner's at six." With that, they walked away.

Lee rubbed his thumb over the warm metal of his keys. He'd always known the Stokes were special.

Lee got into his car and drove the short distance to Nhiari's town house. He'd only been here once before on their date, but nothing had changed. It was a small brick and tile place in the same complex as Georgie's and had two bedrooms. Her car was parked in the carport and he parked in the spot next to it, nerves scrambling around his stomach.

This was it.

Would she forgive him for lying to her? Would she forgive him for shooting her?

Did they have a future together?

The only way to get answers was to knock on her door.

Taking a deep breath, he walked up the few steps and knocked.

The wait was interminable. It was almost midday, so she shouldn't be sleeping any longer, but he couldn't hear her walking around inside.

He rapped again, louder and a little more insistent. This time she called, "I'm coming!" with a little irritation in her voice.

He exhaled and stepped back to give her space. She flung open the door. Her dark hair was tied back in a messy ponytail, she had a plain T-shirt and shorts on and her eyes widened in shock. "Lee." She rubbed her hands over her face, looking as if she'd just woken up.

He smiled. "They gave me parole."

She frowned and stepped back, blinking her disbelief. "What?"

He clenched his hands together to stop himself from pulling her into his arms. He needed to give her a chance to compute what was happening. "Since you contacted Doug a few days ago, they've been putting together the evidence about what I've done to stop Stonefish. With what Rodney's now added to it, they agreed to parole me based on a few conditions." He kept his gaze steady on her.

She tugged on the end of her ponytail. "What conditions?"

"I had to hand over my passport, be available for further questioning, and report to a police station weekly." When she continued to stare at him, he asked, "Can I come in?"

She nodded and stepped back so he could enter her house. The living area was simple but with touches of her. Comfortable sofa in front of a moderate sized television and a coffee table with several books on it.

The photo on the wall was of the waterhole they had swum in. She'd told him on their date that it was her special place.

"Are you all right?" She touched her chest in the same place as his injury.

"Yeah. I need to take it easy for a couple of weeks. No strenuous exercise."

She walked into the kitchen and put on the kettle, getting out a couple of mugs. "Do you want a drink?" She grabbed her phone from the counter and dashed out a text message.

Who was she contacting? "No. I want to talk to you."

Her phone dinged, and she smiled.

"Who was that?"

Nhiari hesitated. "Dot."

"You were checking I was telling the truth."

She nodded.

He couldn't blame her. "Will you talk to me now?"

In answer, she sat on the sofa, wincing a little as she did so, her hand going to her side. Where he'd shot her.

Horrified, he knelt in front of her and reached for her, but hesitated, not touching her. "May I?"

She lifted her top so he could see the slight graze to her skin and the dark bruise spreading from it. Lee brushed it lightly. He had caused this. He had hurt her. Remorse filled him. "I'm so sorry."

She hissed and shifted away. "Why did you do it?"

"Because my mother was going to kill you," he said. "She had a gun pointing at you and would have aimed for your head. I figured I could hit your vest and you would take cover. Sam dragged you away, and it surprised Mother enough that I could get the upper hand." Briefly at least.

"Why didn't you contact me when Rodney broke you out of gaol?"

"Because Lucas said he would kill any police officer he saw. I wasn't risking your life. You're too precious to me."

She closed her eyes and leaned away from him.

How could he make her believe him? "I wasn't double-crossing you. My goal was always to stop Lucas. I could do that without putting you in danger." He frowned. "How did you find us?"

She looked at him. "I put a tracker on your phone."

It was his turn to lean back. "When?"

"That message I sent you at the Ridge."

Surprise filled him and then he smiled. "Payback. Nice work." Then he frowned. "Were you already out there?"

She nodded. "Lucas spoke to my father the day before. He was pretending to be a tour operator. When I heard someone had been asking about the airstrip, I figured he might plan to use it. We were there just in case, but then I remembered the airstrip to the north, and we headed there."

She was so smart. "Good work."

"You're not mad I tracked you?"

"It was sensible," he said. "Though when you turned up, I was terrified for your life. I thought Lucas had killed you when I heard the gun shots."

"Sherlock was faster."

"Remind me to thank him." Lee took her hand in his. "I've done a lot of bad things; I've killed, I've lied, and I've hurt you. But that's all over now. My father's killer is dead, Stonefish is being disbanded, and I've been given a second chance with parole." He looked into her eyes. "And if you'll give me a second chance, I won't waste it. I'll spend a lifetime making it up to you, proving that you are the most important person in the world to me."

"What will you do now?"

He hadn't thought that far ahead, but he should have. "I have my photography," he said. "The coffee table book I told you about wasn't a lie, though now Stonefish is finished, the publisher might pull the contract." He'd call them tomorrow. "And I'm sure I'll be able to get a job around here. I'll do whatever it takes; stocking shelves, herding sheep, picking up litter."

"Lindsay will give you a job if she has one," Nhiari said with a smile.

"Did you speak to her?"

She nodded. "She spoke highly of you."

He bit his lip. "And do you agree with her assessment?"

Her thumb rubbed against the back of his hand where she still held on to it. "I do, but I don't know if we can make it work. You've hurt all of my friends."

"Darcy, Ed and Matt brought my things into town," he said in a rush, trying to stop her from rejecting him. "Tess and Georgie have already forgiven me, and I've been invited out to the Ridge for dinner tomorrow night."

Her eyebrows raised. "Really?"

"Really. Perhaps they realised how much I love you."

Her eyes glistened with tears and she sighed, long and heartfelt. "I love you too."

Elation filled him and he shifted to the couch, pulling her gently into his arms, and sealed the declaration with a kiss.

"You captured my heart the day of our date as well," she admitted when they pulled apart. "I've hated the thought you were manipulating me. My taste in men has always been terrible."

"I'm so sorry, Nhi. I'll never give you pause to doubt me again." He kissed her again.

She nodded. "We'll make it work."
"Yes, we will."

Chapter 22

"We should be going." Nhiari stretched languorously on the bed next to him.

Lee ran a hand down her naked side as the nerves pinched inside him. He kissed her shoulder rather than ask whether they had to go. This was his chance to start making amends, to prove to Nhiari's friends he loved her and was truly sorry for everything he had done. He pulled away. "All right. Let's shower."

They'd both been at the police station most of the day; Lee filling in any blanks Organised Crime wanted to know, and Nhiari catching up on all the work she'd missed while she'd been with Lee. The moment they'd crossed her threshold at home, they'd been in each other's arms as if they'd been apart for weeks.

He smiled as he ran the shower and she stepped in naked. She was glorious, and they hadn't showered together yet. Thankfully, all his dressings were waterproof.

Gently he traced the bruise which was already starting to fade, before he pulled her into his arms.

"We'll be late if you keep this up."

Reluctantly he let her go. "We don't want that."

As Nhiari handed him a towel, she asked, "How are you feeling?"

"Nervous," he admitted. "More nervous than the last time I saw them. This time I know my future, and I don't want to stuff this up." He didn't want Nhiari to have to choose between him and her friends, because he wasn't certain she would choose him.

She hugged him. "It will be fine." She tugged on the end of her braid as she dressed.

Yeah, she was worried too. He would do everything he could to make sure this went well.

***

On the drive out to the Ridge they discussed Stonefish, filling each other in on where Organised Crime was at. The files Andrew had stolen had been helpful in building the case and there'd been a synchronised raid on all known Stonefish properties, both in Australia and Singapore.

"Have you heard from your aunt?" Nhiari asked.

The nausea in his stomach flared. "Yeah."

She glanced at him. "How did it go?"

"About as well as expected." His voice was flat, but he didn't have it in him to pretend.

"You want to talk about it?"

His lips curved. It was one thing he loved about Nhiari. She didn't push. She would wait until he was ready, she wouldn't demand he tell her.

"She was distraught." An understatement considering she'd lost her whole family. "I didn't know what to say. She blames me for not protecting Andrew, and she wanted me to tell her that what the police were saying was untrue." He shrugged. "I couldn't." She vehemently refused to accept anything he said. "Maybe her friends can offer her some comfort." He'd hung up knowing his last tie with his family had been forever severed. He was on his own now.

"None of this was your fault." Nhiari reached for his hand and squeezed it. "They all made their own decisions. You did the best you could."

He didn't bother pointing out Clark's death was his fault. "I thought I'd be relieved when all this ended, but I feel hollow."

"It's consumed your life for almost a year," Nhiari said. "You've lost all your family. You might not have been close to them, but it takes its toll."

She was right. He closed his eyes. "Thanks."

"I know it's not much of a consolation, but you've got me now," she said. "I'm here for you."

His eyes flashed open as incredulity filled him, and he shifted to look at her fully. "You are not a consolation. You're the jackpot. I feel like I've won the life lottery with you, Nhi. I'm so damn thankful you forgave me." How could she even think she was anything less than everything to him?

She smiled as she drove through the gate of the Ridge, her eyes a little glossy. "You're my jackpot too."

Everyone's cars were outside the farmhouse and the campsites were empty. It was getting to the off-peak season, and he'd overheard Amy saying they would close the campsites until the new year, when tourists started travelling north again.

Nhiari met him at the front of her car and hugged him. "Are you ready for this?"

He nodded. "If you're with me, I can face anything."

The sounds of voices, dishes clanking and the scents of something roasting came floating out of the kitchen doorway.

Lee braced himself. "Let's go."

The first person he noticed when he walked in was Amy. She was at the oven, checking the contents and then switched off the gas, satisfied the food was ready.

She turned and spotted him. Her smile was a little hesitant, but she walked over to him and held out her arms. "Welcome. I'm glad you came."

A lump formed in his throat. This woman had welcomed him from the minute he'd arrived as a camper at the beginning of the year. She'd drawn maps to show him where he could go and had invited him in for a cuppa whenever she'd seen him. His vow to stop Stonefish had strengthened after he'd met Amy, if that was even possible.

Swallowing the lump, he moved into her arms and hugged her. "I don't deserve this, Amy. The things I've done to your family… The way I've lied to you… I'm so sorry."

She shook her head and stepped back. "You helped stop Stonefish. We're all safe now, thanks in part to your help."

She was being far too generous. He suddenly realised the kitchen was silent. He looked up, met Brandon's gaze first. He nodded in approval. Perhaps he'd heard Lee's apology.

"It's my turn." Georgie hip-bumped Amy out of the way. "I always said Lee was helping us." She grinned at Lee. "I'm glad I was right." She squeezed him.

Lee chuckled and winced as his wound pulled. "You didn't know when to keep your nose out of trouble."

"I'll second that," Matt murmured.

Georgie spun. "I heard that!" She screwed up her nose and stalked towards Matt in mock outrage. He grinned and snagged her around the waist, kissing her objections away.

Tess was next. She was a little shy, but far more confident than the woman he'd met back in July. "Thank you for saving my life." Her hug was quick, but the smile she gave him filled his heart. These women were going to kill him with their kindness.

"Can we continue my photography lessons now you're good again?" Lara asked, coming to stand next to him.

"I'd like that. You've got a good eye." He glanced at Darcy, who had his arm around Faith. The man nodded his permission.

"Maybe I should go with you." Jordan stepped next to Lara. "Though he was a bit of a shit kidnapper."

Lee laughed then, placing a hand over his chest. "I didn't expect you to be so well-trained," he admitted.

"Sherlock's the best," Jordan declared.

Lee saw the look of love pass between Gretchen and Sherlock. "Yeah. He did a great job of training you, but I promise you won't need protection from me again."

"I bet Lee could add a few new things to your training," Sam said from where he sat next to Penelope, their hands entwined.

Jordan looked interested. "We can discuss."

"Only if you teach me too," Lara piped up.

Darcy groaned in playful protest.

Dot clapped her hands together. "Now that everyone is here, we can debrief. Take a seat."

Everyone obeyed her call and Lee took a moment to compose himself. Nhiari slipped her arm around his waist. "Feeling better now?"

He nodded, blinking back the tears. "You have the best friends."

"They're yours now too. Come on." She pulled him to the table, and they sat in the remaining seats at the middle of the table.

Dot sat at one end next to Oliver, and Brandon sat at the other. "I think I've got the full story about what went down last night, but feel free to add details I might have missed," Dot said.

As Dot outlined the events, Amy dished up and everyone ate her delicious roast lamb dinner.

"Today Brandon accompanied the treasure to Perth with some of the Organised Crime team and it's been delivered to the museum to assess." Dot gestured for Brandon to take up the story.

"There was an armoured car waiting to meet the plane," Brandon said. "We transferred the treasure and took it straight to the museum. Oliver's boss was pretty gobsmacked to see the quality and quantity of it."

"Do we get to keep it?" Lara demanded.

Brandon smiled. "No, La La."

Her shoulders slumped, and she pouted. "But we found it. Lilian wanted us to have it."

Brandon reached to the floor and placed a small bag on the table. "He gave permission for us each to keep one coin." He got to his feet and gave each person at the table one of the silver coins. When he handed one to Lee, Lee's eyes widened. "Are you sure?"

Brandon nodded. "You helped by not letting Lucas take it."

The coin was cool and rough and Lee squeezed it, not quite believing he was included.

"He knows what we went through because of this treasure," Brandon continued. "He gave us a choice; we can take a finder's fee, or jewels from the treasure to the value of the finder's fee."

"How much?" Darcy asked.

Brandon glanced around the table.

"Spit it out, Bran!" Georgie yelled.

"He estimates the treasure is worth about fifty million in today's money." Brandon smirked at Georgie's sound of frustration. "And in cases like these, the finder's fee is about five percent."

"That's two point five million," Tess said.

Brandon nodded.

"Holy shit!" Georgie cried.

"We're rich!" Lara yelled.

Brandon held up a hand. "Hold up. We still have to decide."

"I don't need jewels," Amy said.

He smiled at her. "Yeah, I know Ames, but the way I'm thinking, this needs to be a group decision. Each person at this table has been hurt because of the treasure. Everyone here deserves a portion of the finder's fee."

Oliver shook his head. "I wasn't even here when it was found."

"But your expedition was affected," Brandon argued.

"You earned it," Sam said. "You helped Dot when she needed it."

"We're not family," Gretchen said. "As Lara said, Lilian kept it for her family."

"Bullshit," Darcy retorted. "Every person here is as close as family. You've all done incredible things to help us." His gaze fell on Sam and Sherlock. "You two are my brother's brothers, which makes you mine too. You protected him when he was too dumb to know he was still welcome at home, and then you supported him when he returned and faced Stonefish."

Sam and Sherlock fist-bumped their chests in appreciation.

"As for Nhiari and Dot." Darcy shook his head. "We were stupid not to trust you with everything from the start. You did everything you could to protect us and help us. You've been constants in our life from childhood and are as close as sisters." He smiled. "At one stage, Mum hoped you would become a true sister," he said to Dot.

Nhiari whispered to Lee, "Brandon and Dot dated in high school."

That was kind of sweet.

"As for your partners," Darcy said. "Well, as far as

I'm concerned, it's a package deal. If one of you is family, then both of you are." He met Lee's gaze. "Yeah, even you." He winked.

Everyone chuckled, and Nhiari squeezed Lee's hand. He stared at Darcy, unable to speak. He blinked rapidly and nodded once, but it was all he could manage with his chest so full and the lump so large in his throat.

This family.

They were more than he'd ever dreamed of.

Darcy nodded in understanding and continued. "Gretchen and I spoke earlier, and we both agreed that whatever happens, both Lara and Jordan deserve their share of the treasure, to do with whatever they like."

Lara squealed and Darcy added, "When you're old enough to make sensible decisions."

Everyone laughed at Lara's huff.

"Mum can have mine," Jordan said. "She needs it."

Gretchen sniffed. "No, sweetheart. It's all yours. You were so brave and smart, staying calm when your dad took you." She gave an almost apologetic look to Lee.

"He was incredible," Lee agreed. "Told me they would escape, and they did."

Jordan nodded. "I'll share mine with Cody then."

What a kid.

"So with that settled, what does everyone want to do—take the money and split it between everyone?" Brandon asked.

One by one everyone nodded.

Brandon grinned. "I'll tell the museum."

The money would give Lee time to find a job and figure out what he was doing next in his life. He could contribute to their household. Lee glanced at Nhiari. Assuming he moved in with her. They hadn't discussed what was next.

Around them people were getting to their feet and

clearing the table.

"You OK?" Nhiari murmured.

"I need a moment," Lee responded. "Can we go for a walk?"

She nodded and got to her feet. No one paid them any attention, but Nhiari spoke to Dot and then took Lee's hand and they walked outside into the cool evening air.

The sun had set while they'd had dinner and the stars shone in such vivid clarity above them.

They walked away from the house towards the sand dunes. Finally Nhiari said, "That was something, wasn't it?"

"I never expected…" He shook his head. "They forgave me. They called me family." That was something he couldn't quite get past.

"Well as Darcy said, we're a pair now."

He dragged her close, inhaling her scent and the storm inside him calmed. "We haven't spoken about the future," he murmured.

She stiffened, and he rubbed her back, not letting her go.

"I want to live with you, Nhi. I want to wake up next to you. I want to share your good days and your bad days. I want to make us family. Marry me."

She squeezed him and glanced up. "Of course."

He stepped back, not sure he'd heard right. "Really?"

She chuckled. "Don't sound so surprised. I love you, Lee. You are my family."

He pulled her back into his arms and for the first time, he thanked Stonefish.

For bringing Nhiari and the Stokes into his life.

He glanced at Nhiari and then up at the stars above them.

This was home.

Thank you for reading!

I hope you enjoyed the book. It would be super awesome if you could leave a review wherever you bought it, because I love to hear what you thought of the story.

Keep an eye out for my new series in 2024.

Milton Keynes UK
Ingram Content Group UK Ltd.
UKHW012049260524
443218UK00001BA/27